Wicked Wager: Texas vs. Brooklyn 1

Published by: Brooklyn Girl Ink, LLC

Photos by: Ellandar, Kosmos111, Vectorguy, and Underdogstudios

Edited by: Katriena Knights

Disclaimer:

This is a work of fiction, any similarity to actual persons living or dead, products, businesses, and locations are purely coincidental or used in a fictional manner.

This work of fiction contains adult content: depictions of sexual acts, explicit language that may be objectionable to some readers. This work is intended for adult audiences of 18 and older. Reader discretion is advised.

DEDICATION

To all the nice guys finishing first, I see you.

ACKNOWLEDGMENTS

To God, from whom all blessings flow, thank you for the gift, the desire, the support, and the opportunity. To Damon, this does not happen without you. Love you forever. To Sterling and Semaj, my heartbeats, the best parts of me. To my family and friends, thank you for putting up with my craziness. To Katriena, thank you for making my crazy sound amazing. To Lexie Craig, thank you for supplying me with my new motto, "Hustle until you don't have to introduce yourself" (unknown). To all of my JMC and LIJ people, your love strengthens me. To my Loungers, you guys hold me down and keep me going. Thank you so much for the loyalty and encouragement. To the readers, you will never know how much I appreciate your support. Thank you for taking this journey with me.

Thank you for embracing my crazy,

WICKED WAGER

TEXAS VS. BROOKLYN 1

Dr. Mandisa Avery is a Brooklyn chemist who's lost sight of her life outside the dreams her late mother left her to fulfill. With too many late nights spent in her office working, she's burned out and desperate for a change.

Slade Hamilton is a Texas businessman who adores ranch life. He'd love nothing more than to spend his days tilling his land. However, his inherent need to protect his family legacy from his hateful father keeps him and his future tied to a desk at Logan Industries.

When a lucrative business opportunity forces their paths to cross, Mandisa and Slade must each make a decision: risk it all on undeniable attraction, or hedge their bets to save their hearts and their respective businesses from ruin.

Will they fold, or will they risk it all on a wicked wager?

This novel is a fun and sexy, 80,000-word, erotic romance. It features a hot cowboy from Texas who meets his smart, fiery competition in the form of a concrete princess from Brooklyn. Place your bets on who's going to win this wicked wager.

1

Slade Hamilton stood in front of the large window of his office looking out over the business district in Downtown Austin, Texas. The ever-expanding skyline was one of the things that drew him to this branch of his family's business. From his high-rise on Congress Avenue, Slade could look and see the busy city on one side and the calm of Lady Bird Lake on the other.

As Bull Hamilton's one and only son, Slade could've chosen any of Logan Industries' locations. California, New York, Asia, Europe, or even the coveted headquarters in Houston, where the great man himself ran the company founded by Slade's maternal grandfather. All of those locations were in his reach. But Austin and its freshness, its eclectic mix of the traditional and the new, called to him. It also didn't hurt that the near three-hour trip between Austin and Houston kept visits from his stepmother and father to a minimum.

Slade pulled the knotted tie from his neck and opened the button holding his throat hostage. He pulled in a harsh breath, held it, and let it seep from his lips slowly. Today had gone to hell with gasoline drawers on, and he was more grateful than usual that his father's office was three hours away.

Slade picked up the half-empty tumbler of Scotch and downed his liquid lunch in one gulp. The burn nearly brought tears to his eyes, but the discomfort was nothing compared to what he'd be experiencing once Bull discovered Slade's colossal loss of the StarTech deal.

Six months' worth of work gone like a puff of smoke. Slade was pissed at the waste of his time, but after discovering some of the dirty things Bull expected him to do to close the deal, there was no way Slade could go through with it.

A shrill buzz from the intercom cracked the air. Slade settled the now-empty glass on his desk and pushed the speakerphone button. "Yes, Donna."

"Slade, your father's on line one. Shall I tell him you're unavailable for calls right now?"

For a brief second Slade contemplated Donna's gift of avoidance before he shook his head and capitulated. "No, Donna, might as well get this ass-chewing over with." He picked up the phone receiver and waited for a beat before he spoke. "Bull, what can I do for you?"

"Boy, you know exactly what the hell you can do for me!" His father's voice boomed through the line, making the ache in Slade's head throb more.

"I guess you've heard about the StarTech deal?"

"I gave you explicit directions on how to handle that deal, Slade. If you'd just done what I told you to do, we'd have that damn company in our grip."

Slade rolled his eyes as he listened to Bull's assessment of the situation. Yeah, if Slade had listened to Bull they probably would have owned StarTech. The problem was, Bull's plan included a whole lot of illegal shit that Slade wasn't really inclined to get involved in.

"Bull, it was insider trading. If we'd gone ahead with the purchase of the stock, both of us would end up in handcuffs once the SEC found out."

"*If* they found out," Bull added.

Slade shook his head. There it was—Bull logic. Something was only wrong if you got caught doing it. Even then, if you could weasel your way out of your predicament by denying it or resting the blame at someone else's feet, then you still weren't technically in the wrong.

Slade had spent years attempting to resign himself to Bull's way of thinking and living. There was only one problem, he had this pesky thing called a conscience that wouldn't let him screw people over or do illegal shit just to get ahead.

Tired of Bull's tirade, he placed the receiver down on his desk and let the man rattle on. By the sound of it, Bull had only muddled through the first movement of this familiar symphony. Slade figured he had another twenty minutes before Bull spewed his consistent, "You hear me when I'm talking to you, boy?" and Slade would be expected to answer.

Slade returned to the window and smiled at his beloved city. Its distance from his father's brimstone being its most endearing quality at the moment.

He saw his smile reflected in the window and could almost see his inner child sticking out his tongue and singing, "Na, na, na, na, na, you can't get me," to his angry father. He reveled in that feeling of his petty win until he heard a disturbance from the other side of his office door. A panicked, "You can't just barge in there," coming from Donna made Slade pull up to his full six-foot-four-inch height and step toward the door.

"Donna, who in the hell—"

"Who in the hell indeed, son."

There, big and bold as day, Bull Hamilton stood in the middle of Slade's office. As if this day hadn't already pissed Slade off, it had taken a decidedly sharp turn onto shit's highway.

"I can't believe you fucked this up, Slade! I gave you all the tools you needed to win this damn thing, and you still managed to screw me and my company."

Slade turned halfway from his perch at the office window to give his father a cursory glance. Bull Hamilton wasn't a man to listen to rational thought. He just yelled a lot until most folks around him crumbled in fear. Slade wasn't afraid of his father. He knew how dangerous he could be when he settled on something, but in this, Slade knew Bull had no recourse, so he just turned his back and let the old Texan blow off steam.

"I know you hear me, Slade. What do you have to say for yourself?" Bull continued.

"The same thing I've been saying all along. It was insider trading. I'm not going to prison for anyone, Bull, not even you."

"God, you're some kind of useless," Bull hollered. "We had that stock in the palm of our hands. It was going to be easy money."

Slade was more than a little pissed off now. If he hadn't done his due diligence in his pursuit of the stock, he'd never have stumbled over his father's backdoor deals. "This is your fault, Bull, not mine. If you'd just let me handle the deal my way, instead of cutting corners behind my back, we wouldn't be in this mess. I wouldn't have wasted so much company time and resources on a deal that was doomed from the start."

"Good Lord in heaven. How the hell did I get such a bitch for a son? You whine more than any woman I know. This is business. You go big, you go hard, or you drag your sorry ass on home."

Slade was tired at this point. He'd had this same conversation with his father many times. The result was always going to be the same. Slade wasn't about to engage in dirty shit to appease his father.

He turned around, facing his father, squaring his shoulders. "Listen, I'm tired and really not up for this rant you have planned. How about we just review the previous versions of this conversation and keep pushing? I've gotta head back to my ranch."

"I'm tired of your attitude, boy. Logan Industries is mine," Bull snarled.

"For now," Slade countered.

It was the same old argument again, the real reason behind the chasm between Slade and his father. Logan Industries.

His beloved grandmother hadn't wanted to leave the family business to her wily son-in-law after Slade's natural mother preceded her in death, but Slade was too young to take control of the company when his grandma Ester passed. She'd left it in a trust, and left his father and two others as the co-executors. Bull would be in power for another five years. On Slade's fortieth birthday, the entire company would be handed over to him.

"My mama-in-law was a wonderful woman, but she didn't know shit about business. The fact she left it all to you is proof of that. You botched this up for us, so I'm gonna make you pay."

"Exactly how, Bull? It's not like you can fire me."

"No, I can't fire you, but I can determine exactly where you work in this company. Those two hens your grandmamma named as co-executors to your trust don't have shit to say about general business dealings. Those decisions are left to me. Since you want to act like a bitch, I'm gonna send you to a division where I think someone with your displayed sensitivities would flourish. You're going to Venus."

Slade did a quick mental query. "The cosmetics division?"

"Yup. Right now it's dragging. Needs something fresh to keep it alive, or I'm gonna cut it," Bull answered.

"But Memaw loved that division. She started it up. You can't cut it, Bull."

"Oh, yeah, I can. And if it's not making money, the other executors will have to agree to sell it. I'm turning it over to you and giving you an assignment. There's a rinky-dink cosmetics operation that's based in Brooklyn, New York. It's currently owned by Sadie King. They're tiny, but they've got some impressive sales. I want to buy them, dissolve them into Venus. You've got a meeting in two days with the owner. Lori will pick you up from the airport when you land. Your plane leaves in an hour."

Slade ground his teeth until his jaw began aching. "You made travel arrangements for me? I haven't agreed to any of this."

Bull laughed as he watched Slade. "You will. Because you know I'll sell that son of a bitch for no other reason than to piss you off. This is the only chance you have at saving it. Get me that cosmetics line and the formulas behind all its products or Venus is gone."

Bull stood up with a slick smile on his face. He tipped his cowboy hat in a mock salute and walked out of Slade's office.

Slade grabbed the nearest thing his fingers could reach and launched the empty glass tumbler across the room. When the sound of its shattering pieces erupted in the room, Slade could hear a hearty laugh coming from the opposite side of the door. Once again, Bull had Slade just where he wanted him. Right under Bull's thumb.

Mandisa Avery pored over the spreadsheets in front of her, her eyes crossing as the digits and lines blurred. It was only four in the afternoon, but she'd been inside the tiny office of her Atlantic Galleria store for twelve hours attempting to perfect her proposal. If she could get this presentation together, she'd be able to lure investors to help her realize her mother's dream: a national franchise of her mama's Sweet Sadie's Beauty Supply stores, and its signature cosmetics and body lotion collections, Sweet Sadie's Treats, distributed in all the major retail stores throughout the country.

She had two days before her first meeting with a rep from Venus Cosmetics. Of the three companies courting her, Venus was her favorite among them. They were already in all the chains she wanted to break into, and their brand was known for quality and affordability, two things she insisted upon with her own products.

"Hey, Mandisa, a few of us are heading over to Syn tonight after we close. You down?"

Mandisa wiped her blurry eyes and focused on her friend, Kandi's, face. Kandi may be Mandisa's store manager now, but she'd been looking out for Mandisa's interests far longer than the handful of years she'd worked at Sweet Sadie's. They'd been friends since Mandisa moved onto Osborn Street in Brownsville, Brooklyn, when she was eight. Kandi was queen of the block. Fortunately, they'd clicked from the first time Mandisa had proven herself as an asset on Kandi's double Dutch team.

Back in the day, if you were a little black girl in the 'hood, you either jumped double Dutch or you didn't exist socially. Between Mandisa's mama and all her aunties' instruction, she literally had the double Dutch game on lock. Hell, at thirty-three years old she still had a pristine double Dutch rope made of plastic clothesline—because everyone who jumped double Dutch knew plastic clothesline was the best material for a rope in the 'hood—tied up neatly, resting in the back of her trunk just in case a spontaneous game of Numbers broke out.

"I'd love to, Kandi." Mandisa yawned. "But this presentation is kicking my ass. I've got to get it perfected. I'm meeting with the rep from Venus Cosmetics. Lori Harris arrives in two days. I've gotta have everything in place by then."

Kandi stepped farther into the office, closing the door behind her. She shook her head and crossed her arms over her chest, not even attempting to disguise her disappointment with Mandisa's excuse.

"Girl, you've been working on that proposal since you and Mama Sadie first cooked up this idea all those years ago. I know every detail this rep could need or want is already included in your ridiculously organized slides. What you need to do now is relax, so you don't seem like a desperate beggar when you arrive at the presentation."

Mandisa took her hand off the wireless mouse and sat up straight in her chair, rubbing her temples. Desperate wasn't that far off from the way she felt. Mandisa knew her products were quality. She'd seen to that herself in the lab when she created each item in both lines. Her sales were concrete evidence that consumers loved what she created. If she wanted to continue meeting the demand, she needed to grow her business. Growth equaled the need for capital. She wasn't financially hurting by any means; her stores remained in the black with a sizably impressive profit each year.

Her current success notwithstanding, if she wanted to expand, she'd need to impress an outside investor with not just numbers, but charm. Kandi was right. Mandisa's data was flawless. What she needed to do now was work on her lure.

"Sure, count me in." Mandisa started to return to her work but noticed Kandi still standing there. "You needed something else?"

"No, I'm just surprised," Kandi muttered softly with her head slightly tilted to the side. "I didn't think convincing you to hang would be that easy."

"Damn, Kandi. I know I'm not the most social person in the world, but even I go out and hang on occasion. It shouldn't be that shocking."

Kandi stepped closer to her desk, watching Mandisa carefully. "Not much in the last year and a half. Not since Ms. Sadie passed."

Kandi's statement hung heavy in the air, making it difficult for Mandisa to breathe comfortably. Eighteen months still wasn't enough time to erase the sting of loss Mandisa could never seem to outrun.

"I'm sorry, Mandisa, I didn't mean..."

Mandisa closed her eyes and swallowed hard in an attempt to push her latent grief down. Once she was certain she had it under control, she allowed a small smile to grow slowly on her lips. "It's fine. You don't have to be scared to mention Mama. And you're right. I haven't done anything but work and sleep since she passed. Tonight changes all that. Tonight, Dr. Avery takes a reprieve, and Mandisa gets to come out and play."

"Hey, hey, hey," Kandi sang. "That's what I'm talkin' 'bout."

Mandisa laughed at her friend. If there was anyone in this world who could make Mandisa enjoy herself even when she didn't really want to, it was Kandi.

"All right, slacker, Dr. Avery has to finish up work today if Mandisa is going to party tonight."

Mandisa climbed the circular staircase carefully as she made her way to the bar in the upper-level lounge. Syn was a bi-level club. Downstairs was for dancing and partying. Upstairs was for conversations and cocktails. Her friends were downstairs grinding with the other patrons on the dance floor. Mandisa had done her last two-step when her pretty pumps began pinching her toes. That's what she got for trying to just jump back into the club scene without stretching first.

She pushed through the heavy doors that protected the quiet from the loud bass currently banging on the lower level. As soon as the doors closed, there was an instant drop in volume. It wasn't silent, just a measured groove where people could listen to slow jams as a soundtrack to their conversations, or thoughts.

She sat at the end of the bar and waved to catch the bartender's attention. He was currently serving another customer at the end, but acknowledged her with a slight nod.

"Evening, what can I get you?"

"A whiskey sour."

With impressive speed, he slid her drink in front of her. A quick, "Here you go," and he was turning away.

"How much do I owe you," she asked as she reached into her pocket to pull out a bill.

"Nothing. The guy at the end of the bar says he's picking up your tab for the rest of the night."

Mandisa turned her head to glance at the stranger. Dark hair tapered neatly at the sides and a clean-shaven face. He offered her a wide smile that seemed to reach his sparkling blue eyes.

Her gaze traveled down his square jaw until she took in the size and build of him. *Damn, he's a big one.* The long-sleeved white button-down shirt and the simple black slacks did little to mask the distinct silhouette of his carved muscles.

She continued to move her gaze down the length of his body, appreciating every inch as she continued her perusal. She stopped dead at a large pair of black cowboy boots that made her remember one of her mother's colorful pearls of wisdom regarding men. *Baby, if you really want to know what a man is packing, just look at the size of his feet. If he ain't working with double digits, he ain't worth your time.*

She closed her eyes against the shiver of lust that spilled down her spine. If those boots weren't well into the double digits she'd sell her right arm.

Damn!

"Size thirteens."

The deep rumble of a nearby male voice forced her eyes open. The stranger was sitting beside her. She was so busy daydreaming about how hung he might be she hadn't seen him move closer to her.

"Excuse me?" she managed.

"My boots. I saw you looking at them, figured you were probably amazed at the size of these boats. I promise I won't step on you."

Size thirteens, good gawd!

"I'm Slade, by the way." He offered her his hand and another helping of his bright smile.

"Mandisa," she countered, accepting his hand with a nod.

"Mandisa. What a beautiful name? What does it mean?"

"Sweet," she answered.

"Fitting. It's lovely to meet you tonight, Ms. Mandisa."

"Thank you for the drink, Slade. It was very kind of you. But I can't accept your offer to purchase all my drinks tonight. It's too generous."

He motioned for the bartender to freshen his drink and

returned those beautiful blue eyes of his to her face. "Mandisa, please, it's my honor to do so. And besides, it's all I have to offer in exchange for..."

Mandisa raised an eyebrow in expectation. The smart-assed retort was waiting to fly off the tip of her tongue.

"...conversation."

Mandisa's would-be scowl turned into a full-on smile. This man was smart, charming, and fine as hell. A rare combination in her world as of late.

"I'd be happy to sit and talk to you, Slade. You don't have to bribe me with drinks to do so."

"Not a bribe, darlin', just a way to show my appreciation for your time."

He held out a hand and led them in the direction of one of the empty booths. They sat in the quiet little booth, enjoying the easy conversation and pleasant company. Their waitress brought them another round of drinks, interrupting their conversation for a few moments. When she left, Mandisa returned her attention to Slade.

"Where are you from, Slade?"

The twang in his voice told her he was from somewhere South of the Mason Dixon. It had been there, just below the surface, but when he spoke the word "darlin'" like it was dipped in honey, his accent flourished.

"Austin, Texas." He took a quick swig of the beer and settled the bottle quietly on the table. "Did the yee-haw in my voice give me away? Doesn't usually come out unless I'm comfortable in my surroundings."

"Does that mean you're comfortable with me?"

"Yes, it does." He tipped the long neck of his beer bottle in her direction. "But the more important question is, are you comfortable with me, Mandisa?"

Mandisa couldn't help the smile blooming on her face. It

didn't really make sense, but his easy personality made him so inviting. "Strangely enough, I am."

"Why is that so strange?"

She pulled her eyes away from his and focused on the finger she was running along the perimeter of her glass. "I'm a born and bred New Yorker. We're distrustful from birth. You don't survive in a city like this by letting your guard down."

He laughed a little. The sound small enough not to draw the attention of the other patrons in the lounge, yet powerful enough to shake something loose inside. She felt it. It was a physical sensation of something releasing within the lonely walls of her soul.

I must be hard up if a man's laugh is doing it for me now. When did laughing become so goddamn sexy?

"That's no way to live. You need to come on down to Texas. We're some of the friendliest people you'll ever meet. You'll get to let down your guard and experience life as it was meant to be experienced."

"And how's that?"

He moved in closer. His lean was measured but steady. She didn't even pretend to hesitate. She met him halfway and welcomed the moment his lips touched hers. The firm, determined mutual press of their mouths sparked need inside her. Just as quickly as the kiss had happened, it ended. He pulled away, running a slow finger down the apple of her cheek as he offered a welcoming smile.

"Life was meant to be just like that kiss. Fun, sexy, open, and with the intent of creating happiness and satisfying desire."

He was leaning in again. Their lips met in a rush. She felt the light swipe of his tongue against her bottom lip and decided chasing it was the best idea she'd had all week. Just when she'd found his tongue again, coaxed him into giving her more of it, she heard her name in the distance.

"Mandisa, there you are."

Mandisa pulled away from Slade's kiss when she recognized Kandi's voice. The blessing and curse of having such a unique name was when someone shouted it across a room, you were reasonably certain they were addressing you. She was confident no other Mandisas were sitting in this room tonight.

"Oh, I'm sorry." Kandi stopped short when she reached the booth. "Am I interrupting?"

"No, Kandi," Mandisa lied. "Kandi, this is Slade. Slade, my best friend Kandi. Kandi looked Slade up and down, much the same way Mandisa did when she first laid eyes on him. He was a pretty specimen of big man meat. Mandisa would wager most women would find it difficult not to take a long hard look at the man. "What's up?"

"Anna drank too many martinis, and now she's sick. We're heading out."

Great, I haven't met an interesting man in nearly two years, and one of my girlfriends chooses this moment to get pissy drunk.

Mandisa wanted to groan and kick her feet while she screamed, "I don't wanna." But the girlfriend code of clubbing said we came together, we leave together, so...

"Slade, it was really lovely to meet you, but we've got to get our friend home. I hope you enjoy the rest of your stay in New York."

"I'm sure I will, if you agree to spend some time with me while I'm here. Dinner tomorrow?"

Before she could answer, he pulled a card from his blazer and handed it to her. She opened her small clutch and popped the card inside. Needing both hands to slide out of the booth, she set the purse on the table as she exited quickly. When she looked at him again, she slammed into his powerful stare. He may have phrased it as a question, but between the kiss and the way his gaze locked with hers, they both knew it was a statement of fact she'd be having dinner with him the next evening.

"I'll call you—"

"Mandisa, we really need to get this girl out of here. Sarah just texted me Anna's throwing up at the coat check."

Mandisa huffed and followed Kandi out of the lounge. She stopped when she reached the door and took one more glance backward. Slade was still watching her. His sexy smile still lingering dangerously across his lips as he tipped his hat to her.

You are trouble, Slade from Austin, Texas. Hopefully the best kind.

Slade felt his lips bend into a gratifying smile as he enjoyed watching the round curve of Mandisa's ass sashay across the room. She was sexy, intelligent, and obviously as attracted to him as he was to her. Slade could watch her all night long.

When she turned around and met his hungry gaze with a matching one of her own, he gave her a quick wink and tipped his beer to his lips. He might have been forced to come to New York because of his hateful father, but he was certain he'd be enjoying his destination for one simple reason—Mandisa.

Once she'd gone, he sat in the booth for a few moments remembering what her lips tasted like. They'd shared a brief few kisses before her friend interrupted them, but they were enough to make him want more.

He kept himself amused with thoughts of tomorrow and signaled the waitress to bring his check. Once he'd settled the bill, he was about to leave when the server touched his arm.

"Sir, I think your friend left her purse."

Slade looked down at the small bag Mandisa had held in her hand and cringed. He'd given her his card and basked in satisfaction when she'd placed it securely in her purse. So certain she would call, he'd made no request for Mandisa's telephone number in return.

Not one to belabor regrets, he set about opening the purse to look for a piece of contact information for her.

"All right, Ms. Mandisa. Let's hope you left me a clue."

2

"You still can't get anyone to pick up?" Kandi asked from the driver's seat of the car.

"Nope, I've been calling Syn for the last hour and no one is answering. Dammit!"

"Girl, I feel your pain. That identity theft stuff is no joke. Now you gotta call and cancel everything."

"I'm not worried about identity theft," Mandisa answered. "I only ever carry my ID, a single credit card, and a few bills when I go out. I keep them in my bra or pocket. I left my keys at the store. The only thing in my purse was my last tube of Sweet Sadie's Butterscotch Lip Luster and face powder."

"So, you're sitting over there mad about some cosmetics? All of which you can pick back up when you go to work at one of the five stores you own?" Kandi's questions were laden with suspicion.

"Uh, obviously you haven't looked at the inventory report, Ms. Executive Manger. If you had, you'd know we're out of Butterscotch Lip Luster and won't have any more until the shipment arrives next week. I love that gloss."

"More likely you loved getting next to that sexy-ass man

you were sitting next to with the pretty eyes and broad shoulders." Kandi's smirk was fully visible, making her regret that Kandi could read Mandisa so well.

Mandisa sighed loudly. *No need in lying. Shame the devil, tell the truth.* "Fine doesn't even cover it, girl. Everything about him was sexy. And the way his lips felt—"

"Wait, you kissed him!" Kandi's outburst made Mandisa squeal.

"Girl, didn't you see?"

Kandi shook her head furiously. "No. I was too busy walking and texting with Sarah about our lush of a friend Anna. When I spotted you and called your name, you two were just eye-fucking each other."

Mandisa's insides began to sizzle again with the thought of Slade's lips. A few kisses and some great conversation, and he'd found a way inside her head.

"I couldn't help it." Mandisa's voice sounded strange to her own ears. Light and bubbly, filled with hopeful excitement. She sounded like a smitten schoolgirl. She could wholeheartedly admit that without the least bit of shame.

"He was sitting there looking pretty and smelling like sex and my favorite flavor of ice cream all mixed together, and I just had to lean in and get a taste. Wouldn't you?"

Kandi continued laughing. "I sure as hell would have."

"Well, his number is in that purse, so if I can't find it, I'll never be able to find Mr. Sexy again." Mandisa huffed and let the back of her skull sink into the headrest.

"Chile, you know like I know, you'd better stop chatting with me and keep trying to get someone at Syn on the phone. You can't give up on finding that level of sexy."

Mandisa dialed Syn again. Kandi was right. She couldn't give up on that kind of sexy without trying.

Mandisa sipped from the plastic coffee cup like it contained life's elixir. She was dragging this morning. Between the late night and the early-morning sick calls from two employees at her Pitkin Avenue store, she'd had to cut her sleep short to arrive early enough for opening.

She grudgingly set about her tasks. She and the lone employee who hadn't eaten the funky-looking food from the new takeout spot around the corner, prepped the store for the expected busy day.

It was Saturday. The store was located on the same block as a beauty salon, an African hair-braiding shop, and a nail salon. Sweet Sadie's supplied wholesale items to the owners of those stores and retail products to the patrons. If you lived in Brooklyn, or any 'hood for that matter, Saturdays meant one thing—getting your hair and nails slayed for the weekend and buying the necessary products and tools to keep you looking good until your next visit to the salon.

She was currently helping a woman search for a product she saw on MyTV. Thank God for the DIY gurus that vlogged their tips on beauty and style and the followers like this woman who came to Sweet Sadie's to find their praised recs.

Usually Mandisa would be thrilled to listen to whatever the new craze was. It was one of the ways she kept her stores and products relevant, keeping ahead of the beauty trends by meeting the needs of her patrons. But today this woman's indecisiveness was just getting on Mandisa's last nerve.

Annoyed as she was, Mandisa continued to smile politely, trying to ignore the dull pain the customer's incessant questions kept inflicting. When her employee was free, Mandisa turned the customer over to her and headed to the back for a brief break. She mentally chastised herself as she walked into the storage room. She might've been annoyed by the sick calls and having to come in early, but her sour mood had more to do with Slade's lost number than having to cover the store, and she knew it.

"Slade." The sound of it just slid down her tongue so smoothly. A little sweet mixed with a whole lot of spice. "No sense dwelling on it. That purse, along with his card, has gone to hell."

She looked at her watch and noted they had three more hours until the store closed. She could do this. She had no other choice. When you were the boss, you couldn't opt out, even when you wanted to. Those were the rules.

Slade stared at the folded piece of paper in his hand. He'd found it last night in Mandisa's forgotten bag. He'd looked inside hoping to find some form of identification he could use to contact her. No such luck. Instead, there was a lip-gloss, a compact, and a single piece of notepaper with a telephone number.

He'd picked up his phone to dial it when he'd arrived back at his hotel, but hesitated. The thought crossed his mind that the number possibly belonged to some other man who had shown interest in her last night. Why would she need to write her own number on a slip of paper?

"You can sit here thinking on it, or you can dial it and find out."

Hearing his thoughts out loud pushed him into action. He dialed the number and waited three rings before someone answered it.

"Hello?"

It was a female's voice, but it didn't sound as sultry and thoughtful as Mandisa's.

"Hello. May I speak with Mandisa, please?"

"Are you seriously calling my phone looking for Mandisa?"

"I'm sorry, sugar. I take it I have the wrong number?"

There was a brief pause before he heard the woman's voice again. "Wait a minute. That twang sounds familiar. Is this that sexy Texan that was loved up with Mandisa last night? This is Kandi."

Slade could feel the blood warming his face at Kandi's description of him. "Was that Mandisa's depiction of me, or yours?"

"Both." She laughed, apparently tickled by her answer. "But Mandisa saw you first. Girl code dictates I fall back and let her have you. So, again, Big Sexy, why are you calling me looking for her?"

He shook his head at the mouthful the woman on the other end gave him. He was correct in his assessment. Mandisa was attracted to him.

"Mandisa left her purse on our table last night. I'm trying to contact her to return it."

"Still doesn't explain why you're calling me." Kandi replied.

"The only thing I found in the purse was a compact, some lip gloss, and a folded piece of paper with this number on it. No name, just the number."

"Oh," Kandi sang into the line. "I changed my number when I bought a new phone yesterday. I wrote it down for her before we left the store. She must have left the paper in her bag after she transferred it to her phone."

Slade found himself laughing as he imagined how animated she must be while having this conversation with him. "Kandi, not that it isn't an absolute pleasure talking to you, but is Mandisa around for me to chat with?"

"Unfortunately, no. She's not around today."

"Would you tell me how to contact her?"

"No," she answered quickly. "You're cute as hell, but you could be a psycho. Not about to expose my girl to you."

Slade shook his head. Mandisa was right. New Yorkers really were naturally distrustful. "Honey, I wouldn't hurt a fly. Please, if you don't want to give me her contact info, then do me this favor. Give her my number and tell her to meet me for dinner tonight. There's a restaurant at the Oceanview Hotel off North Conduit Avenue. I'll be there at eight."

The line was quiet for longer than an acceptable pause. "Kandi, you still there?"

"Yeah. I'll give her your message. But just because you're sexy, don't think I won't come for you if you turn out to be some crazed maniac that's got his sights set on my girl."

Slade laughed. He liked this woman. He also didn't take her warning lightly. "I promise. The only thing I want to do is have a meal with her and spend a little time in her company if she's willing."

"All right, Big Sexy. What's your number?"

The heavy base of Jagged Edge's "Where the Party At?" made Mandisa jump and knock the top of her head on a low-hanging shelf in the stock room. She scrambled and answered the phone on the third ring.

"Kandi, what's up?"

"Busy?"

Mandisa looked around at the three unpacked boxes of products waiting to be shelved and sighed. "Not with anything that can't wait. What do you need?'

"A sexy, big man from Texas called asking if you were missing a purse."

Mandisa took a minute to process her friend's words.

Either the poorly ventilated storage space filled with beauty products was getting to her, or Kandi just said she spoke to Slade. "Really?"

"Yes, apparently you left my new number in your bag. He called it hoping to contact you."

Mandisa smiled at the thought of Slade seeking her out. She could feel the excitement bubbling under her skin in anticipation of talking to him again. The idea of Slade calling her "darlin'" like she'd imagined he would placed her in a haze that nearly made her forget she was on the phone.

"Mandisa, are you still there?" Kandi's voice shook her out of her daydream and forced her to focus on the conversation. "He asked me for your number, and I told him no."

"Kandi, you did what?"

"I told him no. Look, if he really is into you, no harm in making him work for it. I took his number down. He's expecting you to call him and confirm your dinner tonight at the Oceanview by JFK."

Mandisa pressed stiff fingers against her temple as she dragged in a heavy breath. "So let me get this straight. You wouldn't give him my number, but you made a date for me with him at a hotel restaurant? What if he's some sort of serial killer? You basically just agreed to deliver me to him."

Mandisa could hear Kandi sucking her teeth through the phone line. "Girl, stop it. The way you were almost sitting in that man's lap last night, it's pretty obvious he ain't all that strange to you. The only thing that man plans on hurting is your self-imposed celibacy."

Kandi was probably right, but that wasn't the issue. "Kandi."

"Mandisa, you need to have some fun. What happened to my girl who partied all the time? The woman that did her damn thing in a lab by day and killed the club scene at night? What happened to the woman who would've met a sexy man like this Slade character and took what she wanted immediately, instead of letting fate get the chance to screw her over? All you do is work and crunch numbers, Mandisa. You don't even spend that much time in your lab anymore."

Mandisa pushed a long, loud breath through her mouth. Everything Kandi stated was true. These were the facts of the situation. That was the woman Mandisa used to be. But then that evil bitch cancer came and stole her mother from her.

"Kandi, you know my mama dreamed of—"

"Yeah, I know exactly what Ms. Sadie's dream was." Kandi's interruption jarred Mandisa, forcing her to pay close attention to her friend's words. "Ms. Sadie's dream was to expand and get her Sweet Sadie's products on the shelves of major retailers. She wanted to do all the work this required. The stores, the products were her life. When did this become your dream, though? Because as far back as I can remember, all you ever cared about was using science to create cool things like sparkly royal-blue eye shadow."

Mandisa kneaded the back of her neck with stiff fingers. Those were loaded questions Mandisa didn't really want to ponder. Would it be a betrayal to her mother's memory, her legacy, to speak the truth?

"Running the stores, growing the stores, was never a dream of mine. But Mama didn't live to see this dream. I'm the only one left to make it happen for her."

"Mandisa." Kandi's voice oozed sympathy tinged with pity. It was a putrid combination of emotion Mandisa hated being on the receiving end of. From the moment her mother's doctor diagnosed Sadie with end-stage ovarian cancer to the day of her mother's burial, sympathy and pity mocked her, always telling her she was about to lose something. Back then it was her mother—now it was her friend's respect.

"No, Kandi. Running and owning Sweet Sadie's was never my dream. If I could give it to someone else and walk away, I would in a heartbeat. But there's no one else that's going to love it and tend to it the way my mother would have, so I have to do it. No one else will ever understand why we do what we do, why these products we sell are so significant to our communities."

"Just don't work yourself to death trying to succeed. Go have some fun with that sexy cowboy."

Mandisa's laughter pinged off the walls of the small supply closet she was standing in. "I don't think being from Texas qualifies him as being a cowboy. You're stereotyping, Kandi."

"Girl, whatever. That man looks like he was born calving, and rodeoing, and doing whatever else they do on ranches and farms in the Wild West. You'd just better take advantage of him and let him do the same to you."

They laughed for a few minutes more until Mandisa heard the chimes above the front door signal someone's entrance into the store.

"Gotta go, Kandi. Someone just came into the store. Since it seems I've got dinner plans to make, I'd better close up a little early and go make myself presentable."

"All right, I'm going. Just make sure you spend the night with that man. If you do, I suppose you'll be limber enough to come in and wow these big spenders looking to invest in Sweet Sadie's tomorrow."

"Girl, bye." Mandisa offered, running a quick hand over her hair and face. She wasn't runway ready. A fitted V-necked T-shirt, black jeans, and a pair of sneakers made up her uniform. A quick glance in a small wall mirror showed her light makeup was still in place since her last refresh. She was presentable, but the next time she saw Slade, she wanted to be more than just presentable. She needed to be flawless.

3

Slade sat in the lobby and waited for his guest. It was ten of eight, and he was beginning to wonder if Mandisa would show up or not. The realization that he was actually concerned about being stood up rattled him.

Slade didn't have much use for women. They were a practicality in his life. He had open and honest liaisons with women who understood up front all he wanted was a little fun and no attachments.

He'd never been worried about being disappointed before. If one didn't show up, there was always something else to do. He wasn't a playboy by any stretch of the imagination, didn't have a different woman hidden in every city. He simply had friends he occasionally slept with when the need or desire arose.

But from the moment he'd seen Mandisa step into that lounge he'd wanted to know her. He'd only been in that damn lounge because Lori, the New York rep for Venus Cosmetics, lived near Downtown Brooklyn. When she picked him up from the airport he'd told her to take him someplace he could drink in peace and get his mind off of the shittastic day he'd had. She'd taken him to Syn, and he'd done just as he said he'd wanted to—enjoyed his drink quietly.

When he spotted Mandisa stepping into the lounge and making her way to the bar, suddenly a quiet night alone didn't seem so inviting. Once he'd actually kissed Mandisa, had the opportunity to feel her smooth skin under his own, he knew he wouldn't be satisfied until he had the opportunity to taste all of her.

Last night she'd seemed like she might not be opposed to that idea. But since he hadn't heard from her since he'd given her friend his number, he was beginning to question if she'd even bother accepting his dinner invitation.

He looked at the entrance once more and then at his watch. Five after eight. Maybe it was time to pack it in and head upstairs to his room.

"Slade."

The sultry heaviness of her voice made him close his eyes as he savored the sweetness of the sound of his name on what he knew to be delectable lips.

He opened his eyes, searching for her in the hotel lobby. "Darlin,' you made it." He stood and tipped his hat for her, pouring on the Southern gentleman act rather thickly. He was in fact a Southern gentleman, but he didn't go around tilting his hat and deepening the twang in his voice for just any little filly. No, this was simply to keep that satisfied look on her face, the sparkle in her eyes.

She found his charm endearing, and somehow knowing that made him want to be this person for her all the time. It was hokey, it was playing to a stereotype, yeah, but it was also bringing the most beautiful smile to the sexy woman standing before him. That alone made it worth it.

"Please forgive my lateness. I had to go home to get ready before I could meet you. I hope I'm dressed all right."

He looked at her. She was adorned in an off-the-shoulder red fitted dress that hugged every form-fitting curve she had, accompanied by a pair of black leather knee-high stiletto boots. Her eyelids sparkled with shimmering shadow that accentuated the lovely dark brown eyes fanned by full midnight lashes. Her lips were covered in a matte red color that dared him to kiss her right now.

The combination of those boots, her curves, and the sexy red lips made his slacks tighten around the semi hard-on the vision of her was creating.

Act right before you screw this up, Slade. Act like you're more than a horny teenager.

"You're beautiful. Let me take you inside and get you fed right nice, darlin'."

Mandisa smiled at him again, the same way she always seemed to when he used that pet name on her. She couldn't stop it. The sound of it just made her face muscles bend her lips into a sappy little grin.

"Is that a Texas custom? You tipping your cowboy hat and calling the ladies darlin'?"

"Yup. We also have two more very important customs in Texas I need to show you." She watched him stand to his full six-foot-whatever-the-hell-inch height and tip his hat again.

He took a slow step toward her. When she didn't back away, he continued until he was standing directly in front of her with hardly enough space between them for air to pass.

He tilted her chin with his finger and bent slightly to bridge the difference in their heights. "The first custom is this. When a beautiful woman that you fancy enters a room, you greet her with a kiss."

He pressed his lips to hers. Soft and tentative at first, as if he were giving her the chance to decide if this was where she wanted to be. He didn't have to worry about that. She had no plans of moving from this spot.

When she met his kiss with a soft purr, he pulled her closer to him, surrounding her with his arms, tucking her into his chest. He deepened the kiss, nipping at the softness of her lips, sliding his tongue inside the heat of her mouth, allowing her to savor the cinnamon flavor of it as she opened wider for him.

The feel of the hard planes of his large body pressed against her soft curves made every nerve she possessed tingle with electricity. She'd known this man less than twenty-four hours. Yet being near him, allowing herself to wallow in the luxurious feel of the broad pads of his fingers on the curve of her neck, stroking her with their hypnotic rhythm, seemed so familiar. As if it was usual, expected.

Kandi's reprimand about Mandisa needing to take a break, to enjoy life, weighed on her. Maybe there was something to Kandi's idea. Maybe she really did need to break loose, get back to her former wild ways, and live a little.

"Mmm, I think I like this custom of yours," she moaned in the brief breaks between their kisses. "What else you Texans got?"

He pressed another quick peck to her lips and held his hand out with the palm side up. "You have a cellphone?"

She reached inside her purse, pulled it out and handed it to him. When he went to wake it from its sleep mode, he smiled at the flashing demand for a password and retina scan.

"You really need a retina scan for your cellphone?"

She lifted a shoulder in a shrug. "Can't be too careful in this day and age." She picked up the phone and lifted it while it scanned her eyes. When the phone was open, she handed it back to him. "What do you need it for?"

He tapped a number onto the keypad and pressed the call button. She heard a light vibration coming from his chest pocket, then he ended the call and locked his information into her contact's list.

"That second custom says, if you find a beautiful woman you want to spend a little more time with, make sure you exchange contact information with her. This way she'll never be able to lose you again."

She took her phone from him and looked down at it. "A cellphone number is all I need to guarantee I'll never lose you…" She looked down at the bright screen again. "Mr. Slade Hamilton?"

He leaned in for another kiss, then pulled his own phone out to secure her contact information.

"Darlin', the way you say my name, like it's dipped in something decadent, is a pretty sure bet I'll always be at your beck and call. Now, what's your last name, Ms. Mandisa?"

"Avery," she offered. "And it's not Ms., it's Doctor. Doctor Mandisa Avery."

Slade quickly lifted his eyes from the screen of his phone and stared openly at her, his gaze slightly clearing the warm haze his kisses had created a few moments earlier. "Doctor?"

She nodded and took a step back, giving him a chance to process what she'd said. There were men in this world, even in the twenty-first century, who couldn't deal with an educated woman. Somehow having brains seemed to be a threat to their masculinity. She was desperately hoping Slade wasn't one of those men, but if he was, now was the time for her to find out.

"Is that a problem?"

"No. Why would it be? It just means I'm in capable hands should I require mouth-to-mouth."

She tilted her head and watched, trying to gauge his truthfulness as his lecherous smile was accompanied by his lifting eyebrows. Not that she'd known him long enough to be able to read his non-verbal cues, but his response didn't give her pause, just made her want to roll her eyes, and so she did.

"Sorry to disappoint, but I'm not that kind of doctor. PhD, not MD."

He waved his hand. "Doesn't matter. You still seem to know what you're doing when you put your mouth on mine."

She stopped for a moment, making an exaggerated appearance of mulling over his findings as she stepped back into his personal space.

She whispered, "I really do. Don't I?" before she ran slow fingers up his chest and circled her arms around his neck, drawing him to her. When their lips met, she pressed her mouth to his, happy to feel the warmth his touch brought to her.

God, this feels so right.

It did, for reasons she couldn't fully understand, she felt grounded in his arms. She pulled away slightly, looking up into the crystal blue of his eyes, getting lost in their tranquil lure. She was standing in a hotel lobby, damn near climbing a perfect stranger, and the world seemed more level than it had at any other time in her recent years.

"Not that I'm complaining about how we're spending the present, but I thought there was gonna be a nice shared meal in our future."

"Does this hotel have twenty-four-hour room service?"

He took a moment to gaze at her, as if he were trying to connect the breadcrumbs she was dropping. "Yes, it does. Why?"

"Because I was thinking maybe we could skip the table and the people in the restaurant and have that meal in your bed."

He stared at her for a beat before he smiled and nodded

his head. "Dr. Avery, I think that's the best idea I've heard all day."

As soon as he clicked the door shut behind him and turned around, removing his hat, Slade pulled Mandisa into his arms. Her warm curves tickling his skin in the most delicious way brought a moan to his lips. Even fully clothed she felt like heaven against him.

He reached down to kiss her, and she leaned back. "Can I use your restroom to freshen up?" He nodded and pointed her in the direction of the bathroom. In her absence, he removed his jacket and boots. He padded over to the bed and took a seat. He reached for the top button of his shirt ready to loosen it. A small creak in the air stopped his moving fingers and pulled his attention to the bathroom door.

"Please, allow me," she crooned. Her voice alone was enough to make his semi grow to full mast. But when he looked up and saw her standing there with her stiletto boots on and a matching demi bra and panty set, he couldn't breathe.

"Jesus."

"I don't think that was exactly the reaction I was looking for." She stepped slowly, taking entirely too long to get within his grasp, in his opinion. When she finally arrived, he had to lick his lips in delight.

He wanted to jump right into the feast, but decided to savor the bounty before him. He took a moment, inhaled deeply, and looked up to meet her gaze.

"Darlin', you do know I'd have been happy spending the night with you, good food, and conversation. Are you sure you want to do this with me?"

She raised a skeptical eyebrow and slowly smiled at him.

"Is this you being a gentleman, Slade, or are you just trying to earn brownie points by being a nice guy?"

"Would you believe a little of both?"

She nodded, then took a moment to lean beyond him, grabbing the purse she'd dropped on his bed before she'd gone to the bathroom. She opened it and pulled out a string of foil condom packets, holding them up for him to see.

"Does this show you how serious I am about spending the night with you?"

He groaned and pulled her closer to him, resting his head on her breasts. "God, woman, where have you been all my life?"

She chuckled as she wove firm fingers through his hair and lightly scraped his scalp with her fingernails. "I don't know if I should be impressed or concerned about your use of religious outcries while I'm trying to have sex with you."

"Trust me, in the Bible belt, we take the name of the Lord seriously. As a good Texas boy I'm only calling on God for two reasons: because I need Him, or because I want to thank Him."

"Which reason are you calling Him now?"

He lifted his hand, securing it at her nape, threading his fingers into the thick loose curls that framed her face and shoulders. "Both."

He pulled her down on top of him, loving the feel of her body's weight against his chest. He slid sure hands down her back, letting them glide down the curve of her ass until his fingers rested on the backs of her thighs. He pulled her up until her legs straddled his hips, loving the feel the heat of her cunt supplied as she seated herself gently on his cock.

He slid his hands down her thighs and moved on to her calves, smiling when he encountered the leather leg of her boots.

"You have no idea how much Texans love boots," he whispered against her mouth.

"The boots are really doing it for you, huh?"

"You in the boots is really doing it for me. Keep 'em on."

The crooked smile on his face and the streak of devilment in his eyes should have let her know she was in for an intense ride. Everything about Slade Hamilton said unpredictable and different. From the way he wore that big-ass cowboy hat with such confidence to the powerful way he walked—even the way his rich voice dripped with sex appeal—Slade Hamilton was a powerful man who played his cards close and kept a woman on her feet. In one smooth motion, he flipped them over, never once interrupting the kiss they were locked in. She was on her back, spread beneath him, happily basking in his heat without the slightest bit of concern for how wanton her spread legs and desperate moans made her appear.

That was Slade. Since that first moment in the bar, he'd made her care less about everything she should be doing and drew her focus to the things that pleased her. His ability to make her forget about the world outside was intoxicating, something that could be dangerous in excess.

She gave herself a mental shake. There was no need to worry about becoming addicted. He'd be gone, back to his life in Texas, in a matter of hours. There would be no time for her system to become fixated on the things his body could do to hers.

Secure in the fact she had this under control, she slid sure hands down his muscled flanks, hooking her fingers into the elastic of his boxer briefs. She tugged, and he rolled from side to side until she got them down far enough that he could kick them off.

When he leaned to the side it gave her the opportunity to see the monster he'd been hiding beneath his clothes. She'd known he was more than a handful when she'd straddled him. The way his cock protruded through his jeans, resting hard and heavy between the lips of her pussy, creating the most delightful friction across her clit was proof enough of her assumption. If he'd left her there, a few swivels of her hips would have gotten her off. But seeing him now, naked, hard, and cut, she was glad she hadn't wasted that orgasm dry-humping him like a teenager.

"Gimme that," she moaned. He made enough space between their bodies for her to slide her hand between them. Discovering her fingers were unable to touch when she attempted to wrap her hand around him made her pussy clench. She hadn't stroked him once, and he was firm and heavy, cock standing at attention, proudly reporting for duty.

She attempted to stroke him, but he wrapped his hand around hers and shook his head. He pulled her hand from his length and secured it over her head. He did the same to her other hand, swallowing both her wrists in one meaty palm. He positioned himself to her side as he used his free hand to glide from her ample bosom down to the soft base of her abdomen.

When his fingers reached her folds, he wasted no time in swirling his fingers around the hood of her clit, coaxing it from behind its silky cover. The feel of his hands on her, rubbing her, sending shocks of electricity from his fingertips to her cunt, causing it to weep with excitement, begging him for more, brought her closer to the climax she could feel building inside.

Her breath came in gasps as she mewled and moaned for

him. When skilled fingers slipped inside her, her moans became an open cry.

"Shhh, darlin'. I promise I'll give you everything you want." He leaned in and kissed her. It was hungry, desperate. He broke the kiss only to whisper in her ear as his fingers continued to stroke her, caressing the spongy knot inside her that threatened to break her apart.

The sound of his voice both soothed and excited her. It stroked her soul just as gently and surely as his fingers stroked her velvet walls.

Sometimes his words seemed like meaningless sounds, others nearly shattered her with the depth of their meaning. Repeatedly he told her how beautiful she was, how fucking sexy she was with the lips of her cunt spread open and dripping for him. How he wanted to bury his face in it and lick every delicious drop she had to offer him. And when one of his fingers lightly slid against her puckered hole and her entire body quivered, he told her how the thought of sliding inside made his dick weep.

She wasn't sure if it was his touch or the filthy things he whispered to her in his sweet voice, but without warning her entire body tightened into one long spasm and then shattered. The tremors of her orgasm were still causing her walls to quake when she heard the distant sound of a foil wrapper being torn open.

She expected him to climb on top of her, but he didn't. He remained at her side, maneuvering her limp body so that she fit perfectly into his big spoon. He wrapped one of her legs over his hips and entered her from behind.

She'd come, he'd stretched and prepared her, but his girth still pulled at the lips of her cunt. She stiffened in anticipation of the pain, but he soothed her by wrapping his arm around her, caressing her clit, and whispering in her ear again. This time his words cheered her, told her how he knew she could handle him, how much pleasure he was going to give her because she was being such a good girl, taking him just the way he liked it.

Logically, his words should have meant nothing. But the way he whispered them with such sincerity, the way each whisper was always accompanied with a gentle touch of his hand or a deep stroke of his cock had her coming again. This orgasm was harder, more intense than the first time, making her seize in his arms, her nails digging into his flesh as she grasped for purchase, needing an anchor to keep her from falling.

As she broke apart for him, he dug deeper, buried himself to the hilt of his cock. His balls slapping against her swollen opening, making her moan with each movement, made her ache with need. He sped up his motion as he ground into her, making her body bounce to the rhythm he was creating. She begged him for more, even though she was shredded by the pleasure he'd already bestowed on her, she shamelessly begged him to continue his destruction of her.

He left her on her side as he moved to his knees. He lifted one of her legs over his shoulder. The move had her spread wide, allowing him to deepen his angle and pivot at a faster pace. The hard ride he was giving her kept her screaming into the pillow beneath her head. When his cockhead scraped across her G-spot in just the right way, she screamed his name a final time, clawing the sheets beneath her fingers while her cunt conformed to the mold of his dick.

He laced his fingers in her worn curls, holding her in place while he snapped his hips, pummeling through her orgasm and triggering his own. He slammed into her one last time before his cockhead swelled, and the first warm jet of cum spilled into the condom.

She turned her head just in time to see bliss soften the sharp angles of his face.

He should always look like this...perfect, peaceful.

Of course Slade hadn't disclosed anything to her that suggested he wasn't otherwise happy. Mandisa had hardly spent enough time with him to know anything more than his name. But in the beauty of their sex, another layer of Slade Hamilton was revealed to her and she knew she wanted him to always carry the serenity this moment seemed to give him.

In their short time together he'd shown her kindness and generosity with his money. But in this moment, when he'd loved her body into exhaustion, he'd shown her that he garnered the most soul-deep pleasure when he was in the midst of giving it to someone else.

Slade stroked her arm softly as he watched her lie next to him in bed. She was tranquil, barely moving, relaxed into the soft bedding surrounding them.

"Mmmm, feels good." She moaned and snuggled closer to him. "I could fall asleep if you keep doing that."

"Good. Means I get to start my day doing what we just did again."

"I wouldn't be the least bit upset if my day started like this night has ended. Too bad I have to be an adult tomorrow morning and attend a work meeting."

Slade could feel the tension moving through her body as she spoke about tomorrow's concerns. She'd been relaxed since they'd come down off their orgasmic high. He'd been barely able to move enough muscles to breathe after the intensity of their coupling, let alone tense up enough that someone else would notice it. There had to be something serious going on at her work for it to intrude on their good time like this.

"What kind of work do you do?"

"I'm a chemist." A heavy breath followed her utterance as if the three-worded sentence was just too much for her to bear.

That bothered Slade. He wasn't exactly certain why, but he knew it just felt wrong to watch her in any form of discomfort. He'd known it when she walked into that lounge last night. It was the first thing that drew his attention to her.

Sure, he'd noticed her physical beauty—he'd have to have been blind not to—but it wasn't the thing that made him want to think of her beyond his initial appreciation for her physical form.

Beautiful women weren't exactly rare finds in his circle. Having money meant you could surround yourself with pretty things whenever you wanted. But Mandisa's beauty was clouded by the weight of something. He didn't know what it was, only that it was real and tangible, as evidenced by the change in her body language now.

For some reason Slade hadn't quite figured out yet, from the very moment he'd noticed her burden, he'd wanted to relieve her of it.

He gathered her in his arms and held her tightly in his hold, hoping somehow his strength alone would be enough to ease her discomfort.

"Problems on the job?"

She nodded her head absently. "Yeah."

"What? Your boss pissing you off?"

"If it were that simple, I'd just find another job," she answered.

"Then what?"

"I am the boss, but that's the problem. I became a chemist because I loved science, loved creating new things with my science. Eighteen months ago, some major changes happened in the company, and I ended up becoming the boss. Running a business is fine for those that really want it.

But I'd rather be lost in my lab than dealing with the crap bosses have to."

Kindred spirits.

He knew exactly what she meant. Logan Industries was his birthright. Something passed down through four generations of his maternal kin. It was the last connection he had to his late mama and her family. On most days Slade wished he could hand the worries of his family's company to someone else. His heart was firmly planted on his horse ranch in Austin, but his body was shackled to an office in the city.

There'd been so many times he'd thought to walk away, just let his father have it all. But then he knew if he did Bull would tarnish it the way he did everything else beautiful in his life.

"Take it from me, darlin', don't let anyone steal your joy. If being the boss ain't what you want, set yourself free."

She turned in his arms then, placing a gentle kiss on his lips, running a careful finger through his hair. "You make it sound so simple, Slade."

"It is."

"I wish it were, but it's not."

"Let me ask you this. If you had a magic wand that could instantly take you away from this situation, allow you to give it all up in the snap of your fingers, would you use it?"

With no hesitation she whispered, "In a heartbeat."

"Then there's your answer. Let it go."

She leaned in and kissed him. Deepening it, allowing the tension in her body to bleed out with each press of her flesh against his. "I'm still not certain it's as easy as you make it seem. But when you say it, I want it to be."

"If there's ever any way I can help you make it simple, you call me, and I'll do everything I can to make it so."

She offered him a smile in return for his promise, and he suddenly felt like the wealthiest man in the world.

"You know what is simple, Slade?"

He gave his head a brief shake.

"Forget what I said earlier about having to adult tomorrow. The decision to spend the night with you, that's as easy and simple as it gets."

Slade burrowed into the soft warmth pressed against him. The front of his chest, groin, and legs were on fire, and his sleep-drunk mind couldn't immediately decipher why. The heat wasn't burning him, so he figured it must be a good thing and snuggled closer to the source.

As he was just about to doze off again, he heard the repetitive sound of a bird chirping. It was cute enough the first time, but as more moments passed the sound picked at his ability to reclaim his precious sleep.

Needing to shut it off, he turned away from the glorious heat he'd been wrapped up in. His body, instantly cold once he'd lost contact with the source of the inferno in his bed, shivered at the loss of heat. He slapped his uncoordinated palm around until it finally made contact with something that felt electronic in his hand.

He lifted it to his face and fought to open, then focus his eyes on what was in front of him. He was conscious enough to realize it was a phone he was looking at. He put it to his ear and said hello, but the sound still continued. He pulled it away from his ear and forced his eyes to focus on the shiny face. When he could see, there was a flashing message across the face of it that read:

10am meeting w/Lori Harris of VC at Oceanview Hotel

Re: Sweet Sadie's

Dammit. Either his father or Lori had put this on his calendar and set that notification. Every alert he had was set to vibrate because Slade couldn't stand the sound of cell-phone notifications pinging all over the place. Being an executive for a company like Logan Industries, his phone was constantly going off. An audible alarm sounding incessantly throughout the day would drive him insane.

He went to unlock the home screen and turn the sound off, but it kept denying him access. Just when he was ready to throw the thing across the room, he felt a warm hand snake over his arm and pull the device from his hand. Mandisa silenced the noise, looked at it for a minute with a single opened eye before tossing the now silent gadget back on the nightstand.

The slight press of comforting fingers drawing circles against his chest calmed Slade. The motion soothed him, lulled him back into the restful sleep the alarm had rudely pulled him from.

Slade slept until he heard a hard vibration against the nightstand and pulled himself up in bed. He didn't have to wonder if Mandisa was still with him. Her lack of comforting heat against his skin alerted him to her absence.

He picked up the phone to read the incoming text, a smile blooming across his face when he saw Mandisa's name as the sender of the message.

Sorry my phone woke you.

Had to leave to get ready for meeting.

Done by lunch. You wanna hang later?

Hell, yes, he wanted to hang later. He typed out a quick response and looked at the time. He had about an hour before he had to be downstairs to meet Lori for this meeting. He picked up the room phone on the nightstand and placed a breakfast order with room service. Hearty food and a fresh batch of coffee were the means he had of coping with this bullshit Bull had placed on his plate. Better to go ahead and get it over with. At least then he could spend some time with Mandisa.

He showered and changed just in time to hear the tap at his door. When he opened it, a young man pushing a cart laden with several covered platters and a pot of coffee was waiting on the other side.

While Slade sat and ate he thought about the fiery night he'd spent buried so deep inside Mandisa. His cock was twitching just thinking about what it felt like to be sheathed inside her. From the moment they'd met, he'd somehow known the two of them would go up like dried tinder once they touched. What he hadn't banked on was how content he'd feel while providing a listening ear to her.

Thinking about her made him lift his phone and find her message again.

Sorry my phone woke you.

Had to leave to get ready for meeting.

Done by lunch. You wanna hang later?

There was something different about the message this time. The words were the same, he was sure, but with coffee and food in his belly, his brain was actually functioning again, comprehending the language in which he was literate.

"Sorry my phone woke you." He read the words aloud and turned them over in his head. "Her phone? That was my phone."

He switched screens, pulling up his calendar to view the events of the day, but there were none. There was no meeting listed with Lori. Was he dreaming? He distinctly remembered being woken out of his sleep by that annoying calendar alarm from his phone.

"Except all of your notification alarms are set to vibrate."

Sorry my phone woke you.

He read the first line of the text again. Why would

Mandisa have a message about a meeting with Lori Harris of Venus Cosmetics on her phone?

"That doesn't make any sense," he mumbled softly into his coffee cup as he thought on the subject. It wasn't until he'd brought a tasty-looking slice of thick-cut bacon halfway to his mouth a rushed thought filled his mind. The only person Lori is scheduled to meet with today was Sweet Sadie's Sadie King. Why the hell would Mandisa be there?

Convinced there had to be some sort of mix-up, he dialed Lori's number and waited for her to answer.

"Morning, Slade. You ready for our meeting with Sweet Sadie's?"

"Yeah, about that. Didn't you say our contact was Sadie King? You have any dealings with her? Can you give me any insight into what I'm going up against?"

"We're not meeting with Sadie King. She passed away a little over a year ago when we first began talks with them about some sort of partnership."

Lori's answer made the food in his gut sit there like a weighted rock. He closed his eyes and pinched the bridge of his nose before he spoke again. "Then who are we dealing with, Lori?"

Lori's reply was quick and light. "Her daughter, Dr. Mandisa Avery."

"Well, shit."

"Excuse me?" Lori countered, waiting for Slade to explain himself. Except he didn't really have an explanation. Or at the very least, he didn't have an explanation that would make this situation sound any less shitty than it was turning out to be.

How fucked was it that the beautiful woman he'd met two days ago, the goddess whose body he'd had the pleasure of worshipping last night and hoped to worship again, was also the woman his father had sent Slade to steal a company from?

"Slade?" Lori questioned him, her concern evident over the phone line. "You okay?"

"Yeah, Lori...never better."

Mandisa fought the smile that threatened to appear on her face as she returned to the very same hotel lobby she'd rushed out of a couple of hours ago. The memory of the delectable things Slade did to her in his hotel room, how skilled he was with his cock, made her shudder.

So not the time for this, Mandisa. Get your head in the game.

She hoped the internal reprimand was enough to school herself into her respectable Dr. Avery persona. Mandisa may have enjoyed hours of Slade Hamilton's touch, but Dr. Avery was the person who needed to rock this presentation.

She tightened her fingers around the trendy designer attaché case in her hand. The slight but discernable presence of her tiny laptop reassured her of her purpose in this building. After the meeting was over she could lose herself in Slade all over again. Right now, however, it was time for business.

Even without having seen Lori Harris prior to this meeting, Mandisa was able to spot her the moment Mandisa stepped into the hotel's restaurant. Coiffed blonde hair pulled into a fashionable roll. Her makeup neatly applied to give off that airbrushed appearance usually attained by a professional's skilled hands.

Like must have recognized like because before Mandisa reached the table, Lori was standing, waving Mandisa forward.

"Dr. Avery, thank you for meeting with me this morning."

"Please, call me Mandisa. And thank you for taking the time to hear my proposal."

Lori nodded as she motioned for the waiter to come to their table. "How about we start this proposal off right with some coffee and breakfast? You can tell me about your company and product, and hopefully by the time the check comes, we'll have something positive to celebrate."

Mandisa wasted no time delving into her practiced spiel. She'd been raised in this company by her mother. There wasn't anything about it she didn't know. The mission of the company, to serve the average woman who didn't have the resources to buy high-end cosmetics, but still wanted to look good, was drilled into her head before she was old enough to wear Sweet Sadie products. Although they made shades that flattered all complexions, the company made a special effort to focus on women of color, because it was so much easier to find drugstore-brand makeup that catered to fairer complexions.

Lori appeared interested in Mandisa's proposal, especially the sales record and the current demand for Sweet Sadie's Signature products. Mandisa knew she'd done what she was supposed to do when Lori stopped sipping her coffee in order to pay closer attention to the laptop slideshow Mandisa was using as a supplemental tool to her presentation.

"Wow, that's extremely impressive, Mandisa. Your Sweet Sadie's Signature cosmetics and body lotions line is exactly the type of thing Venus is looking for. We're one of the top three cosmetics companies in the world, but we still seem to be lacking when it comes to catering to our clientele with darker skin tones. Frankly, we've been looking for a quality product like yours for a long time."

"Does that mean Venus will invest in Sweet Sadie's?"

"Well, we certainly want Sweet Sadie's to be part of the Venus family. But before I can make any offers, or rather counter offers to your investment proposal, my new director wishes to meet with you."

It wasn't the immediate yes Mandisa was hoping for, but it certainly wasn't a no either. She checked this meeting off in the win column of her mental tally and returned her attention to the woman sitting before her. "Do you have any idea when your director would like to meet?"

"Considering he's walking across the room as we speak, I'd say right now."

Mandisa turned around to look toward the entrance behind their table. The first thing she saw was a familiar cowboy hat. Panic began to settle in her stomach when the owner of the hat's face came into focus. When the man was finally standing at their table, Lori stood to make introductions.

"Dr. Mandisa Avery, the new director of Venus Cosmetics, Slade Hamilton."

Mandisa watched Slade tip his hat to her, then Lori. Lori gathered her things, then left the two of them alone.

When he sat, they both just stared at each other. This was surreal. It couldn't be happening. She'd spent the night letting this man take her to sexual heights she hadn't experienced since...well ever, and now he was sitting across from her ready to do business.

"Mandisa," he began.

"You son of a bitch. You played me. You set me up from the moment I walked into that fucking lounge."

He held up both hands as he shook his head. "I had no idea I'd meet you in that club. I certainly didn't know you were the person I'd be meeting with to discuss an investment deal."

"You must really think I'm stupid." She spat the words

across the table in a quiet but furious fashion. "You really expect me to believe you didn't know who the hell I was at Syn? That you didn't target my ass, plan this entire seduction to give you a better advantage in business negotiations?"

"Mandisa, you can't really believe that."

"Exactly what am I supposed to believe, Slade? This is too much of coincidence to be accidental. You planned this shit. Unfortunately, the joke's on you. The dick was sublime, but there isn't a man alive whose meat is good enough to fuck me out of my company."

"Enough," Slade shouted as he slammed his hand down on the table, bringing the attention of the other patrons and restaurant employees to their heated discussion. He cleared his throat, and when the nosy Nellies in the restaurant returned to their own conversations, Slade lowered his voice to resume his explanation to Mandisa. "I did not seduce you with any ulterior motive. The only thing I wanted was to spend time with you."

He let some of the anger bleed out of his voice as he reached his hand across the table to gently caress hers.

"I promise you, when I took you to my bed last night, I had no idea who you were. Everything that happened between us in that room came from a sincere place, darlin'."

There it was, that damn word, the one that always felt like silk every time he directed it at her. She wanted to hold on to her anger, but slowly it ebbed away. "You really didn't know?"

He shook his head. "I didn't."

She took a deep breath and leaned into the back of her chair. "What do we do now? Can we even do this deal now?"

"We can," he answered. "I'm just not sure you'll actually want to when you hear what I'm offering."

"What do you mean?"

"Mandisa, you're looking for an investor. It's not really

Venus' style to invest in other companies. We don't want partnership, we want ownership."

"What?"

"We want to purchase your company and bring you and it on board to the Venus family. Sweet Sadie's is a success because of your formula. We want to bring you on as the lead chemist in a new line targeted for people of color."

"So, instead of owning my own company, I'd just be another employee at yours?" If the way she flinched when she finished her sentence was any indication, he understood how she felt about that without her having to say it. "Why would I come work for you when I can just continue to work for myself?"

"Because according to the conversation we had last night, you don't really want the burden of running your mother's company anyway."

"You know what, Slade? Fuck you!"

He smiled, his charm seemingly unfazed by her directive. "Been there, done that, hope to do it again. But that's not the point. The point is you told me last night that running this business was never something you wanted. It was always your mama's dream. You just wanted to use your science to make things."

She rolled her eyes and crossed her arms over her chest before she spoke. "I told that to Slade, a nice man who was showing me a good time and allowing me to relax. I wasn't talking to the director of a company that's looking to buy me out."

"As luck would have it, those two men are one and the same. Mandisa, last night I told you I wanted nothing more than to take all your worry away. That I wanted to show you how peaceful and fulfilling life could be when you're focused on the important things. We didn't know I could help you then. Let me do it now."

She watched him, watched sincerity paint his features and twinkle in his blue eyes. It was there last night when they were naked, eating burgers and fries in his bed, and she'd believed him.

But can I trust him now?

"Slade, you can't just whisk me away and magically take away my life, my responsibilities."

"Darlin', you don't know this about me, but I can pretty much make anything happen if I put my mind to it. Let me show you there's another way, a better way."

"What are you suggesting?"

"Spend some time with me. Come down to Austin, let me show you all the reasons why I love my city. Let me take care of you. If you aren't fully convinced that selling your business to me is the best thing you could do for yourself afterwards, then I'll bring you back home. No harm, no foul."

If only it were that easy. The idea of spending her days with Slade, not worried about spreadsheets, account balances, inventory, and government regulations regarding the creation of cosmetic products was tempting. Considering how magical their night spent together had been, the idea of running off to his quaint little ranch, living a simple life, appealed beyond good reason.

"Slade. I can't do this. I have a life here, a business. I can't just leave."

"You have employees, a manager perhaps? There has to be someone you can trust to look after your stores. Let the people who work for you do their job, and you go have some fun. Three weeks. That's all I'm asking. It's not an eternity, and it's not enough time to do any damage to your business."

He was right. Kandi was phenomenal at her job. She could handle all five stores for any length of time, but that wasn't the issue. Mandisa belonged in Brooklyn running her mother's stores.

"Slade, it's a ridiculous idea. Nothing you say or do in Texas is going to impact my decision. I'm not selling Sweet Sadie's."

"You really do underestimate me, darlin'. How about we make a little wager? You come spend three weeks with me in Austin. I'll show you all the city has to offer. I'll even take you to visit my little spread of land and my horses for a few days. You completely extract yourself from Sweet Sadie's. The only time Kandi will be allowed to contact you will be in emergent situations. When those three weeks are up, if I've made my case, and you love everything about what I'm offering you—"

"A lowly job versus the ownership of my own company?"

He shook his head. "Your freedom," he answered. "If you don't absolutely love being free of all of this and just getting back to the science, getting back to the thing you love, then I will double your asking amount of investment capital for the same percentage you originally offered."

Double?

She'd asked him for a five-million-dollar investment for fifteen percent of her company. Could she really afford to turn down the ten million dollars winning this bet would yield?

"What's the matter, darlin'? You scared you'll lose?"

Three weeks in Texas with him, and she'd walk away with ten million dollars in hand for Sweet Sadie's. It should've been the easiest decision of her life, but it wasn't. The decision was hers to make, but somehow, she felt Slade's powers of persuasion might be dangerous enough to become a problem for her.

She shook her head. She couldn't overthink this. Her company needed this money, and it was being laid at her feet. All she had to do was say yes.

"So what's your answer, darlin'?"

4

"I really don't understand why you're tripping about all of this."

Mandisa rolled her eyes silently as Kandi braided extensions into Mandisa's hair. Of course her friend couldn't understand why Mandisa was so upset. Kandi lived life as it came. She didn't plan too far ahead, and she didn't dwell on the past. Unfortunately, life didn't afford Mandisa the luxury of living without cares.

"Kandi." Mandisa sighed. "He's a perfect stranger. A man who could turn out to be a threat to everything my mom built. I can't just take him at his word that he's not trying to screw me."

"I don't think you really have to worry about that, considering he's already screwed you."

Mandisa huffed in frustration. This is what she got for sharing the details of her evening with Slade with her friend.

"Mandisa, I think you're making more of this than there needs to be. You may not know every detail about Slade's life, but at any time when you were with him, did you ever feel unsafe?"

Mandisa had experienced a myriad of emotions and sensations while in Slade's presence: levity, excitement, curiosity, desire, necessity. "No, I didn't feel unsafe with him."

"What about when he took you back to his hotel room? Were you worried for your safety then? What did you feel when you two were in bed together?"

Musing over Kandi's last question left a heavy pause in the air.

"Mandisa?" Kandi asked as she stopped braiding and walked around to kneel in front of a seated Mandisa. "Hey, did something happen last night? Did he do something to you, Mandisa?"

Mandisa shook her head quickly. "Not in the way you mean. He was a perfect gentleman." Warmth traveled from the center of Mandisa's chest, beaming outward to the rest of her body as she called up memories from the few hours spent in Slade's arms. "It's so strange, Kandi. I've known this man less than five days, yet when we were in his hotel room, it didn't feel like meaningless sex. He was tender, considerate, passionate, all the while taking care of my needs, not seeming at all concerned with his own."

"And you have a problem with this why?"

Okay, out loud she did have to admit her concerns sounded ridiculous. How many women, herself included, had she heard voice their desires for a man to treat them the way Slade treated Mandisa?

"That sounds like lovemaking to me," Kandi added. Her lips lifted in an impish grin.

"Honestly, Kandi, that's what it felt like." If she were honest, that was the thing that made the entire experience unsettling. She was expecting a quick roll in the hay accompanied by a couple of simple orgasms. What she'd received was a total mind-body experience that touched the recesses of her spirit every time Slade brought her to climax.

Mandisa looked up at her friend to see a soft smile on Kandi's face. It was familiar, beaming with all sorts of affection and encouragement that Mandisa needed at this moment.

"Mandisa," Kandi continued. Her words were soft and measured, intended to calm and soothe. "Don't you think you deserve this? After everything you've been through since you found out Ms. Sadie was sick, don't you deserve something light and fun?"

Light and fun she could do. However, this thing with Slade didn't feel all that light. She shook her head, trying to silence the doubts running around her mind. Kandi was right, Slade had been nothing but a gentleman. She didn't have to worry about her safety—not her physical safety, anyway.

"Come on and finish braiding my hair," Mandisa whined playfully. "I'm not going anywhere for the next three weeks without a protective style."

Kandi gave Mandisa's shoulder a playful push and returned to her perch behind Mandisa, quickly returning to the intricate braiding pattern she'd been in the middle of creating. Mandisa allowed the repetitive movements of Kandi's fingers in her hair to lull her into needed calm. *All of this is going to turn out fine. Everything will be okay.* Now if she could just believe the mantra she was chanting in her head, all would be right with the world.

Slade waited in the private hanger, glancing every few moments at his watch. He seemed to be doing a good deal of that when it came to Mandisa. Waiting and patience weren't really Slade's strong suit. He'd made her a good offer. He was confident in that. Slade always made good business deals. It was never his objective to cheat the person or entity sitting across the table from him. Although he knew the idea was sound, he also understood Mandisa was going to fight him tooth and nail for this.

He couldn't blame her. This was a family business, something she worked on with her late mother. He understood the sentiment. He understood what it was to want to be close to the loved ones you'd lost by clinging to the things they'd left behind. He was doing the very same when it came to Logan Industries. The difference? He actually enjoyed his job and the company. Mandisa didn't really seem to be sharing the same experience.

He also couldn't see the sense in her maintaining so much stress to keep a cosmetics business running. He enjoyed looking at pretty lips and eyes just as much as the next man, but was it truly worth sacrificing so much for?

He didn't like the idea of Mandisa being stressed. Slade couldn't pinpoint why her stress level was such a concern, but remembering their conversation in bed made him want to help her any way he could. This buyout was the best way he could help her.

"Whatever you're thinking about looks about as fun as a root canal."

Slade's smile was tugging at his lips before he had a chance to lay eyes on her. "Glad to see you made it, darlin'." He stood up slowly, and tipped his hat to her. "Forgive me, but I can't seem to remember what I was thinking of. The sight of you just resets my brain."

He allowed his hungry gaze to slide down and then up the length of her body and took the vision she made in. A trendy pair of white tennis shoes whose tops were covered by the bottoms of her jeans adorned her feet. Long thick legs covered in dark-wash denim accented the deep curves of her hips, thighs, and ass. The dark fabric of her jeans in perfect balance with the red fitted T-shirt that read "Brooklyn Strong" across her full bosom. The entire outfit was the perfect mix of comfortable and sexy.

He pulled his eyes up to her face and noticed she'd changed her hair from the shoulder-length coils he'd loved running his fingers through to what appeared to be an endless amount of small, long braids that fell nearly to her waist.

"You changed your hair." He couldn't help but smile when he said it. Every nuance of this woman seemed to make him smile uncontrollably, even something as usually benign to him as style of hair.

She raised her hands to it, fingering the small braids, making the electric-blue highlights within the dark hair color visible to him.

"Box braids," she answered. "It's a protective style. Taking care of my hair can be a little cumbersome when I travel. Having it braided up makes it easier to take care of while I'm away from home."

Slade nodded, as if he'd understood anything about what she was referring to, and moved closer to her. He leaned down, his smile pulling wider as she stepped into his embrace and moved up on her toes to meet him. Circling a hand around to the small of her back, he pulled Mandisa to him until he could feel the welcome weight of her body against him. The moment their lips pressed together, Slade savored the sweet and spicy taste of cinnamon as Mandisa pushed her tongue inside his mouth. Smart, sexy, and in full command of what she wanted, this woman was beginning to become addictive.

"You ready to show me a good time, cowboy?"

He nodded and was about to speak when his phone began vibrating in his pocket. He held up a finger to excuse himself when he saw his father's name flashing across the screen. "Why don't you go on up and get comfortable on the plane? I'll join you as soon as I'm done with this call."

She kissed him again, then headed toward the plane. He waited until she was safely inside before he answered.

"What do you want, Bull?"

"Is the deal done? I called Lori, but she couldn't give me an answer. Said you'd taken over the negotiations yourself."

"I did. This sale deserves a light touch. I can't just bulldoze in. The owner isn't looking to sell. I've invited her down to Austin to see our facilities firsthand."

There was a pause, his father inevitably turning his wheels, figuring out all the angles on the situation. "You thinking if she sees what we have to offer it will sway her to play ball?"

That wasn't the only thing Slade was hoping for with respect to Mandisa, but Bull didn't need to know all that. "Pretty much," Slade answered.

"All right. You bring her down to Texas, wine and dine her, and get this deal done. I don't have to remind you what's riding on this, Slade. Get me this company and formula, or Venus is gone."

The phone call ended with a click, and Slade was left with Bull's threat ringing in his ears. His protective instincts began to spark. Everything in him screamed for Slade to protect what was his. As he climbed the stairs to the plane, it didn't escape his notice that when his total focus should be on Logan Industries, he wasn't thinking about his business at all. Instead, his only concern within that moment was the woman waiting for him on the private plane.

Mandisa was pulled from sleep when she felt the weird pressure change in her ears. Annoyed by the sensation, she burrowed closer to the solid and warm cushion of Slade's shoulder.

"We're descending," he whispered as he placed a gentle kiss atop her head. The deep timbre of his voice sending tiny shocks of electricity through her system made her nerve endings buzz. There was just something soothing about the sound of this man's voice. Maybe that was how he'd convinced her to go along with this crazy wager of his? His voice had probably hypnotized her.

She smiled at the ridiculous notion, but aside from Slade using some kind of voodoo on her even as she sat on the descending plane, she couldn't explain why she'd agreed to this nonsense. Okay, double her asking amount was definitely an incentive to travel down to Austin with a stranger she hardly knew. However, the way her body instinctively pressed closer to his wasn't about the money he'd offered her for Sweet Sadie's. It was intuitive, something her body just knew to do, like breathing, without thought.

She cracked her eyes open and peered at the window across the aisle. It was still dark outside. They'd left at one in the morning New York time. Four hours later, a shift in time zone, and they were meeting the still-dark morning sky of Austin, Texas.

She followed Slade down the runway steps and accepted the hand he offered her when she reached the bottom.

"Welcome to Texas, darlin'." His voice and smile, just as big and bold as everything else on him, welcomed her.

"What'cha think?" He spread his arms wide and turned in a broad circle.

She took gentle fingers and massaged her newly braided scalp gingerly. "Well, considering we're on a tarmac that looks pretty much the same as every other runway, not much. I do have one question, though."

He waited in expectation, nodding, encouraging her to continue.

She pulled her phone from the back pocket of her jeans and slid a finger across the screen to wake it. A brief glance at the illuminated background, and she returned her gaze to him.

"It's barely five in the damn morning. Why the hell is it already eighty-five damn degrees? This doesn't make any sense."

His grin didn't falter as he hooked a finger in her belt loop and pulled her to his chest. "If you're hot, Mandisa, all you gotta do is tell me. Ole Slade knows just how to put out your fire."

That crack was so disgustingly corny, but damn if her pussy didn't throb and get slick from just his words. Too embarrassed to admit this man had her panties wet without even touching her, she closed her eyes and rested her head against his defined pec while she took a deep breath.

Either she was going to get some control over herself, or she'd be too busy laid up with Slade, tasting every delicious inch of him, to see any of his precious Austin.

Getting through the airport to the passenger exit was relatively easy. Having the kind of company money to fly privately had its benefits, she presumed. As they walked through automatic airport doors, Slade headed toward a black SUV idling at the curb.

Slade opened the trunk, tossing their bags in the back, quickly returning to open the door for her. She sat down in the back passenger seat and smiled briefly at the quiet man sitting in the driver's seat.

When Slade opened the opposite door, the driver leaned out of his window, tossing Slade an annoyed flick of his hand. "One of y'all is getting in the front. I'm not your damn chauffer, Hamilton."

Slade leaned into the passenger door and shook his head. "Darlin', I'd normally ask a lady to take the front seat, but since I don't want this ill-tempered rascal's bad mood to rub off on you, I'll spare you the inconvenience of sitting next to him."

After Slade closed the door, she watched the driver as he scowled at Slade, who was slowly sauntering in front of the SUV.

When Slade was seated, he turned around halfway to address her. "Please forgive his manners, sweetie. Did he at least introduce himself before he started scowling?"

She smiled and leaned forward to make eye contact. "I'm the one whose manners are failing. I did enter his car without introducing myself." She offered him a hand before saying, "I'm Mandisa Avery." The driver looked at Slade for a moment, then pressed the dome light of the vehicle on before turning his attention fully to Mandisa.

"Aaron Nakai," he stated, shaking her hand firmly.

The amber light in the car illuminated the russet tone of Aaron's skin, the midnight-black eyes and the straight strands of hair that were gathered in a haphazard ponytail traveling endlessly down his back.

He was beautiful. There was really no other way to describe him. His features were all carved and masculine, but there was a delicate loveliness and quiet strength that seemed to shroud him. Just from a single glance, it was obvious he was a man who could handle himself, but Mandisa was certain there was something more to him gauging by the intensity behind his coal eyes.

"Hurry up and strap in, Hamilton." His voice was gruff as he pulled his attention from Mandisa and focused on Slade. "I was up at ass o'clock to pick you up on time. The least you could do is hustle a bit."

She watched as Slade leaned back into his seat, turning his head briefly to the side and winking at her as he mouthed, "*Watch this.*"

"If I promise to have Indira send you a pack of her special blend coffee, will that help you pull your head out of your ass?" Slade's offer seemed to fall on deaf ears, but he didn't seem worried about Aaron's silence.

Aaron was still and quiet for a moment longer before Mandisa watched him turn his head toward Slade. From his profile, she could see his eye widen slightly. *Damn, that must be some good coffee if it can get this man to stop scowling.*

"Make it two and we're even," Aaron grumbled quickly. He put the SUV in drive and pulled off into traffic without saying another word.

Damn, Slade was good. Even if this Indira's coffee was laced with the most addictive drug there was, the promise of it shouldn't have been enough to completely dispel Aaron's obvious annoyance at Slade. Slade's talent of knowing just what to say at the perfect time was the ingredient necessary to make this deal worth something.

Slade's smile caught Mandisa's eyes and forced the edges of her lips to bend in kind. It was good to know she wasn't the only one who succumbed to Slade's powers of persuasion. Apparently men and women alike couldn't resist the big Texan's charms.

She snuggled back into the cushions of her seat. As she closed her eyes in preparation for the ride a cold chill ran the length of her spine.

Laugh now. She heard the words ringing in her head as clearly as if she'd spoken them aloud. The only reason she knew she hadn't was the lack of response from the other occupants of the vehicle. *But will it be that funny when he's using his charms on you to swindle you out of your company?*

And just that quickly, all those doubts that plagued her up until the moment she'd stepped on the plane in New York were back.

Welcome to fucking Austin, indeed.

5

"Welcome to the Havenheart Ranch," Slade boasted proudly as he helped Mandisa out of the SUV. Once she was on her feet, she turned around in a circle to take in the scenery around her.

Mandisa was instantly uncomfortable at the sight of his home. She was expecting a plush apartment somewhere. Something that felt rich, pretty, and superficial, reminding her of who he truly was and why she was there with him. What she met instead were endless peaks of proud hills and bottomless valleys that cradled calm water. A ranch filled with reddish-brown earth, verdant grass, golden blades of hay, and other ranch-type elements a city girl like her only saw on television show backdrops.

She turned again in the circular driveway to face his home, again divested of her assumptions when a modest two-story house sat where she'd assumed a sprawling mansion would be. His house wasn't small. She'd wager there were at least four or five bedrooms in it, just from her current view. However, it looked like something out of a common suburban neighborhood, with nothing gaudy or attention-grabbing about it.

Everything from the warm beige and brown earth tones of the exterior to the colorful garden along its perimeter invited its guests to relax and take refuge inside. The soothing scenery instantly put Mandisa on edge. She immediately distrusted anything in this man's world that encouraged her to let her guard down.

Never trust when things are too nice. Nice is an illusion.

"What do you think?" Slade's question pulled her from her musings. She was just about to answer when the front door to the house opened, and a short, middle-aged African-American woman whose smile and eyes were marked with wisdom and knowledge ambled out onto the porch. She was petite, but Mandisa could detect the cloak of confidence she wore as she stood at the top of the front porch stairs with her hands mounted firmly on her hips.

"Is that my Slade?" she asked, her smile brightening, curving her lips even deeper than before.

Slade grabbed Mandisa's hand and pulled her toward the porch. "Sho' is, Mama Indy, and I brought a friend."

Slade hopped up the few stairs and only released Mandisa's hand to wrap both arms around the older woman, swooping her up into a giant hug that lifted her off her feet.

"You silly man, g'on put me down." It was obvious to anyone witnessing the scene that the woman Slade referred to as Mama Indy had no real fire in her reprimand.

Slade gently settled the elder woman back on the porch, placing a sweet peck on her brown cheek. "You miss me, Mama Indy?"

She laughed. "'Course I did." She patted his arm lovingly before she turned her sights on Mandisa. "Now who is this pretty young lady with the beautiful smile?"

It wasn't until Mandisa played the woman's words over

quickly in her own head that Mandisa realized her lips were, indeed, curving into a happy smile. How could Mandisa not smile? The scene between the two people before her was so tender and loving, not unlike the many Mandisa had shared with her own mother.

"This is Mandisa Avery. We met in New York, and she's here to spend a little time with me and possibly do a little business." Slade turned to Mandisa, stepping slightly to the side. "Mandisa, this is my former nanny and my surrogate mother, Mrs. Indira Price. She's one of two women responsible for raising me."

By the twinkle in his eye, Mandisa could feel Slade's sincerity when he spoke of the matron. Mandisa offered her a hand in greeting, only to have it shoved away. In a split second, she found herself enclosed in strong, thin arms that held her in place as the elder woman rocked Mandisa in her arms.

"You're a friend of my Slade's. Makes you family. Family gets hugs."

A little thrown by the woman's friendliness—New Yorkers didn't share personal space with strangers; they had to ease into that sort of physical affection—Mandisa fell into the unexpected comfort of her captor's arms.

"I'm a friend of Slade's. How come you never greet me with hugs?" The warm spell of the embrace was broken when Aaron spoke from behind them.

"'Cause you're trouble, and I don't invite trouble into my home."

Aaron waved a dismissive hand as he walked up to the porch and dropped a loud smack of a kiss on the matron's waiting cheek. "You know you love me, old woman."

"Call me old again, and I'll take my shotgun to your hide."

Aaron threw both his hands in the air and backed away

slowly into the house, leaving the three of them alone on the porch.

"Y'all chil'en come on inside and get some of this here food I cooked up."

Mandisa hadn't even thought about food, but the moment they all shuffled into the house, the distinct smell of blended spices and bacon—oh, God, real bacon—and something baked and buttery called to Mandisa through the air.

"You hungry, darlin'?" Slade's question barely registered as Mandisa looked at a full spread of enticing food waiting at the breakfast table.

"If I wasn't before, I am now." Mandisa followed Slade's lead and moved over to the slush sink to wash her hands. Hands now clean and dry, Mandisa sat down, taking her eyes briefly away from the food to see Aaron pulling his napkin from the table and spreading it across his lap.

"Can't wait to dig in to this food, Mama Indy. You got any of your special blend coffee around?" Aaron picked up his fork as he spoke, filling his plate with eggs and thick-cut bacon, the kind you couldn't buy in a pack but had to have sliced from a slab at a butcher. Mandisa's mouth watered. Bacon was her weakness. Her mother used to make slab bacon on Sunday mornings before church. It was salty, and tasty, and everything that was perfect about a good cut of bacon.

When Aaron went to stuff his fork into the mound of food he'd shoveled onto his plate and attempted to lift it to his mouth, Indira stood with her arms crossed and her eyebrow lifted. The silent cue was all Aaron needed to drop his fork back onto the plate and fold his hands patiently in front of him.

"Now let us bow our heads." Indira led them into a brief prayer of thanks, and then silence ensued. The only noise from any of them was the minor clang of the metal cutlery touching the ceramic dishes.

When Indira placed another plate of warm, freshly made biscuits in front of Mandisa and motioned for her to take another, Mandisa had to put up her hands in surrender.

"I can't, Mrs. Price. There's just no room."

"You call me Mama Indy. None of this Mrs. Price stuff," she rebuffed. "At least have a cup of my coffee before these boys drink it all."

Mandisa smiled and nodded, conceding to the offer of coffee. She really didn't have room for another morsel of food, but she'd take a few sips of the coffee to appease this treasure of a woman.

Mandisa added cream and sugar to her cup and grabbed the handle of the ceramic mug. When she lifted the cup halfway to her lips she felt the weight of Slade and Aaron's gazes locked on her.

"Is there something wrong? Do I have food on my face?"

The two shook their heads in tandem and waited silently. Too full to concern herself with their weird stares, she shook her head and took the first sip of the coffee.

Mandisa wasn't much of a coffee drinker. She'd occasionally order one of those iced designer coffees that she couldn't pronounce from the local chain, but even her uncultured palate recognized she was sampling greatness.

"Dear God, that's good." She pulled her lips unwillingly from the cup at the demand of her lungs and their miserable need for the breath she was holding. The flavor was rich, yet smooth. There wasn't a hint of the usual bitterness she experienced when she purchased a cup of coffee. "For the love of all that is holy." Mandisa paused a minute to take another sip. "What is in this? There's gotta be some sort of controlled substance in this. It's like crack. I can't stop drinking it."

The scene in the car where Slade was bartering with

Aaron, using Indira's "special blend" as a boon, made so much more sense now. This nectar of the gods masquerading as coffee was addictive.

Mandisa heard laughter filling the room. She presumed it was coming from the two men sitting at the table with her, but she couldn't truly be certain because her nose was almost completely in the mug as she tipped it high to get every drop she possibly could.

When Mandisa finally put the cup down, Indira appeared again, asking if she wanted more. "I do, but I really can't. Will there be any later?"

"For you? Anytime you want it." She offered Mandisa another warm smile and motioned for Mandisa to follow her. "Let's leave the cleaning to these two while I show you to your room."

Halfway in a food coma, Mandisa didn't resist when Indira moved her along the halls and up the stairs until she was standing in the middle of a large bedroom equipped with a fireplace and four-poster bed to boot.

Damn, do Texans do everything big?

"This is the guestroom closest to the master suite. Slade requested I get it ready for you. If you need anything and I'm not around, you can just walk down to the end of the hall, and you'll find him."

"You don't live here with Slade, Mrs…Mama Indy?"

The older woman gave her a dismissive wave. "Chile, no! Slade is a grown man. He doesn't need his mama up under him. I live in a guesthouse on the east bank of the property. Aaron is Slade's foreman. He picks me up every morning on his way to the horses and drives me home at the end of the day. He lives on property too."

Mandisa attempted to answer, and a huge yawn escaped her mouth. "Please forgive me," Mandisa managed to utter at the tail end of the long sigh. "I guess the nap I caught on the plane wasn't enough."

"G'on and get yourself together for bed. I'll bring you lunch if you want it. If not, you can join us for supper around six in the evening."

Before Mandisa could nod her acknowledgement, Indira was on her way out the door, and Mandisa was looking for her bags. Once she was showered and settled into the plush mattress of the bed, the warmth she'd felt from the food and fellowship downstairs started to recede, and a slow chill began to build inside her.

She was in a lovely room, at her host's request, receiving the royal treatment from his family/staff, and here she was feeling hollow and displeased as she curled up in this bed alone. *Maybe he did only bring you here for work. Maybe whatever you two were doing in New York was a one-off.*

"God woman, how ungrateful and flaky can you be? You said you didn't want him thinking he could sex you out of your company. Now you're mad because he seems to be honoring that? Get it together."

She balled up her fist and punched the innocent pillow next to her, getting in another shot when she heard a knock at the door.

"It's Slade. Can I come in?"

She scooted up in the bed, crossing her legs Indian style beneath the comforter as she gave Slade permission to enter the room.

"I won't keep you long," he murmured as he walked over to the side of the bed, sitting gently beside her as he reached for her hand. "I just wanted to make certain you were settled in."

"I am. Your home is lovely." Her words were quick, and for some reason she couldn't find the strength to look him in the eyes. He knew her, saw too much of her whenever she gazed at him. She didn't want him to see how disappointed she was that he didn't want her, just her company. "Thank you for bringing me here."

She felt his soft touch travel from her hand, up the length of her arm, until his fingers were lifting her chin and she couldn't hide from his questioning eyes any longer.

"I've set up a visit at Venus' labs here in Austin. Thought you'd enjoy getting to see some of our facilities."

And so it begins.

"If we get out there by early afternoon, we can make it back in time for supper."

He's not wasting any time getting down to business.

"One of our chemists will be on hand to answer any of your questions about the facility and its capabilities."

She held her hands palm side up with fingers spread in a halting motion. "Can we take a pause for minute, Slade!" She winced at the shrill sound of her voice. She didn't think she'd intended for it to sound so harsh. But, damn, could she get a minute to breathe before he was shuffling her off to his lab?

However unintended, the sharpness of her tone broke through, and he dropped his fingers from her chin. A tight line appeared at the center of his brow as he peered down at her. "Mandisa? What's wrong?"

"I'm sorry," Mandisa began slowly. She closed her eyes to get her bearings back. She wanted to tell him he was pissing her off by rushing her into business matters she wasn't ready to address. She wanted to explain that the idea of focusing on business so soon after experiencing the warmth of his family tainted the wonderful feeling the morning's events had left her with. But when she thought about all those things she felt, all those things she wanted to reveal to him, she was left raw and exposed.

He's already putting his plan in motion. Don't show him a weakness he can exploit.

"I'm just a little tired after the trip and the meal. Could we maybe take a rain check on the tour today? Maybe in a day or two when I'm a little less tired and more focused, we can head out?"

Slade watched her carefully, as if assessing the truth in her words. Too afraid he'd pick up on the real reason behind her outburst, she snuggled down into the covers and closed her eyes.

After a moment or two of silence, Slade's weight shift on the bed and the warmth of his lips pressed against her cheek.

"Whenever you're ready, darlin'. Just get some rest."

A few moments later, she heard the quiet click of the door signaling his departure. She released a long breath of relief and let disappointment flood her. Yeah, she'd known there was going to be some business occurring on this trip, but she'd also hoped for some pleasure too. Unfortunately, between being placed in a separate room and Slade's desire to jump right into the business flow of things, it didn't look like there'd be much pleasure on this trip at all.

6

Slade stood outside of Mandisa's door puzzled by the events he'd just witnessed.

What the hell was that?

Mandisa claimed she was tired, but it wasn't fatigue he'd seen in her eyes. Fear, anger, disappointment, distrust, colored every inch of her, and for the life of him he couldn't understand why.

From the moment he'd met her, he'd gone out of his way to let her know nothing happened without her freely given consent. What on earth could make her distrustful of him after the wonderful time they'd had around the breakfast table that morning?

His body was tired from the back-and-forth travel over the past few days. However, his mind was still buzzing as it tried to lock in on the uneasiness he'd sensed pouring off Mandisa. Resigned to tabling it for later, Slade walked away from Mandisa's door and down the stairs. He made a quick stop at the kitchen counter and grabbed a treat, then headed straight for the stables.

He needed to see his other lady, the one he neglected all too often to handle something Bull dropped in his lap. He walked straight to the back of the barn until he'd reached the last stall. A long, amber-colored face framed with blonde hair bobbed up and down when she acknowledged Slade's presence.

"Hey, Queen-Sorrel. You miss me, girl?"

His red lady nodded and nuzzled into the gentle stroking Slade offered her. Time in Queen-Sorrel's presence always calmed Slade. Damn if he didn't need her. Slade pulled a sweet treat out of his pocket and held it just beneath the horse's mouth. With quick precision, she snatched the apple out of his opened palm, and he knew all was right in their relationship.

The pride he felt for this horse bordered on unhealthy at times. But Slade couldn't help it. She was perfectly made for him. He'd known it the moment he saw her ten years ago. She'd just called to him. She was big and brilliant, with as much grace as horses much smaller than her. She, like him, was blessed when it came to height and breadth. At seventeen hands, she stood taller than most American Quarters. Her solid build was a source of comfort for him. With her he could let go. He never had to worry about being careful how he handled her, or aware that he was bigger and stronger than everyone else around.

She'd been the reason he'd purchased this ranch and all the horse stock with it. Walking away from Queen-Sorrel just wasn't something he'd been able to do, then or now.

She nudged him with her head, the signal that she wanted to go out and play a bit. As tired as Slade was, he knew it made more sense to rest and then take her for a ride. But like always, whenever his lady asked for something, he had to indulge her. He reached inside the stall and gave her long neck a smooth stroke. The sound of footsteps coming his way made him pause long enough to see Aaron entering the stables.

"It must be real nice knowing all you have to do to get out of the shithouse with your women is bring them a kiss, a sweet treat, or a shiny bauble."

One corner of Slade's mouth lifted as Aaron spoke. He leaned close to his horse and whispered soothing murmurs in her ear. He pushed away from Queen-Sorrel's stall and faced his foreman and best friend. "Why? You jealous?"

"Hell yeah," Aaron answered. "I'm here all the time with Mama Indy, and she treats me like I'm fertilizer on the bottom of her shoes most days."

Slade waved a dismissive hand at his friend. Both Aaron and Mama played at fighting. But the truth was they each adored one another. It was just their way to fuss with each other all the time. It was the one reason Slade left Aaron in charge of his ranch. It wasn't just because he was an excellent horseman. And he was, Slade had no doubt of that.

Aaron had been Slade's best friend from the moment they'd met as boys. Each of them possessed an abiding love for animals and adventure that cemented their bond instantly. Before coming to Texas for law school, Aaron spent most of his life on a horse ranch much like Havenheart. There wasn't a better man Slade would trust with his horses and his land. But Slade kept Aaron here, paid him handsomely to take care of what Slade loved most—Mama Indy.

Slade had lost two of three women he'd loved. His birth mother when he was a small child, and his grandmother when he was just shy of manhood.

His grandmother had taken him in when his mother died, spared him from the hell Bull no doubt had planned for him. She'd loved him and spoiled him as any good grandmother should. But Indira Price was the one that loved him, nurtured him, and tanned his lily-white hide when he had more piss and vinegar in him than sense. That old woman was the last living piece of his heart, and when he couldn't be at the ranch like he wanted, there wasn't a man he'd trust more than Aaron to look after her.

"It's always so damn easy for you," Aaron chided.

Easy was relative as far as Slade was concerned. Yeah, he didn't have a problem gaining the interest of a pretty woman. But what did that matter when he still came home to an empty house?

Slade gave himself a mental shake at that thought. He wasn't ready to settle down with anyone. He liked his freedom too much. But lately, it was getting harder and harder to work himself into the ground when he didn't have a reason for it.

Saving his grandmother's company was his motivation now. But one day soon, Slade feared that reason was going to fall short. What would he do then? What would be his recourse?

"Stop calling my mama old, and she might not spit in your lemonade when you come 'round begging like you're wont to do."

"I wouldn't put it past that she-devil to actually spit in my damn drink." Aaron chuckled. "So, what's the deal with the city-chick you brought back with you?"

"Bull sent me to New York to buy out a small chain of beauty stores. He just dropped the shit in my lap at the last minute. Threatened me with my grandmother's company if I didn't comply."

Aaron shook his head. "Man, how long you gonna let this man yank you around for Logan Industries? Is it really worth being on Bull's leash like you are?"

"Five more years and it's mine."

"Let's hope you survive that long," Aaron quipped.

Slade playfully pushed at Aaron's shoulder and motioned

for him to hand Slade Queen-Sorrel's tack. Aaron moved the few paces to pick it up and handed it to Slade, and then moved over to prepare the gelding a few stalls away for a ride as well.

They rode to the western bank of the property where the serene flow of one of the many streams on the ranch greeted them. They tied the horses off and sat at the edge of the stream. Being out here never ceased to amaze Slade. Being here, living in concert with the land and nature, did wonders for his often-battered spirit. Coming here always gave him just enough strength to continue moving forward with whatever life was throwing at him that particular day.

"So, you gonna tell me about this Mandisa woman?" Aaron's nudging pulled Slade out of the tranquil moment he was enjoying. "Don't think I haven't noticed you never answered my question to begin with."

Slade knew Aaron hadn't forgotten and was only granting Slade a few moments to reconnect with his land before throwing him back into Bull's chaos.

"She owns that small chain of beauty stores and is the creator of a proprietary formula that is revolutionizing the cosmetics world. Bull wants it. I'm tasked with getting it."

"So you brought her here to seduce her out of her company? Bull can't expect you to do that."

Slade shook his head. If only it were that simple. If only Mandisa were some anonymous fuck that he could hit and quit. Unfortunately, her presence was somehow more meaningful than that. The truth was she was threatening to complicate his life in ways he couldn't even verbalize at this moment.

"The seduction happened before I found out she was the person I was sent to New York to see. We met blindly in a lounge my first night in town and spent the next locked inside my hotel room. It wasn't until the morning of the meeting that everything became clear about our true identities."

Aaron let out a low whistle as he shook his head. "Damn, Slade. You just can't do anything easy."

"Tell me about it. I was sitting in a bar, pissed as hell at my evil-ass daddy, and in walks this irresistible creature that I'm determined to make my way to knowing. We hit it off. We both wanna have a little fun without any attachments. I mean, there wasn't any of the usual song and dance. I tried it, but all she wanted was to spend time with me instead. I should've seen it was too perfect when the only thing she asked of me was a good time and burgers and fries in bed afterward."

Slade picked up a few pebbles at the bank of the stream and tossed them one at a time in quick succession to vent his frustration. It didn't help. The more he thought about the mess he'd found himself in, the more pissed he became.

He was furious. At exactly what he couldn't say, but he knew he was mad. He was sure it had something to do with his father forcing him into this deal in the first place. But he knew there was more beyond that.

Those first two days with Mandisa, when neither of them knew anything beyond each other's names, were perfection. They were filled with amusement and intrigue—two things he hadn't associated with a woman he was attracted to in… well, never. There was this strange, or at least strange to him, innocence about their interactions.

Yes, they'd shared amazing sex, sex that had shattered his previous concepts of what good sex felt like. But the way they clicked—the way it felt natural to him to have her in his arms and at his side—there was no complexity to that. It was plain, simple, pure.

And in a matter of hours, his father's nonsense had

muddied that connection. All he'd done was mention visiting their Austin lab, and Mandisa had shut down.

"You still haven't answered my question," Aaron offered. "Why is she here on the ranch? I understand you needing to wine and dine her, but you could've done that at your loft downtown. Why bring her on your land where your family is?"

Slade didn't turn away from the stream. He didn't trust himself to keep the answers to Aaron's questions out of his features. If he turned around, Aaron would know the secret thoughts Slade was having, thoughts he didn't even want to admit to himself.

"Slade. We've been friends for a really long time. You've kept your circle small for a reason. Don't let Mandisa make you forget that."

Slade ground his jaws together as he turned to face his friend. There was something about Aaron's tone that was grating on him. "You telling me not to get involved, Aaron? We both know it's a little late for that."

Aaron stepped closer, slapping a hand on Slade's shoulder. "I'm just saying be careful. Make sure this is something worth the fallout that's probably going to follow this hellified situation your daddy's put you in."

Slade relaxed a bit. He could see the sincerity in Aaron's eyes. As much of a hard ass as Aaron could be, he didn't do shit just to spite folks. He wasn't built like that. His friend was attempting to help.

"Mandisa seems like a nice person." Slade waited for the other half of Aaron's declaration to arrive, his skepticism evidenced by his lifted eyebrow and crossed arms. "No matter how nice she is, my first loyalty will always be to you, Slade. I'm sure she's as wonderful as you believe her to be. I'm just telling you not to mix business and pleasure. As fine as this woman seems, if you guys get together while you're trying to do this deal, you'll never know whether she's with you for the deal or for you."

Slade gave a brief nod of thanks to his friend. It felt good to have someone watching his back, even if Slade didn't completely agree with everything Aaron said. His friend was right about one thing, though. If anything ever came of this connection he shared with Mandisa, it would always be tainted by this deal. He didn't want to question Mandisa's motives, and he certainly didn't want her to feel the need to question his.

Whatever the hell Slade ended up doing, he needed to be very careful. He couldn't lose this business deal, but he wasn't sure he could lose Mandisa either.

If only I could figure out how to keep them both.

Excitement lit up Slade's insides as that thought took root. Maybe he'd been looking at this thing all wrong. He'd brought her down here to convince her to sell him her company. But maybe the more effective solution wasn't to focus so much on the business.

"Shit." Slade's biting comment rang in the air. Why hadn't he seen this before now? They'd spent the morning laughing around the table, and then he barged right into her room, telling her he was taking her in to see his lab. The hot-to-cold switch probably threw her for a loop.

"Everything okay?" Aaron stepped closer to see if Slade was all right.

"Yeah. Talking to you just made me realize how I put my foot in my mouth with Mandisa before I came out to the stables."

Slade turned toward their horses and untied Queen-Sorrel. By the time Aaron caught up to him, he was already in his saddle and turning his horse in the direction of his house.

"Where the hell you going, Hamilton?"

"Aaron, I think you're right. Trying to focus on the business aspect of our relationship while we're sexually involved may be problematic. I'm going to see if I can rectify that right now."

"What are you going to do?" Aaron's question rang out through the air, posed to a retreating picture of Slade mounted on his horse.

With a bright smile plastered across his mouth, Slade clicked his tongue and used his heels to gently alert Queen-Sorrel of Slade's desire to move. As the horse moved forward, Slade turned his head slightly over his shoulder to capture Aaron's confused gaze. "I'm on my way to see a woman about a horse."

Mandisa walked to the stables after watching Slade bring his horse inside and was surprised when he nearly collided with her.

"Damn, cowboy. Where're you off to in such a damn hurry?"

"Funny enough, I was coming to see you."

"Huh?"

Mandisa wasn't sure she'd heard him right. In her current state of mixed emotions it was completely believable that she'd misheard or misinterpreted something he'd said. That was exactly what she'd done this morning. She'd completely overreacted. Her nap had given her time to think sensibly.

After she'd woken, she'd stood at the large patio windows and looked out over the horizon of his beautiful land. She'd been focused on a thick spread of lush, green trees when she'd seen him riding his horse back toward what she presumed were the stables.

Now, eager to apologize, Mandisa jogged quickly down

the stairs and headed in the same direction she saw Slade riding in. Back at the house, alone in her room, saying I'm sorry seemed much easier. But standing here directly in front of him, she couldn't find the words to express her regret.

"I was just coming to ask if you'd want to go riding with me sometime." His words were a good deal slower than the hurried pace he'd just displayed.

When he steadied her, he stepped back and motioned for her to follow him out of the stables. He was silent as they walked back toward the house. His quietness intriguing to her, she followed his long gait with quicker steps to keep up with him.

"So what's this about riding?"

"I'd like to make sure you get the full ranch experience. You can't really do that on foot, or car," he added. "The roads only give you a small amount of access out here. Some of the terrain can only be covered on horseback. If you want to start later this evening, there should be enough light after supper for us to take a slow ride for a couple of hours. We can take dessert with us and talk a little by the stream. Or we can start first thing tomorrow. Whenever you feel up to it. I'd just love to spend some alone time together showing you some of my land."

She couldn't help the smile broadening on her lips. Coming from a concrete kingdom such as Brooklyn, she didn't have much frame of reference for exactly what this scenario entailed. But just the thought of him sharing something he obviously felt passionate about with her kept her cheeks lifted until her smirk turned into a full-on grin.

"I hope that smile means you're interested."

"It does." The satisfactory way his face lit up told Mandisa Slade was happy with her answer. "What do I need to do?"

"First, we should probably go downtown and get you a

few things. As much as I'm loving those denim shorts you've got on, walking around all day with that exquisite skin exposed can cause damage. You'll need to change into your denims. Never go out during the day without some sunscreen on." He stepped away from her and scanned his gaze from the top of her head to her sneaker-covered feet and shook his head. "You'll need a hat, preferably one with a wide brim. You'll need to get some boots, too."

She shook her head. "What for? It's hot as hell here?"

"The terrain here can be difficult. Tennis shoes aren't really going to give you the traction you need to walk safely around the ranch. If cowboy boots aren't your thing, we can get you a pair of construction boots instead. I'd just hate to see you sprain one of those lovely ankles, or worse."

Mandisa shook her head as she sat down on the porch steps. "I'm a concrete princess from Brooklyn, Slade. Why the hell did you think it was a good idea to bring me here?"

His smile brightened, as if he'd been waiting for her to ask him that very question. He didn't seem the least bit disturbed by her smart-assed comment. "Because I wanted you to get to know me."

Slade motioned for her to move over. When she made space for him, he sat close to her, allowing their hips and legs to touch. He moved his arm around her shoulder and pulled her even closer to him.

"If concrete makes you more comfortable, I can take you to my downtown loft." He lifted her chin with his finger again. It was a simple touch, but so much intimacy accompanied it. It forced her to look him in the eye, allowing him entrance into her soul. "But I brought you here to the ranch because my apartment is where I stay when I need to be near work. This ranch is my home. It's the place I get to be me, amongst the people and creatures I love."

"Slade—" She attempted to interrupt him, but he leaned down and pressed a soft kiss to her lips, ensuring her silence.

"I'd hoped you'd see my actions and realize you're being here wasn't all about a potential business deal."

She leaned in and kissed him, needing so desperately to connect with him at that moment. "I want to believe that. It's just very hard to forget that you want my company. It makes me second-guess everything you do and say. It makes me feel guarded. I don't like that feeling being associated with you."

He moved his hand from her shoulder and laced his fingers with hers, and then used his other hand to span the horizon of his land. A sea of greens, browns, and golds spread out much farther than her eyes could see. The land was so vast. It was a bit overwhelming to think of how small they were in comparison to the huge patch of earth that made up Havenheart ranch.

"This land was the first thing I purchased that had any real value to me. I had to work for it. I had to save for it. The fight to get it forced me to put my heart and soul into it. If you get to know it, you'll know me. It's as simple as that. The only question that remains is do you want to spend time getting to know it and me?"

"You and these damn questions." She purposely deepened her East New York accent as she spoke, and watched as he laughed. He always laughed when her Brooklyn surfaced. For some reason he appeared to find it endearing. Whatever. She hadn't been joking. Slade was always throwing these contemplative questions at her that made her analyze everything she felt or thought. Not really caring to dig deeper into why it made her heart jump a beat or two whenever he suggested getting to know him better, she simply laid her head on his shoulder and smiled.

"Yeah, I think I'd like to get to know you both," she whispered.

Slade was about to lean in for another kiss when a gentle buzz coming from the back pocket of his jeans halted his motion. He lifted a single finger up, begging Mandisa's pardon as he lifted his phone to his ear.

"Hamilton."

"I just saw Bull's car coming up from the east road." Aaron's voice was low and stern, its timbre sounding an alarm without the slightest rise in volume. "Does he know about your guest?"

"Somewhat, but thanks for the info. Would you mind taking a trip downtown for me? Mandisa needs a few things."

"Not a problem. I'll get one of the hands to cool down my horse and meet her on the back porch in a few."

Plans settled, Slade was about to pull the phone from his ear to end the call when he heard Aaron's voice again.

"And, Slade."

"Yeah?"

"Remember Bull tends to use what you care about against you. Might be wise to keep Mandisa away from him while he's here."

A cold chill spread through Slade. One glacial peak after another turning his insides to ice made Slade shiver. Aaron wasn't wrong. Bull would use anything he could to control Slade. That was how he'd ended up in New York meeting Mandisa in the first place. He glanced over at her, the lovely smile she offered him thawing some of the frigid anxiety blooming inside him.

"Noted." His response was short and exact, causing Mandisa to pull slightly away from him as he ended the call.

Damn if just the thought of Bull couldn't spoil a perfectly good moment.

Slade grabbed Mandisa's hand and brought it gently to

his lips. "Darlin', I'm afraid that was work. Something's come up that I have to handle right now. Would you mind going inside and waiting for Aaron to take you shopping? He'll send for you when he's ready."

Slade saw the fog of disappointment begin to cloud her eyes. He leaned in, pressing his lips to hers, continuing the kiss until she moaned, giving him leave to slip his tongue inside and taste her warmth.

Whatever the fuck Bull had come to say had better be important as hell. Missing out on any time with this woman was not something Slade was going to take lightly.

"I promise," Slade spoke soothingly. "If there were any other way I'd take you myself."

She nodded and kissed him again, running her fingers through the hair at his nape. "I know. I'll go inside while I wait. See you at dinner."

He leaned back on the porch and watched her get up and walk through the door. He heard the gush of breath leave him when the door closed behind her. She was away from Bull, far enough that he could protect her.

Slade sat for a few moments on his porch. Preparing himself, he took a deep breath, trying to hide the tension attempting to take root in his body. The few minutes of meditation he attempted to steal were interrupted the moment he saw Bull's signature black limousine cresting the top of the hill that would bring the old man through Slade's front gates.

When the car slowed and then stopped in front of Slade's home, he stood and walked down the steps. It wasn't a show of respect, a son eager to meet his father. No, this was an act of protection.

Slade wouldn't allow Bull to set foot in his home. The furthest the man ever got was the front steps.

In Slade's mind, he'd built this house to keep the things

and people he loved near. It was his refuge, his place of peace. Bull didn't get to infiltrate that no matter how hard he tried.

"Here we go," Slade muttered to himself. He waited the few moments it took for Bull's driver to exit his seat and walk around the car to open it for the old buzzard sitting inside.

"What'chu want, Bull?" Slade made certain his tone was laced with as much disrespect and loathing as he could muster. Bull knew Slade's rule. If he wanted to pester Slade at the office, he could do that all day. But here, on Slade's land, he didn't turn up without an invitation. As far as Slade was concerned, there would never be cause for an invitation to be extended to Bull. Bull knew this, and he usually complied with it. His presence here could only be for one reason—Mandisa.

"You need to learn some respect, boy, when you're speaking to your daddy."

"I'm a grown man on my own land. I'll speak how I want to uninvited guests that show up on my doorstep. Again, what do you want, Bull?"

"I assume she's here." Bull took a moment to scan the front of the house, as if he could see through the walls.

"Bull, what do you want?"

The man took an exasperated breath as he realized there was no getting around Slade's question.

"I want to sit down and talk to her. I don't trust you to not fuck this up."

"Not gonna happen. You told me to take care of it, and I am. She's not dealing with anyone else except me."

Bull laughed, the shrill sound making the inside of Slade's teeth itch. The old man removed his broad cowboy hat and wiped his sweaty brow with a pressed handkerchief he pulled from his lapel pocket.

"Now, son, I think you know me well enough to understand that when I want something, I get it."

Slade straightened to his full height. It was the one thing his daddy had blessed him with. It also meant Slade was able to shut down Bull's condescending bullshit by making the older man look up to him. Three inches didn't seem like a lot. But when it allowed you to put someone like Bull in his place without saying a word, it made all the difference.

"Bull, I'm certain you also remember who I am. You know when I'm pushed, I will do anything I can to stop you."

Slade could tell the old man was thinking back over some of their more famous battles. As much as Slade hated everything about the way his father did business, he'd learned some things from him too.

For instance, Slade never walked into a meeting not knowing his opponent's kill switch. And although he'd held out on using it, he had the very thing he needed to destroy Bull. Years of watching, waiting, and listening had yielded Slade undeniable proof that would topple Bull's empire and bring the man to his knees. Unfortunately, ending Bull would also destroy Slade's family's legacy.

Revealing Bull's insider trading deal with StarTech.It would be a last resort. Landing Logan Industries in the middle of a media and legal shitstorm wasn't something Slade was willing to do yet. But he'd use it to protect those he cared about, Mandisa included. If he needed to pull the trigger, he'd let that particular bullet fly.

"Just remember, I am the head of Logan Industries," Bull warned. Slade didn't need a reminder. It was a fact that ate away at the lining of his stomach more than Slade cared to admit.

Slade moved off the porch and stepped closer to Bull until he was standing directly in front of his father.

"You are the temporary CEO of *my* company. In a handful

of years, I'm going to take the reins of my company, and I'll have a decision to make. I can let bygones be bygones and find a prominent place for you at L.I., or I can throw you out on your ass. So, you can keep pressing this issue and pissing me off, or you can make the best of this situation and just let me handle it my way. Decision's yours."

Bull swallowed as his eyes narrowed into tiny slits. He wasn't happy, that was obvious to Slade. But the truth was, Slade wasn't all that concerned about Bull's happiness. Especially since Bull had never cared one iota about Slade's.

Bull nodded and stepped back toward his car. "Five years is a long time, Slade. A lot could change by then. You'd take care not to push me too far. You know what I'm capable of when I'm pushed."

Slade watched Bull slither back to his limousine. He watched Slade until the driver closed his door. Slade didn't move from the spot he was standing on until he saw Bull's car pass through the large wrought iron gates that sat at the edge of his property. When his father was gone, the tension in Slade's muscles began to relax a little. Slade was very aware of Bull's track record. The man left a bleak path of destruction wherever he traveled.

"Not this time," Slade muttered. He pulled his phone from his pocket and typed a quick text to Aaron.

Need info. Bull seems hungry for this deal. More than usual. Find out why.

Two seconds later Aaron's reply flashed across Slade's screen.

Will do.

7

Mandisa waved at Mama Indy on her way in the house and made a quick detour upstairs for her wallet. She stepped into the walk-in closet, picking up one of two purses she'd brought with her. She made a quick check inside for her wallet and headed toward the door. When she reached it, she heard a harsh voice that sounded like Slade. Concerned, she walked closer to the balcony door, and opened it slightly to listen without detection.

"What'chu want, Bull?"

"You need to learn some respect, boy, when you're speaking to your daddy."

"I'm a grown man on my own land. I'll speak how I want to uninvited guests that show up on my doorstep. Again, what do you want, Bull?"

Slade's voice was off. It was rough, heavy with anger and annoyance, so unlike his usual light tone. Since she'd met him, Slade had been nothing but kind to Mama Indy and everyone else he encountered on his ranch. The way he spoke to his surrogate mother, the care and regard Slade held for the elderly woman was obvious in all his interactions with her. Mandisa wondered what could cause such a shift in Slade's kind personality, make him demonstrate such blatant acrimony for his father.

She was about to lean in closer to hear more of their conversation when she heard a knock at the door.

"Mandisa, it's Mama Indy. Aaron's out back waiting to take you shopping. It's best not to keep that sulking brute waiting. He can get a bit testy."

Unwilling to let the matron catch her snooping, Mandisa stepped away from the balcony door, storing away what she'd heard in her "to-be-discussed-later" file. She was still attempting to comb through the unanswered questions her discovery poured into her head when she grabbed the doorknob to the bedroom door.

"Everything all right, Mandisa?"

Mandisa nodded briefly, forcing a small smile onto her lips.

"Yes," she answered. "I wanted to make sure I had my wallet in the right purse."

"I understand that, but I'm certain if Slade's sending Aaron with you, Slade will be covering the cost of your trip to town."

Mandisa didn't doubt Mama Indy's assumption. Slade took care of all her needs, with or without her request. Maybe it was time she began doing the same for him?

Once the two made it downstairs, Mandisa waved goodbye to Mama Indy and opened the back door to find the same black SUV she'd arrived in waiting for her. Aaron was leaning against the passenger door, texting on his phone. When she closed the door behind her, he lifted his head and pushed his phone into his jeans pocket.

"Hope I'm not interrupting."

Aaron shrugged a shoulder and opened the door for her. She shook her head in jest and climbed into the SUV.

This is gonna be fun.

By the time Aaron sat next to her in the driver's seat, Mandisa was belted in and ready for the trip. When the sound of the turning engine filled the cab, she looked out the passenger window to get another look at Slade's property. It didn't matter which direction she looked, it was all beautiful. Strong, vibrant, and welcoming, his land mimicked the sensation of a comforting hug, an invitation to come in and rest a while.

When they made it back to the main road, Mandisa pulled her attention from the receding tree line that surrounded the perimeter of Slade's property and focused on Aaron. "So, how long have you known Slade?"

He spared her a brief glance and returned his gaze to the road. Save for the quick moment of eye contact, she'd have believed he hadn't heard her. There was no reaction, not the slightest twinge to make her believe he'd actually heard or understood her words.

"We grew up together on his grandmother's ranch. After my dad died, there weren't a lot of options for my mother and me. When Mrs. Logan offered her a job with good pay and living quarters, my mother moved us here from Arizona. My mom passed a few years after moving here. Mama Indy took me in. Been here ever since."

"You've never left Texas in all that time?"

Aaron shook his head. "No. Had the chance to leave when I was going to law school. But my family is here. Couldn't see my way to leaving them. I went to a local school instead."

Mandisa kept her head turned and her gaze focused on Aaron as he spoke. "A lawyer, huh?"

She could see a smile creeping up on the corner of his mouth. "What? Dusty ranch hands can't be lawyers too?"

She shook her head. “Not at all. I’m just wondering who or what was so special that you would spend all that time and money training to be a lawyer, then give it up to be a ranch foreman.”

His smile bled away and the muscles around his jaw began to tighten. “As I said, my family needed me.”

“Your family meaning Slade and Mama Indy?”

He tapped the steering wheel with his thumb as he drove, still looking out at the open road before them. “Slade and I have been through too much to be just friends. He’s a brother. Both our moms died when we were young. Mama Indy raised us both.”

The sound of the sweet woman’s name brought a smile to Mandisa’s lips. “Sounds like Mama Indy is great with taking in strays. My mom was like that too. All the neighborhood kids came to her for mothering.”

Mandisa had been an only child by birth, but the truth was she’d shared her mother with every kid in Brownsville who needed a positive mother figure in their lives. It had been frustrating at times, but the truth was, when she’d lost her mother, those same kids came back to help her grieve such a terrible loss. Kandi was proof that you didn’t need blood to be siblings, to be family.

Mandisa glanced slightly out of her peripheral vision during the exceptionally long pause that followed Aaron’s last response. He wasn’t a man of many words, and that made Mandisa nervous. Did she fear Aaron? No. But the silence made her wonder just what was going through the stoic Native American man’s head as they made their way along the road.

“Why are you here?”

The direct, yet strange question pulled her out of her musings and forced her to turn her head in his direction. She was still trying to gauge if he was being a smart-ass or if she should take Aaron's query seriously when he repeated the question again.

"Why are you here, Mandisa? Is it for Slade, or the deal?"

She crossed her arms and leaned her head against the headrest, gauging how much of her inner Brooklyn to unleash before she opened her mouth. Depending on the severity of the situation, Mandisa could get Brooklyn loud and crazy in the blink of an eye.

"Is this the part where you tell me to leave your friend alone and never return to these parts again?"

Aaron shook his head, his long curtain of midnight hair flowing in waves with each movement. "I have no power over whether you go or stay. I'm just trying to gauge your reasons for coming to Havenheart."

She nodded, slightly impressed by Aaron's candor. "The truth?"

She waited a bit while she gathered her thoughts. She was certain this was some kind of test—she just couldn't tell which way she was supposed to answer his question. His face was impassive, giving nothing away to help lead her in the right direction.

Mandisa looked out the passenger window once more, watching the blanket of vegetation gradually pass by as they made their way into the city limits. She continued staring at the landscape, wondering why this simple question seemed so difficult for her to answer.

Of course she was here for the deal. She'd be crazy not to try to win this bet with Slade. But there was more to it. The disappointment that filled her when she believed Slade had wanted only business dealings between them was proof of that. The zing of electricity she experienced any time he touched her also served as proof that this was more than just a business wager. Slade was more than just a business associate. She returned her gaze to Aaron and could see him give her a cursory glance from his profile.

Tired of trying to figure out the right thing to say, she simply spoke from the heart. "Both," she answered. "I'm here for both Slade and the deal."

She could see the slight lift of the corner of Aaron's mouth turning into a smirk as he processed her answer. The tiny gesture coaxed a matching smile onto her own lips as she accepted the truth of her statement. Yes, the money was a nice draw. Nevertheless, there was something about Slade that sweetened the deal even more.

"Well, I'll be damned." Aaron's voice boomed inside the vehicle. "An honest woman, and from New York City, no less."

She should have told him to kiss her ass, but his smile and brazen reaction to her answer made her giggle. She curtailed her laughter long enough to look over at him again.

"So I take it I passed whatever little test you were throwing at me?"

"Not so much as a test. More of a gauge. If you can admit to me that the money is just as interesting as the man, then I know you're being honest. I know you're considering him. That's all that matters to me."

She nodded in acceptance of his estimation. Aaron had no worries. Consideration of Slade was all she seemed to be able to do since she'd met him. Her mind, her focus should have been completely on business. Still, Slade was the only item on her brain's agenda since she'd laid eyes on him in that lounge back in Brooklyn.

She smiled to herself as she thought of the people Slade surrounded himself with. First Mama Indy and now Aaron. Each of them so obviously dedicated to Slade it made a welcomed warmth spread through her.

Mandisa gave another brief glance to the man seated next

to her in the SUV. He'd pulled no punches, made it plain what the purpose of his question was. Truthfully, she couldn't be upset about that. How could she? She knew there was a woman in Brooklyn who had and would do the same for her to anyone who appeared to be easing his way inside Mandisa's circle. Sharing traits with her best friend, Kandi, was a definite way to earn Mandisa's respect. If she wasn't certain of it before, Mandisa knew it now—Aaron was someone she'd get along fine with.

Slade sat at the kitchen table reading his tablet and sipping on a cold glass of homemade sweet tea. He was about to scroll to the next page when the sound of Mama Indy's voice halted his motion.

"Was that your daddy's car I saw out in the yard earlier?"

"Yes, ma'am."

He took another sip and set the glass quietly down on a coaster. Many years of living with Indira Price had taught him to appreciate when someone else does the cleaning for you by keeping things tidy. This included picking up after yourself and keeping water rings from cold drinks off her table.

"What did he want?"

Slade didn't look up from his tablet. He simply shook his head and answered, "He didn't want anything, Mama."

Slade heard the running water at the sink suddenly stop. Soon Mama Indy was sitting across from him at the small kitchen table. "Slade? How long you and me been doing this dance?"

"What'chu mean, Mama?"

"I mean, I ask you what Bull wanted, and you tell me

nothing, 'cause you think you're protecting me from worrying about Bull's nonsense."

Slade grabbed a cookie from the table and shoved it whole into his mouth before answering. "Not sure I know what you mean, Mama."

"Slade?" Her sharp voice let him know she meant business. He'd caught hell one time too many as a kid to not heed the warning that came with that sound.

"Mama, Bull is threatening to sell off Venus. In order to save it, I have to get Mandisa to sell me her company."

Mama Indy shook her head and folded her arms across her chest, another sign that she wasn't pleased with Slade's behavior. "Please tell me you didn't bring that nice girl down here under false pretenses. I know I raised you better than that, Slade."

"Mama, Mandisa is here because I want her to be. The business thing is important, but it's secondary."

She squinted her eyes as she watched him carefully, measuring his truthfulness, looking for his tells. When she appeared satisfied Slade was being truthful she leaned forward and placed a weathered brown hand over his.

"Bull has taken a lot from you, Slade. He's always forced you to play his game to get the things you deserve. Don't let Mandisa be another thing that you lose to him."

The sweet drink in Slade's mouth turned bitter with her warning. He closed his eyes for a moment, and a highlight reel of Bull's transgressions against Slade played on a loop. Bull's treatment of his natural mother while she was alive, her subsequent death resulting from that ill-treatment, and the most recent loss, Macy.

"Slade, be careful." Mama Indy's voice pulled him out of the deluge of memories flooding his mind.

"I already told you I wouldn't let him near Mandisa," Slade answered.

The older woman shook her head and continued. "I'm not talking about your daddy, Slade. I'm talking about you. You have a tendency to rush into things, things that aren't necessarily right for you. You see something, and you don't stop until it's yours. That quality can be a good thing. But it can also hurt you if you never take the time to ask yourself if you should be chasing the thing in your sights."

Slade couldn't deny her statement. He had run in head first in several situations without thinking about the consequences. And he'd suffered tremendously every time.

"You're the best judge of character I know, Mama. Are you saying you don't think I should try to see where this thing goes with Mandisa and me?"

She stood up and gathered his face into her soft hands, leaning down to press a loving kiss to his forehead. It was her way of soothing him. As a child when he'd scraped a knee, or Bull had done something to send Slade away in tears, she'd always console him by granting him a warm kiss on the forehead. It was his signal that everything was going to be all right.

"That young lady is not Macy. She may be here about business, but she's here for you too."

He laughed quietly, her motherly adoration the remedy to the dark thoughts beginning to swirl in his head. "How could you possibly know that, Mama? You've spent less than a handful of hours with her."

The matron waved a dismissive hand at Slade and walked over to the kitchen counter. "If you know what you're looking for, it don't take a whole lot of time to get to know folks. The fact that Mandisa doesn't take her eyes off you when you're in the same room tells me she's more concerned with you than any business deal. She tracks you across a room, watches you hard when she thinks you're not looking. Her face lights up with just the sound of your voice."

Mama Indy turned away from him, grabbed a knife from the counter top, and began slicing vegetables in preparation for their evening meal.

"You know what else I notice?" she asked. Her voice was filled with just enough mirth to know whatever her observation, it was going to be at his expense. "I notice that you do the same thing. Watch her when you think no one is looking, light up like a Christmas tree when you hear that gal's voice. Macy didn't do that for you, or to you. Macy only lit up when you pulled something new out of a box for her."

If that ain't the truth.

"Mama, things are still very new with Mandisa, and they're complicated by business matters. I don't know where it's going. Hell, it may not go anywhere. Her home is a four-hour plane ride away from here. I know I like her. I also like spending time with her. That's all I plan to do while she's here. As for Bull, I won't give him the opportunity to destroy this."

Mama Indy stopped chopping vegetables long enough to look over her shoulder at Slade. Her face was weathered by time, and there was a weariness about her eyes that made the son in him worry for his mama.

"It's always disturbed me how easily Bull could hate his own child. I did my best to protect you as a boy. So did your grandma. But no matter what we did, we still couldn't stop that man from hurting you. He's a hateful man, Slade. Just be careful. He's mean. If he can't get to you, he won't have a problem going after her."

Every word she'd just spoken was absolute truth. Bull was an evil old man who'd do anything to get his way. It wouldn't do to take him lightly, not with Mandisa's wellbeing hanging in the balance.

"I'm working it out, Mama. I've already got Aaron

working on something for me. I can protect Mandisa. I'm just not so certain about Logan Industries."

"That business ain't worth your soul, Slade." She shook the knife in the air, punctuating each word with a hard jab as she spoke. "Don't lose your soul to the devil trying to save a thing. Whenever you're ready to not be at Bull's mercy, you just need to speak the words, and it'll be over. Until then, I'm scared you're fighting a losing battle, son."

His blood began to boil when he thought about it. Slade had been playing Bull's game since he was a child, and he'd yet to definitively win. He'd thrown the old man a few times, had even managed to win by default. But never, not once in all their years of battling, had Slade delivered a knockout that would leave his father destroyed. And if Slade was honest, that was what he really wanted—Bull defeated and devastated. Just the way he'd left Slade for all these years.

"I know you think I can just let this go, but I can't," Slade replied. "You and Aaron keep telling me to let it go, but it's my legacy that old buzzard is trying to destroy."

"Your legacy is what you make it, baby. That business does not define the beautiful boy I raised. It doesn't begin to represent the fine man you've become. The reason Bull is always able to win is because he goads you into being something you aren't. I'm not saying to give up, or to stop fighting him. I'm saying fight him your way, not his."

8

"You two enjoy yourselves." Mama Indy's salutation rang out through the air as she waved through the open window of the SUV. Aaron pulled off, and the two disappeared down the road.

On the front porch Mandisa watched and waved until the taillights of the vehicle disappeared from her view. She leaned back into the cushions of the porch swing, patted her full belly and sighed.

"I don't know how many more of those wonderful meals my gut can take. I swear I'm gonna burst."

"Does that mean there's no room for Mama Indy's coffee?" Slade stood in the doorway holding a coffee tray in his hand.

"If you know what's good for you, you'll hand over the coffee nice and easy, cowboy."

The look on his face, the perfect mixture of amusement and fear, tickled a small giggle out of Mandisa as the big man shuffled to her side.

"You know, most folks don't really use the term 'cowboy' out here. Most would call me a rancher."

"Really? Well, I can stop calling you cowboy if you'd like. But cowboy is so much sexier."

His smile softened his features as he said, "Cowboy it is, then."

Mandisa took a long sip of the sweet concoction, letting its warmth travel through her body, soothing away the minor chill brought by the evening sky.

"I swear to all that's holy Mama Indy must put freebase in this damn coffee." She was only slightly aware of the choking sounds Slade was making beside her.

"Did…you…just…" Slade's sputtered speech made her smile lazily across her coffee cup. "…accuse my elderly mama of lacing her coffee with drugs?"

Mandisa nodded her head. "Slade, this stuff is as addictive as the rock dudes are slinging on the corners in Brooklyn. Does she buy it? Grow it? I just know I need the connect so I can re-up when I go back home."

Slade put his cup down and leaned back into the cushions of the chair as he shook his head. "I swear I just stepped into an episode of *The Wire*."

"Nah, *The Wire* took place in Baltimore. I'm from Brooklyn. Remember that."

She felt him inch closer to her on the porch swing's bench. The familiar heat adding to the cozy feeling Mama Indy's coffee began when Mandisa took her first sip. Taking a final mouthful of the brew, she gently placed her cup on the end table next to her and reclined until she felt the hard press of his shoulder beneath her head.

"Can we not move from this spot…ever?"

She felt the slight shift of his weight send the swing into a slow back-and-forth lull. She opened her eyes slightly. The bright moon sat proud in the sky above them, casting a romantic glow across the land and the porch. Her eyes walked from Slade's crossed ankles, up his powerful legs, flat stomach, and expansive chest and arms until his face came into view. Cast in the same amber glow as the rest of their surroundings, he looked majestic, celestial.

"Hmm, you like it here?" he asked before he pulled her closer into his side, bidding her to rest in his embrace.

Liked was an understatement. "What's not to like? Mama Indy's food is phenomenal, the house is spacious, and the land is beautiful. It's like being on an exotic vacation."

She could feel the rumble of his chuckle as it moved through his chest, tickling the side of her cheek as it rested just above his heartbeat.

"Texas? Exotic?"

"To someone from Brooklyn, yeah. Don't get me wrong—there are some beautiful areas of Brooklyn. It's not all a dangerous war zone like the media would have you believe. But it's a different kind of beauty. Where you have land and greenery spread out as far as the eye can see, Brooklyn is hard planes and concrete. Brooklyn is a mix of old buildings with eclectic histories and people. Each neighborhood and its architecture tells a different story about the inhabitants that have called it home from generation to generation."

She felt the slow stroking of his fingers drawing circles on her upper arm. The contact, although muted by the fabric of her shirtsleeve, sent tiny spikes of electricity across her skin.

"You know, if we're going to go riding tonight, we should probably get to it, Mandisa." The low rumble of Slade's voice made her skin tingle with need.

She was looking forward to riding with him. Had been all day as Aaron had dutifully taken her on a day trip into town when Slade was called away from the ranch on business. But sitting on his porch, watching the heavens and all their nocturnal celestial bodies, Mandisa couldn't bring herself to leave this moonlit oasis. "Would you be terribly upset if we just stayed right here?"

"You don't want to go riding?"

She could hear the unspoken, "with me," dangling in the air. She placed a gentle hand over his and allowed it to rest. "I do want to, but I'd like to talk to you first."

Slade must have noticed the serious tone of her voice, because he sat up, effectively disengaging his hand from under hers as he turned to face her. "Everything okay?"

It wasn't. The brief beginnings she'd overheard of the conversation between Slade and his father still bothered her. She knew she was probably overstepping, but she couldn't shake the feeling that something was terribly off in that scenario. "I wanted to talk to you a bit about your father."

She watched Slade fight to keep his features expressionless. The blank stare of his wide clear eyes was fixed on her. She swallowed hard, hoping to dislodge the discomfort of his heavy gaze.

"What could you possibly have to say about my father, darlin'?"

"Before I left with Aaron to go shopping, I had to go upstairs to my room to get my purse. I overheard you and your father talking to one another."

He shifted in his seat, his back straighter, his gaze more focused. "What exactly did you hear?"

"Nothing, just the first few sentences of your conversation. Mama Indy came to tell me Aaron had arrived before the two of you could get into it. But Slade, the few words I did hear pass between you seemed very strained…angry. I don't ever think I've ever heard you sound so hard, scary. It was obvious to me something isn't quite right between the two of you. Is everything okay?"

Slade pulled his palm down his face, wiping away some of the tension resting on his brow. "Mandisa, my father and I don't really see the world the same. We're complete opposites in almost all aspects of our lives. What you overhead was just us being us. I'm flattered that you're so concerned, but really, there's nothing to worry about."

"You're certain?"

An easy smile played on his lips, and he leaned forward, placing a quick peck on her mouth. "There's nothing wrong. Bull and I butt heads all the time. This is nothing new. Don't you worry about it."

He moved in closer, placing warm lips on the sensitive curve of her neck. Sparks of fire ignited underneath her skin, causing her to moan in pleasure as his mouth moved up her neck until it met the soft flesh of her earlobe.

"Now, are we gonna sit here all night talking about my daddy issues, or are you gonna ride with me?"

She pulled away from him slightly, stood up, and climbed on Slade's lap, straddling him, planting her cunt directly over the print of his crotch. "I want to go riding, but just not the kind you were planning on."

Mandisa could see intrigue twinkle in Slade's eyes as he caught on to her true meaning. His lips curved into a perfect smile mixed with excitement and amusement. She ran a tender finger across his lips, loving the easy way he had about him. Slade never seemed too worried about anything, a trait she wished she could adopt. He just let life happen, let it be whatever it was going to be and enjoyed the ride as he went. How sweet must this man's life be? How sweet could hers be if she'd only take a lesson from him?

His easiness was one of the things that attracted her to him. Well, aside from the god-like body and his amazing skills in the sex department, his ability to let things happen called to her. It made her want to let herself go when it came to him. She wanted to not think about any of the circumstances surrounding their meeting and her arrival here. She simply wanted to experience him.

She wasn't certain if she could live this way permanently, but for her remaining time in Texas she planned to just enjoy Slade and all he had to offer.

Slade's hands traveled up her thighs and curved around her ass, pulling her down on his crotch as he pushed his hips up, grinding his semi-hard cock between her pussy lips. She pressed her lips hard against his, demanding entrance and sighing with relief when he finally complied.

The absolute fire that blazed from the simple touch of tongue against tongue made her body burn. Mandisa needed Slade in the worst way, and all these damn clothes he'd made her put on in preparation for their horseback ride were preventing her from getting what she needed from him right now.

Why can't clothes just fall off from a simple kiss like they do in the movies?

"Can anyone see us out here?" She spoke quickly in between their kisses, too needy to stop and have a proper conversation.

"The bunkhouse where my hands live is down the road on the other side of the stables. If someone wanted to look, they could. I doubt it, but the possibility does exist."

She tempered their kissing for just a moment to digest what he'd said. "You care if anyone sees us out here?"

He shook his head, then moved his hand up to cup one of her breasts. "My land, my house. I do what I please. Anyone else has two options: enjoy the show or leave."

He moved in closer, threading his fingers through her braids, angling her head to expose her neck. He bit into the soft flesh there, sending shivers through her body, pulling a low moan from her lips as the light stubble on his face added to the myriad of sensations.

"Condoms?" Her question hung in the air for a few moments before he pulled back to look up at her.

"In the house," he groaned. "I packed some in my knapsack to take with us on our ride. But…" He leaned in to kiss her again, nipping at her bottom lip with his teeth while he lifted his hips, pressing his cloth-covered flesh into her mound. "…you distracted me."

She smoothed a slow hand down his chest and abs until it was resting on his crotch. She gave it a gentle squeeze and watched Slade close his eyes in response.

"So if I want this, I either have to go in the house or go riding?"

He pressed himself into her palm. The sight of him with his bottom lip tucked between his teeth as he moved his hips to get more friction from her grip made her clit throb.

"Sweetie, ain't a chance in hell of me being able to ride a horse right now. I'd hurt myself."

She cringed at the image his words created. Him hurting that beautiful cock of his was not on her agenda. She needed it, had plans for it, and none of those plans included pain. Well, not the bad kind of pain.

She pulled herself up from his lap and stood on her own feet. She began unbuttoning one button after another down the middle of her shirt until both flaps of the material parted, leaving the black lace of her bra exposed to him. When he remained sitting, she placed both hands on her hips and let her lips curve into a sexy smirk.

"What? You need more of an invitation?"

Her words broke the spell, and he shook his head and slowly rose to his feet. He grabbed her hand and before she realized what he was doing, he bent down and lifted her over his shoulder. He made quick work of getting them through the door, making one brief stop to grab a knapsack resting on a hall chair. With the bag secured in his hand, he continued up the stairs, ignoring her squeals and pleas to be released. When he reached his final destination, he dumped her on the bed like a sack of potatoes and began pulling his shirt over his head.

"I don't quite fancy trying to peel you out of those jeans right now. Strip," he growled.

She laughed. Apparently she'd poked the beast. She toed off her boots and went to work unbuckling her belt and removing her fitted jeans. She'd seen Slade all gentle and tender, and it was one of the sexiest experiences of her life. But seeing him now, standing at the side of the bed, muscles rippling, all brooding hulk, looking as if he was about to devour her, made her shiver, and her clit throb.

Her clit begged for attention that she couldn't resist giving. She closed her eyes, let her hand slip down her stomach until it reached the valley between her legs. She spread them slowly, allowing her fingers to slide down her slick folds. All they'd done was some petting and kissing, and she was so close to climax she was afraid to graze her swollen nub with the slightest touch.

"God, woman," he growled. "I swear you're trying to kill me."

The bed dipped with his weight and soon Slade joined his fingers with hers. She was just about ready to explode when he pushed her hand aside, spread the lips of her pussy with his determined digits. The motion was so quick it startled her, making her open her eyes to watch him as his dipped his head and licked her from her clit to the twitching hole of her cunt.

"Fuck," she hissed. She couldn't say anything else once he began his assault. His skilled tongue robbed her of breath, making her dizzy from the unique mix of pleasure and lack of oxygen she was experiencing. The sensation was so good, so intense, she was caught between smashing into him or pulling away. Her body finally decided for her as the first peaks of orgasm began to crest, making her grip the dark strands of his hair tightly and ride his face.

Her body locked in blessed tension, her legs wrapped around his neck. There was some distant concern about suffocation, but her climax was so powerful, she could hardly be concerned with nonessential things like breathing.

When her body finally returned partial control of her limbs to her, she relaxed her hands in his hair and fell limp against the mattress. She was falling fast into comforting blackness, her eyes blinking rapidly at the vision of him rummaging through the knapsack he'd brought with them. Losing the battle, she closed her eyes again for a brief moment when she heard the crinkle of foil and a quick, "Sorry, darlin'," coming from Slade.

She glanced at him, unable to process exactly what he could be sorry for. He'd blissed her the fuck out with a few swipes of his tongue, and if the determined look on his face was any indication, he was about to blow her back out with the same savage intensity he'd graced her with only moments before.

He pressed inside her in one swift motion, balls slapping against the puckered skin of her ass. Her walls pliant from her recent climax muted the stretch, but taking all that girth and length in one pass made her cry out. Her pleasure laced with the slightest twinge of pain, the burn of her abused pussy lips gave way to indescribable satisfaction.

Slade spread her legs as far as possible, holding them open with the firm grip of his hands. Mandisa didn't bruise easily, but she knew without a doubt there would be proof of Slade's lovemaking in the morning. Good thing he'd forced her to buy more jeans. Her shorts would definitely alert the entire ranch as to what occurred between them under the cover of night.

He was brutal, his cock nearly splitting her in two. She was splayed and devoid of any shame as she begged him to continue his assault. He was destroying her in the worst way, and she was so wanton all she could do was beg him to keep her on edge, beg him to keep her cunt dripping, beg him to own her body like no man had before him.

He leaned down to kiss her, demanding entrance into her mouth, sharing the unique flavor of her previous climax that still coated his tongue. He ravaged her mouth while his cock hit her spot in just the right way, and within seconds, her body was tensing again, muscles locking down on his masterful cock in complete abandon. She knew she was screaming her pleasure, but his kisses swallowed her cries, filling the room with muted moans from a voice she almost didn't recognize as her own.

And before her body could come down from this new height, he braced his weight on his arms and plowed into her. He was ruthless, animalistic. His muscles rippled and strained beneath her touch. His body was coated in a thin sheen of sweat, while a vale of unadulterated bliss covered his face. His quick pace faltered as she felt him swell within her. One last thrust, and he kissed her fast and rough against the delicate curve of her neck, his teeth sinking into her bare flesh, marking her.

She whimpered, the aftershocks of her own climax rocking her as he pushed through his. She'd have to remember to be upset about the bite mark she knew would result from this. But right now, as that bite prolonged her orgasm, kept her coming on his dick, all she could do was whimper and mewl like a helpless babe.

Seconds later he released her, kissed her gently where his teeth had borne down on her flesh. He stroked her still-sensitive nipples, then shifted his hand down to the cavern between her legs and gently stroked the near-raw flesh of her cunt.

"So sorry, baby. I just needed..."

Still dazed by the pleasure he'd given her, she lifted her head to look at him and spoke the only words her brain could muster. "So good."

He let out a rushed breath and gathered her into his arms, holding her tightly against his chest, planting a smiling kiss on her forehead before they both succumbed to sleep.

The bright and disrespectful sun poked at Mandisa's closed lids. When she finally surfaced to consciousness, she could feel the hard, familiar planes of a large man's body pressed against her flank. After a week of waking up with Slade plastered possessively against her, her body immediately recognized the luxurious comfort of his skin.

Slade leaned down to kiss her, but she blocked him with her hands, turning her face into the pillow.

"I haven't brushed my teeth yet. Morning breath isn't sexy."

He gave her a hearty laugh, pulling her hand away from her face and stealing a kiss despite her protest. "Everything about you is sexy, even your funky morning breath."

She scooted out of the large bed and sauntered across the room to the dresser where she pulled out a T-shirt and a pair of panties. She took a quick shower, brushed her teeth, and tied her braids into a neat ponytail before she emerged from the bathroom.

She found Slade stretched out across the bed with the covers falling just below the perfect curve of his meaty ass.

She made sure to grab a firm handful and slap one of his cheeks when she climbed back into the bed.

"Don't start something you can't finish," he mumbled into the pillow.

"Oh, I can most definitely finish it."

He lifted his head and looked over at the alarm clock resting on the nightstand. Shaking his head before he dropped it back on the pillow he groaned, "Not before we both need to be dressed and downstairs at Mama's breakfast table."

"Well, if you'd had my things placed in your room, then you wouldn't have to waste time walking all the way down the hall to shower and get dressed. We could've saved time by showering together."

Slade looked up again. Mandisa expected to see amusement in his eyes, perhaps a fun retort waiting on his tongue. But what she found were those soulful eyes penetrating her consciousness, looking deeper, venturing beyond the smiling façade she held in place.

"I hope you're not upset about me asking Mama to fix this room for you. I didn't want to presume you wanted to be down the hall with me. I wanted you to have the option to say no if you wanted to."

Damn it. Again, he'd been able to read her without any difficulty at all. Was she really that much of an open book? Was she that transparent? Or was it just as she'd assumed in the car with Aaron, that this was Slade's superpower?

"I'd be more than honored to have you down the hall with me, darlin'. As long as it's what you want too."

She gave up a brief chuckle before she spoke. "Maybe once Mama Indy leaves tonight. I don't think I want her seeing you move my things into your room. Don't want her thinking thoughts about what we might be doing in there."

Slade let out a loud howl of laughter. "If you only knew

Indira Price the way I do, you'd know you have nothing to worry about."

He brought his lips to hers in a quick kiss before he stood. "Get some rest. We'll figure out sleeping arrangements later."

Slade stole another kiss before stepping into his jeans. He grabbed his shirt, socks, and boots in one hand and headed out the door with a quiet click.

Mandisa closed her eyes as Slade exited the room. She snuggled into the still-warm linens that were covered in Slade's delectable scent. She wrapped herself up in those covers and luxuriated in the comfort she found within them.

There had been brief moments of doubt that fought to rear their head when she'd arrived on this land, but Slade had snuffed them out with a tender kiss. She refused to allow doubt to intrude on this. She'd come here with the purpose of enjoying herself. Right now, that meant enjoying the promise of sharing intimate space with Slade again. Mandisa would worry about everything else later.

Mandisa was startled by her ringing cellphone. Realizing she must have dozed off after Slade's departure from her room in the early morning, she pulled herself up in the bed and smiled when she saw Kandi's name flashing across the screen.

"Hey, girl, you're violating the terms of my bet with Slade. What's up?"

Kandi's full-bodied laugh jumped across the phone line and settled somewhere deep in Mandisa's heart. Damn, she'd missed hearing Kandi cackle like a hyena.

"Actually I'm not," Kandi offered. "I called the great man himself and asked if I could call you and check on you. He says I can call you when I want to chat, but you're not to dial my number unless it's an emergency."

"You did?" Mandisa was a bit puzzled. She wasn't exactly certain when Slade and Kandi talked. Slade allowed few things to disrupt their time together. "When did this happen?"

"Earlier today. So, how's the farm?"

"It's actually a ranch."

"And the difference?" Kandi asked.

"A ranch has more livestock, focuses mostly on animals like horses and cattle. A farm focuses more on crops. They have animals too, but smaller animals like chickens and pigs."

Mandisa heard Kandi suck her teeth, a Brooklyn girl's way of calling bullshit. "And just how do you know this, Miss Concrete Princess?"

Mandisa had to laugh, herself. A week ago she wouldn't have known the difference; all this open land would have looked the same to her. But after spending time with Slade and his small family, they'd taken the time to educate her on their way of life. Not to mention, she'd made the exact same mistake a few days after arriving here and was quickly corrected by Mama Indy.

"Let's just say Slade's mother is a wonderfully knowledgeable woman about such matters."

"Wait, hol'up," Kandi interrupted. "You've met his mother?"

"Yes, and his best friend too. They both live on the property."

"On the property? You mean, in the same house?" Kandi asked.

"No. I mean on the property. They each have their own homes spread out on the land. It's huge down here, Kandi. You could fit East New York, Brownsville, Flatbush, and

Canarsie within these gates, and there'd still be some room left over."

"Damn, Mandisa. Sounds like an episode of *Dallas* up in there."

Mandisa couldn't hold her laughter. Kandi's way with words had long since been a source of amusement for her.

"So it sounds like the cowboy is showing you a good time." Mandisa could hear a slight touch of uncertainty in Kandi's voice, turning her statement into a question.

"Yeah, he is. He and his people have been really gracious hosts." Mandisa was telling the absolute truth. In little more than a week's time, Mandisa had been made to feel like she belonged on the land.

If she wasn't spending time with Slade, she was with Mama Indy, watching the woman make one fabulous recipe after another. The old woman seemed happy to have someone to share stories with about Slade and Aaron growing up and getting into so much trouble together. She'd even taken to sharing some of her secret ingredients with Mandisa. Emphasis on the some. Mandisa still hadn't managed to find out what the hell that woman was putting in her coffee to make it so damn good.

If Mama Indy was too busy to entertain her, even the broody Aaron was eager to step in and share some of his time. He'd shown her around some of the more remote parts of the land that Slade hadn't gotten around to yet.

One day she'd followed him around the ranch like a lost puppy when Slade had been summoned to his offices for work. When they'd come back to the house for lunch and he'd removed his hat, giving her a closer look at his beautiful midnight hair, she'd given him a few tips about helping to manage some of the split ends she could see.

He hadn't the slightest idea what she was talking about. So she'd mixed up a natural egg-and-mayonnaise deep conditioner and applied it to his hair. He'd growled the entire time she washed, then conditioned, then rinsed his hair. However, when he saw the results, the smooth shine that gleamed when the light hit his strands, a small smile broke free on his lips.

These people were becoming an expected and welcomed part of her life. Thinking of the soon-approaching end date brought a twinge of sadness to her. Needing to lift her spirits, she brought the discussion around to safer topics. "How's Sweet Sadie's doing?"

"As well as always," Kandi answered quickly. "Why? Don't you trust me?"

"Of course I do." Mandisa never would have left if she didn't. Kandi was the only person she'd trust with her mama's stores. "I still have to ask, though. This is the first time I've been away, Kandi. I miss the stores. I miss you. Just want to make certain everything's okay."

Kandi's brief silence made Mandisa worry. She never wanted her friend and work partner to think Mandisa didn't trust her. But as a responsible owner, she couldn't just turn off being concerned about the welfare of her business either.

"Everything's fine, Mandisa. The stores are doing great, and the staff and I are okay. Don't worry yourself." Kandi was quiet again. Not long enough to worry Mandisa, but still long enough for her to notice the loquacious woman wasn't carrying their conversation as she usually would. "I just called to make sure you're giving this a chance, Mandisa. That you're not sabotaging yourself out of having a good time."

"Have I really been that bad, Kandi?"

Mandisa knew the answer to her own question. Of course she'd been that bad. She'd worked herself into exhaustion making her mother's business a success. Kandi had hounded her endlessly to step away from it all before the pressure took its toll. But her warning fell on Mandisa's deaf ears until Slade walked into the picture.

"Never mind," Mandisa replied. "Don't answer that. I promise you'd be proud of me, Kandi. I haven't thought of work once since I've been here. I've been spending so much time with Slade and his family, work hasn't even entered into the equation."

"Good," Kandi answered. "That's all I wanted to know, that you're having a good time. I'll chat with you next week. Go have some more fun for me."

Kandi ended the call, leaving Mandisa to think on her words. Mandisa was absolutely having fun—too much fun. This was a working vacation, yet she hadn't done any work since she'd stepped on this land.

Yes, she and Slade had agreed to take time out to acquaint her with him and his beautiful home. However, she did come here with a purpose—to get needed capital for her business. To finance her mother's dream.

Mandisa had been so busy falling in love with Slade's land, and deeper in lust with him, she'd completely dismissed her responsibilities to her company.

A woman should never set her dreams aside for a man, Mandisa. As soon as she does, she loses herself and becomes nothing more than an extension of him.

Mama Sadie had drilled that into her head from childhood.

If I'd done that when your daddy walked out on me, I'd have had nothing. Where would the two of us be if I'd followed his dreams instead of my own? Don't let a man, or that silly emotion love, make you stupid, little girl. Always have your own.

Unable to shake her mother's teachings, even when they felt counter-intuitive, she threw her legs over the side of the bed and walked to the closet to pull out some clothes. She dressed in a pair of black slacks and a button-down shirt and added a pair of wedged booties to finish the outfit.

She walked downstairs into the kitchen, finding Slade, Mama Indy, and Aaron already at the table. They each stared at her with incredulous gazes. She assumed they were each attempting to figure out what kind of crazy she'd succumbed to, wearing any type of high heels on a horse ranch.

"Going someplace, darlin'?" Slade's question filled the silent room.

"Yeah, and I was hoping you'd accompany me too."

"Really? Where'd you have in mind?"

She smoothed her hand over her slacks, removing wrinkles that weren't there. A stalling tactic she'd learned when dealing with her late mother's disapproving stare.

"Your labs," Mandisa answered. "I was hoping you'd show me around your facilities today."

Slade flinched just the slightest bit as he took a sip from his coffee mug. He shared a strange look with Aaron and Mama Indy, one Mandisa hadn't yet catalogued, before he returned his gaze to her.

"If you're sure you want to visit Venus' labs, I can certainly make that happen for you. Just give me a few minutes to change out of my denims and into more appropriate attire."

He wiped his mouth with the napkin resting on his lap and then he stood. Without another word, he walked out of the room, leaving a chilly draft behind him that made her shiver.

She rubbed her arms with her hands, trying to get some of the earlier warmth back in them as her eyes collided with those of the two-remaining people at the table. There was something unspoken between the two of them, something neither of them seemed inclined to make Mandisa aware of.

Too concerned with keeping things on track, Mandisa

pulled her eyes away and focused on the food before her. She loaded up her plate and dug in.

There was nothing like a healthy plate of food to keep one's head down and mouth too busy to speak. If she was fortunate, she could keep shoveling food into her mouth until Slade returned. If she did, there'd be no need to worry about why she suddenly felt as if Mama Indy and Aaron, two people she'd become so fond of in such a short time, were disappointed in her. And more importantly, why that disappointment mattered.

9

Slade pulled into his reserved parking spot at Logan Industries and cut the engine on his SUV.

He looked over to the passenger seat to find Mandisa smoothing the creases of her pants. If his guess was correct, all her twitchiness meant something more was going on behind this impromptu visit to the office besides her need to see test tubes.

"With respect to proprietorship, I had to let the Assistant Director know you were coming. Other than that, no one knows who you are or your purpose here."

She nodded her head slowly, now picking invisible lint off the smooth material of her pants.

What the fuck is it with her and these damn pants?

He placed one of his hands over hers to keep her from fidgeting. She still wouldn't look up at him, but she threaded her fingers with his, squeezing tightly.

"Darlin', what's wrong?"

She shook her head as she kept her eyes focused on their joined hands. "Nothing," she answered.

"Mandisa, I might not have known you long, but even I

can tell when something isn't right with you. What's going on? Are you having second thoughts about this? You do know you don't ever have to walk inside one of my labs unless you want to."

She took a long but silent breath and raised her head and eyes to him. She was composed. To the average person, she looked put together, ready for whatever was waiting. To him, she looked tense. As if she was exerting too much effort to keep the mask in place.

"Slade," she answered with a calm smile across her lips. "I'm fine. I've enjoyed every minute of my time with you on the ranch. But we did make a deal. I can't possibly make a decision about selling to you until I see what kind of facilities you have."

She turned away from him to open the car door, but Slade refused to release her hand, keeping her planted in the seat. He leaned in, touching his mouth to hers. He needed the connection they'd shared only hours ago not just to anchor him, but to somehow remind her they mattered more than this damn business deal on the table.

When he pulled away, there was warmth in her eyes again, less of the cold emptiness that seemed to be attempting to settle in. Satisfied his Mandisa was back, he opened his door and walked around the car to open hers.

She smiled at him again as she took his hand and let him help her out of the vehicle. They walked to the elevator. Mandisa watched the illuminated numbers above the elevator door while Slade watched her.

When they arrived at the appropriate floor, a low tone dinged to announce their arrival. The doors opened, and they were greeted by a middle-aged man standing with a clipboard in his hand and a pocket protector securely lining the breast pocket of his lab coat.

Bill Johnson was everything one would traditionally

expect when meeting a fifty-year-old scientist. Black, wire-rimmed glasses, a starched and iron-pressed long lab coat covering an equally stiff suit, and a facial expression that let the rest of the world know he was smarter than most stupid mortals. Everything about Bill said, "Don't touch me, I'm sterile."

Every time he saw this man, Slade wanted to laugh, but his good manners made him give Bill the respect he deserved. "Mr. Hamilton, it's a pleasure to see you again sir."

Slade took the hand that Bill offered and shook it before turning to Mandisa. "Dr. Bill Johnson, please meet Dr. Mandisa Avery. I'm trying to court her to head up our new line. Please help me convince her that Venus is where she needs to be."

Bill smiled at Mandisa and offered her an excited hand as well. "Dr. Avery, it's a pleasure to meet you. Mr. Hamilton has told me a great deal about you. I've also followed up on several of your accomplishments in the chemistry world. It is truly an honor to meet you."

Mandisa smiled and returned his eager handshake. He could tell she was readying herself to speak, but Bill jumped in again before she could utter a word. "I read your study in *Chemistry Now*. Let me just say it was the most forward-thinking concept on waterproof mascara that I'd seen in the last twenty years. That study caused so many cosmetic houses and lines to change their formulas on the chemical level."

Slade fell back while Bill and Mandisa discussed things he had no knowledge of. Bill escorted them to some sort of anteroom where they removed their jackets and then donned lab coats, disposable caps for their heads, booties for their feet, and protective goggles to shield their eyes. Slade followed Bill and Mandisa, watching her as she delighted in all the equipment and scientific bells and whistles Bill had to show her.

Apparently, the lady knew her stuff. Although Slade hadn't the slightest idea what she was talking about, Bill seemed to hang on her every word. Not just Bill, either—all the other worker-bee chemists clamored around to get a glimpse of the apparently *famous* Dr. Avery.

Since the moment Slade's eyes fell upon the lovely sight of Mandisa in that lounge, he'd known she was something special. Her aura stood out like a beacon while he muddled in the depths of his anger at Bull. Her light had literally called to him, and it was obvious that even in her professional community, her radiance still drew people in.

Slade leaned against a far wall in the back, giving her room to move around without his big frame hovering over her. A spark of pride ignited within him as he thought of all of Mandisa's qualities.

Beautiful, kind, funny, sexy, brilliant, and mine.

It took a moment before the words in his head caught up with his consciousness. The realization sent a chill through him. When did he begin thinking of this woman as his? Neither of them had asked for any kind of commitment. Lord only knew Slade wasn't ready for one. But he couldn't deny the pride that swelled within him as he watched her in her element. He couldn't deny how possessive he felt when it came to her.

Thoughts of another woman he'd once felt that strongly about filled Slade's mind. A dull ache began to throb in time with his heartbeat. The pain was bearable now, but ten years still hadn't cured him of it. Slade shook his head, trying to free himself from the past's painful grip. Mandisa wasn't Macy. She'd given no indication that she'd betray him the way his ex-fiancée had.

Mandisa was loyal and dutiful, probably two of the

reasons Slade couldn't seem to get enough of her. The fact that she was here, trying to make her mother's dream into an empire, trying to add to that existing legacy, was selfless and noble. Macy wouldn't know nobility if it smacked her on her plastic-surgery-altered rump.

Slade had sworn never again after the debacle with Macy, but staring at Mandisa now, watching her glide so effortlessly from one workstation of the lab to another, "never" seemed a lot less permanent than it ever had before.

Slade allowed the idea of more than their prescribed three weeks together to filter through his mind. What would it be like to have her with him all the time, with no expiration date looming in the near future? Was that something he wanted? Would she even consider it?

Slade remained fixed in his far corner of the lab, continuing to watch Mandisa move from section to section. His mind was still attempting to process this unexpected realization when his senses detected the sour smell of burned cigar.

Slade's body instantly tensed against the repugnant odor. He knew no one was stupid enough to light up a cigar in the lab. It was the remnants of a recent moment of indulgence in a disgusting habit.

He didn't need to look to see who it was. Only his father would think it appropriate to walk into a place of business reeking of his vice. "What do you want, Bull? How did you know we were coming here today?"

Bull remained silent for more than a beat before he stepped close, leaning against the same wall that was currently holding Slade up.

"Slade, I keep telling you, boy, there's nothing you can sneak past me. I have eyes and ears everywhere." Slade could feel his anger rising inside of him. If the amused look on Bull's face was any indication, Bull noticed too. "You might want to check that attitude of yours. You can't kick me out of here."

Slade swallowed hard. There was truth in Bull's statement. The high-rise building housed several subdivisions of Logan Industries, including Venus Cosmetics, and its labs. Slade couldn't run him out of this building the way he could the ranch.

"Is that Dr. Avery? She's a pretty thang, ain't she?" Bull noted.

Slade tracked his eyes across the room when he realized Bull's distraction had caused him to lose sight of Mandisa. When he found her again, she was back in the anteroom, removing the protective gear and exchanged her lab coat for the blazer she'd arrived in.

Slade left Bull where he stood and headed for the anteroom to catch up with Mandisa. Protective gear removed, he was turning around to lead Mandisa out of the labs and away from his father when he heard Bull's rough voice coming from behind him.

"Ms. Avery," he called, grabbing Mandisa's attention. "Might I have a word?"

Mandisa turned around, giving a brief smile to Slade as she looked around him to see the source of the voice calling to her.

"Hello. I'm Bull Hamilton, Slade's daddy and the CEO of Logan Industries. It's such a pleasure to meet you."

Slade watched as Mandisa graciously accepted the hand Bull offered in greeting. He could feel his blood begin to boil as he watched the exchange. When the old bastard pulled Mandisa's fingers to his lips and pressed them against her knuckles, Slade had to grip the doorknob to keep from closing his fist and slamming it into Bull's face.

"It's an honor to meet you, Ms. Avery," Bull cooed when he finally released Mandisa's.

Mandisa nodded and watched Bull carefully, as if she were taking in all his attributes and assessing him carefully.

"Actually, it's Dr. Avery," she countered. "And it's a pleasure to meet you too, Mr. Hamilton."

The side of Slade's lip curved into a sinister smirk. Gracious and the epitome of class, she still managed to check Bull on his shit.

Thatta girl.

"Doctor, please forgive me. In my experience, doctor means someone who has attended medical school."

Slade's body relaxed as he watched Mandisa cross her arms against her chest and lift a perfectly arched brow in question.

"The original etymology of the word doctor is 'one who is learned, or who has learned the most in their discipline. One who is qualified to teach.' There's no mention of the practice of medicine at all. With a PhD in chemistry, I'd say that I'm definitely afforded that designation."

Slade almost hurt himself trying not to laugh. Bull's face was turning an uncomfortable shade of pink. Obviously shaken by Mandisa's ability to both put him in his place and remain perfectly professional at the same time, Bull simply swallowed hard and nodded.

"Well, I did not know that, *Dr.* Avery. I guess you learn something new every day."

"If we're lucky," Mandisa countered, "we indeed do."

Bull cleared his throat, obviously still uncomfortable with Mandisa's ability to handle herself. Slade just shook his head. This wasn't even heavy lifting as far as he was concerned. This exchange with Bull wasn't even something this brilliant woman had to work hard at. She was the perfect mix of kick-ass sassy and smart that made her a threat in the boardroom and bedroom. Too bad Bull hadn't known that before he stuck his foot in his mouth.

"Is there something we can do for you, Bull?" Slade hoped he normalized his tone enough to keep the obvious hatred he had for his father out of his voice. Mandisa didn't need to know the history Bull and Slade shared. She didn't need to become involved or tarnished in any way by his father's black soul.

"Well, I'm staying in Austin for a few days. I was hoping to convince Ms...." Bull stumbled over the word as he took a quick look at Mandisa. "I mean, Dr. Avery, to join me for dinner."

There was a familiar gleam in Bull's narrow eyes. It made Slade's pulse beat in an erratic rhythm. Slade felt himself take a step closer to Mandisa, crowding her, needing to make some form of contact with her.

Slade didn't take his eyes off Bull when he spoke. "Dr. Avery's calendar is very busy. I don't think she'll have time to have dinner with you."

"I think the lovely doctor is capable of telling me what her schedule will allow. Aren't you, darlin'?"

Slade felt his body tense and tightened his already closed fist. He could see from the smile dancing in Bull's eyes the man was enjoying this confrontation. He could also see Bull had a lecherous plan sparking in his head.

"Ah, thank you for the offer, Mr. Hamilton," Mandisa interjected.

Slade felt her hand press against his arm lightly, a simple gesture that drew some of the tension out of his body, bringing his attention to her instead of his father.

"Slade and I already have plans for the next few days with respect to your labs and business negotiations. There isn't much leeway for extracurricular activities. I'll have to take a rain check."

Slade let a spark of pride bend his lips into a celebratory smirk as he stepped closer into Bull's space. "You heard it for yourself—the lady's calendar is full. I'll make sure to have my secretary update you on any developments regarding Dr. Avery's decision on Logan Industries' purchase of her company."

Slade slipped a hand to the small of Mandisa's back and gently guided her toward the door. He needed out of there in the worst way, and he wasn't about to let her suffer in Bull's presence alone.

The silent ride down the elevator drew out the few moments it took to reach their parking level. Slade instructed Mandisa to wait at the curb for him while he retrieved the car. He needed a few minutes to get his head together before they headed out.

He sat in the car, took a deep breath, and fought hard to bury the anger he always walked away with whenever Bull invaded Slade's space.

When are you going to get over this, Slade?

It had been more than a decade since he'd cut all personal ties with his father. They still had to work together, but Slade didn't have to deal with him outside of Logan Industries business.

Slade's mother would be rolling over in her grave if she could see the two of them now. But Slade refused to be like his saintly mother, constantly forgiving sins from an unremorseful heel of a man. What did all that forgiveness get his mother? A broken heart and an early grave. Slade wouldn't allow Bull to kill him the way Bull had Slade's mother. He wouldn't go down without a fight.

He shook himself free of the memories stoking his anger, turned the ignition, and pulled out of the parking spot. When he stopped the car in front of Mandisa, he placed his easy smile back on his face, hopped out, and opened the door for her.

The wary smile she wore gave Slade further incentive to

get his head back in the game, become the easy Slade she knew. That Slade was fun, that Slade was desirable. Mandisa didn't need to deal with this Slade. The Slade that harbored all this hatred was an ugly, dangerous man that few people needed to witness. Nothing good ever came from that Slade rearing his head.

He made certain to keep his carefree cowboy façade in place when he leaned across the console and dropped a quick kiss on her lips. "Ready to go, darlin'?

"I will be as soon as you tell me what that bullshit in the lab was about."

Mandisa crossed her arms over her chest and pursed her lips as she waited for Slade to answer her question. She could see the turmoil flaring in his eyes as he tried to figure out how to answer her.

"Mandisa, honey…"

She held up a hand and watched him carefully as his words trailed off. "Just stop, Slade." She knew he was about to hand her a load of crap, so she just stopped him mid-sentence. She didn't know what the hell had happened, but for damn certain she knew something was amiss between the senior and junior Mr. Hamiltons. She hadn't imagined all that tension between the two men.

"I'm a Brooklyn chick who's spent way too many years in the 'hood learning to decipher non-verbal cues to ascertain intent. You intend to lie to me, and you should know, I'm not really with that. So, what the hell did I step in the middle of?"

He pulled his gaze away from hers and focused on pulling out of the parking lot and getting on the road. He drove silently for a while before he finally cleared his throat and spared her a brief glance.

"My father and I haven't really seen eye-to-eye in a good while. That was just Bull attempting to run this deal his way. In all his years in business, he still hasn't learned the art of allowing the second party in a deal to decide in their own time. I just didn't want him pressuring you to commit to a decision you weren't ready to make."

The muscles in his face had relaxed enough that she believed there had to be some truth to what he was saying. But Mandisa wasn't naïve—she could sense this hostility between father and son impacted more than their business relationship.

Mandisa unfolded her arms and leaned back into the cushioned seat. Whatever this problem was between Bull and Slade seemed complicated. Too complicated for her to deal with in the few days she had left in Texas. Too complicated for her to get involved with, considering she wasn't more than a visitor in Slade's life.

Just let it go, girl.

She nodded, accepting his explanation, ignoring the voice that kept nudging her to dig deeper, discover as much information as she could regarding Slade and his relationship with his father.

Your visit isn't about their family drama—it's about winning this damn bet and earning capital for your mother's company. Just let it go.

"So, what do you have planned for the rest of the day? You know, since my calendar is so full. I would hate to have knowingly lied to a man who could end up being my boss. I'm certain you told your father I was busy because you'd already scheduled something for me."

Slade laughed. It was a genuine, hearty laugh that told her he understood she was calling bullshit, and he wasn't stupid enough to try to deny it any longer.

"Now that you mention it, I do have something I want to

show you. I've been meaning to take you somewhere special since we arrived. Today, we're going to make that happen."

A skeptical arched brow was her only response.

"Trust me, you're going to love it."

She gave a flat chuckle. "I'd better."

10

Mandisa wrapped her arms around Slade's waist as they rode Queen-Sorrel through what seemed to be endless fields of greenery.

When they'd left his lab, he'd offered to take her "up the road," as he called it, to a private dining room. She'd nixed that idea, wanting to be rid of her business suit in the worst way. He'd suggested they hit up some of the microbreweries in the area on Rainey St. as an alternative. But once he told her they were usually packed to capacity during the afternoon and evening hours, she begged him to take her back to his ranch for lunch and some of Mama Indy's coffee.

After eating at Mama Indy's table, enjoying both the food and the company, the evening sky was pressing upon them. They changed into riding clothes, said quick goodbyes to Slade's family, and headed directly to the stables.

Mandisa had ridden a few times since she'd arrived. She wasn't going to win any prizes, but she was beginning to become comfortable with the beautiful creatures Slade loved so much. He'd walked only one horse out by the time she met him. He climbed up, settled himself effortlessly in the saddle, and then offered her a hand. With quick ease, she was seated behind him, and they headed away from the main road and into a thicket of trees.

She wrapped her arms around his waist. Soothed by his warmth and the serenity of their surroundings, Mandisa leaned into Slade, resting her cheek against his strong back, allowing the mild rhythm of the horse's gait to lull her into relaxation.

She didn't recognize this part of his land. It was covered with tall trees whose branches and leaves acted as a lush veil, shielding whatever and whomever it protected from the intrusion of outside eyes.

Mandisa snuggled closer to Slade, savoring the calm his nearness and their surroundings offered. She wasn't clueless —after that blowup at the lab, she knew exactly why Slade had brought her here. He either wanted her to forget, or he wanted to divest himself of his memories instead. She'd wager his motivations rested somewhere dead center of both those objectives.

Whatever was going on between Slade and his father, she felt its hold bleeding away from his relaxing form. The earlier tension seeped out, leaving him calm and loose as he sat in the saddle.

She felt him pull the reins of the horse, bringing her to a soft stop. "Don't fall asleep back there. Wouldn't do for you to fall off. If you get hurt, you'll have to extend your stay while you recuperate."

He slid off the horse with ease and held his hands out, beckoning Mandisa to lean forward. With his hands firmly planted at either side of her waist, he took on her weight, guiding her off the horse until her feet were safely planted on the ground. Slade joined one of his hands with hers and used the other to swing his saddlebags over his shoulder.

He led her into the thick foliage, pulling back branches

and leaves until they were in the middle of a clearing. Just as the last rays of the day's sun dipped beneath the horizon, Mandisa saw the twinkling of slow-moving water in a placid stream.

"Slade..." Mandisa didn't have words beyond the whisper of his name. It was more of a tether to reality for her as the perfection of the scene unfolded before her.

She felt Slade step behind her, enfolding her in his arms, the heat of his body permeating her flesh, seeping deep into the fabric of her soul. She closed her eyes and shook her head slightly. This was too much for her. It was sensory overload. To feel so much in such a short time left her raw and desperate for the man holding her.

Slade leaned down and pressed a warm kiss to her cheek before stepping away from her and pulling her to a spot under a tree near the stream's edge. He released her hand, pulled a blanket from his bags, and spread it across the ground. He sat down, leaned comfortably against the large tree, and crooked his fingers to beckon her.

Without thought or hesitation, she walked the few steps to the blanket and sat down between his legs, allowing him to encircle her in his arms. The moment was perfection. No sounds passed between them other than the soothing hum of the water sliding across rocks as it ebbed and flowed.

They remained that way, locked up in each other's arms, allowing their surroundings to add to the fullness of the moment.

"This feels so right," he whispered. His voice was so quiet she had to wonder which of them he was addressing, Mandisa or himself.

"Hmm?"

"This...you...us," he answered. "It feels right for us to be together here. Don't you agree?"

Without question she did, but could she allow herself to

admit that being here with a perfect stranger, doing nothing but sitting by a stream made everything in her life seem right?

"All vacations feel that way, Slade. That's why we love them."

"This isn't just vacation fun, Mandisa. This is more than that, and I think we both know it."

She leaned away from him, turning slightly to meet his gaze. "Slade, we both knew this was temporary. I've got little more than a week left here, and I'm going back to Brooklyn."

"But what if you weren't, Mandisa? What if you decided to stay?"

Mandisa didn't understand what he was asking. Not really.

"Whatever you decide about this prospective business deal between us, I'm not ready to let this thing go. I'm not sure if it's something that can last forever, but I know it needs more than a few weeks before we walk away from it."

She turned around completely, sitting cross-legged as she faced him. The crisp blue of his eyes sparkled like the water in the stream. His eyes calmed her, called to her in ways nothing else had.

"Slade, I live in Brooklyn. You live in Texas. We both have busy careers. How can we cultivate this into more?"

"There're planes, buses, cars, web cams, phones—all sorts of apps and devices that will allow us to see each other either virtually or in person. I'm just not ready to let this—or you—go, Mandisa."

Mandisa reached for his hand, stroking the strong digits of it with her thumb. "Is this about what happened with your father earlier?" She wasn't certain how the two could be related, but she knew more than most the stupid things a person could get into when motivated by anger.

"Partly, but not in the way you think. When I saw you in

that lab I was elated to watch you in your element. Seeing you move around my facility, imagining you there permanently, working with me to create something magical in the cosmetics world—it all just felt so real. It was right. Then later when my father attempted to horn in on your time. I got possessive."

"But why? He's your dad, not a contender for my affections."

She watched Slade nod, seeming to agree with her statement. "I know that, but I just didn't want to share you with anyone else. Especially not when I have so precious little time left before I have to let you go." A look of discomfort that fell over him, the uneasiness slightly etching the lines of his face. "I realized I don't want to let you go. I want to keep you, keep us. I want to make certain no one has the privilege of touching you except me."

"But Slade—"

"Mandisa, I know all the reasons it doesn't make any sense. But I also know when we're together, nothing—and I do mean nothing—feels as good as this. Give it a chance."

She closed her eyes, needing to break away from the power of his cerulean gaze. Everything the man said was one-hundred-percent correct. None of what he was asking made any sense. They didn't know each other well, they were here for more than pleasure, and there was so much to lose if things went south.

If things went wrong, both their businesses could be negatively impacted, his less so than hers, but still, there was so much risk.

She opened her eyes again, prepared to let him down, prepared to do the sensible thing. She was familiar with sensibility. She was a scientist. She didn't deal in dreams and whims. Yet when her gaze met his again, Mandisa couldn't think of the myriad of logical reasons she should back away from this man and his offer. She forgot all the practical points she was going to make to counter his very emotional proposal.

All she could remember was the way it felt to have her body pressed against his. A perfect mixture of safety, desire, and freedom she'd never experienced before. Not even when she was in her lab doing what she loved had she ever felt so at peace as she did resting in his arms.

"Slade, we don't..." She couldn't continue. Whatever lie she was about to speak into the atmosphere died as soon as she heard her own voice. His gaze locked with hers, and everything inside her begged her to capitulate, to give him what they both wanted.

She sat up on her knees and crawled slowly to him, stopping when she was straddling his legs, seating herself in his lap. His eyes were so bright with expectation, tinged with just the slightest bit of vulnerability.

The look he gave her crushed her, decimated the scientific detachment she wanted so desperately to use as a barrier to him and his ability to infect her rationalism with his optimism. Logic told her to walk away, to run. But looking at this sexy man bare himself to her wrecked her, made her want to latch onto the thin thread of hope he was offering.

"Why can't I say no to you? Why can't I do what I know is the right thing when it comes to your ridiculous requests?"

Slade didn't answer Mandisa. He must have known she was speaking more to herself than him. He brought their foreheads together until they touched gently while he smoothed a tender hand over the top of her head, resting his fingers at her nape.

"Slade, you have to promise me this won't affect our wager. That this won't impact whatever business deal comes out of this bet. I have employees who depend on me."

"And I don't?" His answer was a little raw, either from annoyance or their physical closeness.

"Yes, this could negatively impact you too, but I have more to lose than you. I can't screw this up simply because you fuck me senseless."

A cocky grin spread across his face, making her heart beat just the slightest bit faster. He slid a lone finger down into her cleavage, slipping one button after the other open as he continued his downward trail.

"I do fuck you senseless, don't I?"

He reached inside her shirt and underneath the underwire of her bra, pulling one globe and then the next free of the satin material. He rolled one pert nipple into a perfect peak between his thumb and pointer finger, drawing an involuntary moan from her.

She couldn't deny his taunt. He did fuck her senseless, made her do all sorts of ridiculous shit like agreeing to spend three weeks with him when three days had been enough to turn her world upside down.

Slade moved to the opposite nipple, bringing it to the same pointed perfection, making her moan even louder. Mandisa reared back, her body instinctively bucking against him, searching for the right amount of friction to soothe the growing ache between her legs.

He let his hands stray from her tender breasts and move down her sides, to her waist. He unbuttoned her jeans, sliding his hand beyond her navel, past her mound, and into the wet crease between her pussy lips.

"I need you out of these jeans, darlin'."

She kicked off her boots, and they worked in conjunction to free her from the prison of the denim material. He motioned for her to return to her perch above his lap and slid his fingers between her dripping folds.

One fingernail scrape against her clit and electric waves

sparked from her core and traveled throughout the rest of her body. She pushed her hips toward his thick fingers, seeking the pressure she needed to chase the orgasm already building inside her.

He teased her, rubbing gentle circles around her clit, denying her the speed and force she needed to complete her climax. She moaned again, biting her lip to try to quiet the sound.

"There's no one out here but the two of us," he whispered closely in her ear. "No one can hear you, no one can see you. Let go, baby." He bit her earlobe, immediately licking the tender flesh to sooth it. "Let me have all those wonderful sounds you're gonna make while you fuck yourself on my fingers."

He slid his fingers farther down, sinking into the depths of her cunt first with one then two fingers, making her cry out in delight as he twisted and stretched them inside her. His middle and ring fingers inside her while his thumb rubbed against her clit had her slick walls trembling, tightening around his digits, milking them for every bit of pleasure they could give her.

She was hovering over the brink of orgasm when she felt the middle finger of his opposite hand breach her mouth.

"Get it wet for me," he commanded, and she complied willingly. She allowed his finger to enter her mouth, curving her tongue around it, bathing it like she would his cock had he blessed her with it. When he was satisfied, he removed his finger and slid his hand down her back until she felt his wet digit slide down the crack of her ass. He wiggled it until it rested comfortably between her cheeks.

Mandisa's quick breath must have relayed her apprehension. She'd never engaged in anal play before, never allowed herself to be breached there.

"Sshh, darlin'. Trust me."

Her body relaxed at his coaxing. Slade always took care of her—this would be no different. She steadied her breath as he circled the tight flesh. She didn't know if it was his actual caress or just the idea of him touching her in two secret places at once, but all the sensation she was experiencing seemed to be heightened.

He quickened his pace, forcing her to push back and forth between his hands, chasing the sparks of orgasm the dual stimuli were giving her.

She could feel herself succumbing to his ministrations. She needed an anchor, something to keep her grounded as he pleasured her. She crushed her mouth to his, burying her fingers in his hair, biting down on his bottom lip as her climax struck her, splitting her down the seam of her cunt. When she began to feel her orgasm ebb, her muscles relaxing into a mild quiver, he pressed the tip of the digit he'd been circling around her back entrance and pushed inside.

The breach was painful. Her skin felt stretched beyond capacity upon his entrance. But soon the pain subsided, the sensation morphing into something seductive and desirable. Her muscles tightened again, latching onto what should have been the end of her orgasm and throwing her right back into another cresting wave of pleasure.

Muscles locked, all she could do was scream. The sound was rough, raw, burning the inside of her throat as it escaped into the air.

And through it all, he kissed the skin of her lips, neck, face, and any other part of her he could reach as her body splintered into a million pieces above him.

When she finally stopped coming, he gently removed his fingers from her cunt. His mouth bowed into a satisfied smile as he admired the traces of her wetness remaining on his digits. With a spark of devilment in his eyes, he painted her mouth with it. He licked her lips clean, pulling her trembling body closer to him until she collapsed against his chest. When she was safely in his arms, he slowly removed the tip of his finger from her ass and circled the abused flesh until any remaining discomfort dissipated.

"I swear…swear to God you'd better be worth…worth this, Slade."

He laughed slightly, rocking her, petting her, lulling her into dazed comfort. "I promise, darlin'. I am."

11

Slade dropped Mandisa off at the house and told her to go on up and get ready for bed. Cooling Queen-Sorrell was going to take a few moments—after their romp by the stream, he wasn't sure Mandisa could stand on her own two feet for much longer.

He walked his horse back to the stables and began their practiced cooldown. He stroked and brushed her, talking her down into a relaxed state. When he'd checked her hooves and was satisfied his girl was comfortable in her stall, he put away her tack and made his way toward the doors of the stables.

His phone vibrating in his back pocket stopped his forward motion. He pulled the phone free of his denims and was surprised to see Aaron's name flashing across his screen. "Hey, Aaron, is everything all right?"

Aaron wasn't much of a talker. He texted Slade more than anything, but calling during the evening hours was reserved for emergencies. "We've got a problem. I'm pulling up in front of the house now."

"Drive to the stables. I'll come meet you out front."

Slade walked out of the stables just as Aaron was bringing his truck to a full stop. Slade opened the passenger door and hopped inside.

"What is it?"

"I know why Bull is so eager to get this deal in place. It's the last chess piece he needs to steal your company from you."

Aaron's words felt like a punch to Slade's gut. Slade watched his friend carefully, assessing Aaron, looking for anything that told Slade he'd possibly misheard his foreman. Aaron's steady, brooding gaze told Slade there was no mistaking what he'd heard.

Aaron wasn't just Slade's friend and foreman. He wasn't just the man Slade trusted with his life. Aaron was a brilliant corporate attorney who would serve at Slade's side once Slade took over Logan Industries. Research, and finding things out that most people didn't want you to know, was his specialty. If he was bringing this news to Slade, it was true.

"How?" Slade's question sliced into the air. Fortunately, Aaron had been around Slade long enough that he was more than prepared for Slade's pending meltdown, if it came to that.

"He can't sell or buy your company outright—his contract precludes that. But there's nothing to stop him from selling individual sections of the company if he can make the company profit from it.

"C.E. Stuart, Inc. is Logan Industries' biggest competitor in several markets. We're mostly neck and neck in all categories across the board. However, there are two categories where we best them by a wide margin. Finance, which was your division before Bull sent you to Venus, and cosmetology."

"The picture is beginning to form, but I need details, Aaron. How does this tie in to Mandisa?"

"Apparently, Stuart has been after Mandisa, her formula, and her stores for the last year. She's turned them down every time."

Slade groaned loudly. His son-of-a-bitch father was a slick bastard. This plan was ingenious. He could sell off blocks of Slade's company and not worry about the consequences.

"All right, he sells significant pieces of the company. Even if we end up going under because of his sneaky dealings, how does that benefit Bull? He doesn't own stock in the company. He earns a salary. He can't touch Logan's profits. As nasty as Bull is, you know he's not doing this simply to fuck with me. He's gotta get something out of it too."

Aaron nodded and handed Slade a slip of paper. He reached up and turned the dome light of the car on for Slade to read it.

"He has to bring Mandisa, her work, and her stores along for the ride as part of Venus. Once he does that, Stuart'll make him president over several divisions in their company. The deal could net him millions and allow him to fuck you over all at once."

Slade read as Aaron spoke, fire burning in his veins as each word verified everything Aaron said. If he were sitting in the driver's seat instead of Aaron, he'd have slapped the steering wheel to let out some of his frustration.

Again, his father was attempting to steal from him. God, Slade was so tired of fighting this man. If it were solely about him, Slade would be tempted to give it all up to cut all ties with Bull. But the thought of leaving Mandisa in his grip made his skin tight and his ears throb with the heavy thud of his racing heartbeat.

"Aaron, you're the one with the brilliant legal mind. How can I stop him? I can't let him manipulate Mandisa into something she's already decided against. The trust doesn't allow me to take control for five more years."

"I don't have an answer for you yet. I hadn't gone to law school yet when Bull took over. I've never actually seen the trust. Do you have a copy?"

Slade shook his head. "The house attorney took care of it. I can call him tomorrow and ask him for it."

Aaron shook his head. "No, he works inside the company. You must assume everyone that works there is either in bed with Bull willingly or by force. I have some friends down at the courthouse. If I can find the judge who presided over the estate case, then I might be able to get what we need without tipping our hand to Bull."

Aaron placed a firm hand on Slade's shoulder, giving it a hard but reassuring squeeze. "I'll find a way to protect you, Slade. You're my brother. No one gets to torment you but me."

Slade nodded. The notion that Aaron had his back brought a mild sense of relief. Aaron was a miracle worker. If there was the slightest bit of wiggle room in all this legalese, Aaron would find it.

"All right, I'm going to the house," Slade announced. "Mandisa is waiting for me. I'll see you in the morning."

Aaron shook his head. "No, you won't. I'm on my way to New York."

"Why?"

"In my digging, I found out Bull is sending one of his cronies to New York. I just want to make sure he's not up to anything that will cause any trouble for Mandisa. She's blameless in all of this. She shouldn't have to suffer for something she had no part in."

Slade swallowed down the guilt that arose from Aaron's statement. He was right. Mandisa didn't deserve to have her company stolen from her. What was worse, he'd put her company in harm's way by enticing her to sign this deal with him.

"You gonna tell her what's going on?"

Slade focused his gaze on some fixed point out the passenger window. "No, not yet. I want to wait until I have more information. Until you can tell me definitively if you can stop Bull or not."

"Slade, that woman cares for you. If she finds out you knew her company was in danger and you didn't tell her, it will crush what you have."

Slade kept his eyes positioned on his window. He didn't need to see the disappointment in Aaron's eyes. Hearing it in Aaron's voice was more than enough to sour Slade's stomach.

"If I tell her now, she'll leave." Slade cleared his throat after he spoke, attempting to free his voice from the neediness he'd heard in it.

He was too close to building something important with Mandisa. They'd agreed to give the connection they had a chance beyond the three weeks she'd be in Texas. If she knew it was his father attempting to screw her over, she'd walk away from him without the slightest glance backward. He couldn't allow that. If he could protect her—and their relationship—lying by omission didn't seem like all that bad a choice.

"Don't let Bull cost you another woman you love, Slade."

Slade tried to shake the sense of dread Aaron's words brought. He couldn't think of adding Mandisa to that list of people Bull had stolen from Slade. "I never said anything about loving her, Aaron."

Aaron laughed. It was a strange sound coming from the usually stoic man, making the hair on the back of Slade's neck stand at attention. "It's obvious to anyone that sees the two of you together how much you love her. It's also obvious by the way you attempt to keep her at your side all day every day. And let me tell you, even if Mandisa hasn't noticed the way you're micromanaging her time and schedule, Mama and I certainly have. Slade, you can't keep her with you by keeping her with you. She has to make the choice to love you or not."

There was too much truth in his friend's statement, more than Slade could admit. The only thing he could face at this moment was the fact that he needed Mandisa with him. He wasn't willing to lose her.

"My decision is made, Aaron. Keep me posted on your trip to New York."

As Slade went to open the passenger door he heard the flat tone of Aaron's voice. "Be careful, Slade. Bull didn't become the monster that he is overnight. One bad decision at time eventually culminated in the raging psycho we know today. Don't let your past losses lead you down the path of destruction."

Aaron's warning soured Slade's stomach, making him swallow the bitter taste of bile backing up into his mouth. He breathed in slow deep breaths through his nostrils to settle his uneasy gut and gave his friend a final nod as Slade slipped from the truck.

He took careful steps back to the house, needing as much time as possible to shut up that damn angel on his shoulder. With each step, its voice became less pronounced, and he could ignore it a little more.

Sometimes you had to fight fire with fire. That was the only way you could win. He'd show Bull once and for all that Slade's life wasn't up for grabs. He just had to make certain he didn't fuck around and become his evil sire in the process.

Mandisa was drifting somewhere between sleep and consciousness when she heard Slade enter his bedroom. Within moments she heard the en-suite shower running, and images of miles of sexy, taut skin, encasing carved muscle danced beneath her eyelids.

She wasn't certain if it was just a Texas thing, but lord knew Slade Hamilton was a delicious specimen of a man, and she was grateful he was hers for the taking while she was visiting.

Mandisa still had a smile on her face when she felt his side of the bed giving way to his weight as he climbed in next to her. He gathered her into his arms and dipped his head for their usual goodnight kiss.

"Hmm, a smiling woman in my bed. To what do I owe that pleasure?"

"I heard you in the shower, and my mind started conjuring up images of you in the water."

"The thought of me in water makes you smile?"

She chuckled, loving the feel of his hardening cock lying heavy on her hip.

"No, the thought of you *naked* and in water makes me smile."

She could feel the rumble of his laughter underneath her palm as she slid it down his chest, moving slowly until her fingers were tickled by the treasure trail of dark hair lightly sprinkled on his abdomen.

She delighted in the moment her hand reached and then cupped his sex, causing his laughter to morph into a low, sexy growl.

"Damn, woman. Whatcha got in mind?"

She let his question linger in the air unanswered as she disappeared under the plush duvet and buried her nose into the crevice where his thigh met his pelvis. She took a deep breath, inhaling the pleasant scent of clean and spice from his shower gel.

She wiggled her way between his legs, pushing them gently apart to make room for herself. That first lick ran from the soft skin of his sac all the way to the tip of his cock, making him spread his legs even farther, beckoning her to dive in to the feast she was making of him.

She circled her tongue around his proud cap and dipped her tongue into the well of his slit, scooping up the pearl of pre-cum that was resting there. She heard moaning again, at first thinking this was a new sound coming from Slade, but then noticed something different about it. His moans were deep, soulful, always expressing his need or satisfaction. This moan was the kind that came from deep within when you were devouring something delectable, when you were satisfying a longstanding craving that had been long denied. This moan wasn't Slade's, it was hers, and she wasn't the least bit ashamed of it.

She slid down Slade's cock, eager to taste as much of him as she could at one time. His length and girth made it impossible for her to deep-throat all of him, but damn if she wasn't going to try to choke on him if she could.

One hand tightly fisted around the root of his cock, the other gripping his heavy sac with just enough pressure to add to his pleasure and not cause him harm, she bobbed up and down, creating a frantic rhythm between her mouth and hand, essentially wringing the pleasure out of Slade one stroke at a time.

He moaned, moving his hips in tandem with her rhythm. She could tell when the pleasure was just this side of torture when his thrusts became erratic. The thought of her bringing him to his brink like this made the walls of her cunt contract. They'd talked about her taking him until he burst inside her mouth, about her desire to swallow all his essence. But until this moment, Slade had refused to do it until he could provide her with test results giving him a clean bill of health.

After more days than she cared to count, he'd presented her with those results two days ago. Now, with his fingers buried in her braids, holding her mouth in place, as he fucked her throat raw, she was nearly at the brink of her own orgasm as she thought about tasting his. She cupped her tongue on the underside of his cock and dropped her jaw as far as she could while Slade fucked her mouth until he spilled inside her, yelling as each jet of his come pulsed out of him.

Without thought, she closed her lips around him, creating a tight seal. She moaned when the first taste of his release landed on her tongue. The taste of his essence making her spasm, she pushed shaking fingers between her swollen pussy lips, dipping them into her wetness before circling her throbbing clit. A few strokes, and fire lanced through her. His leaking cock trapped in her mouth, pushing into the recesses of her throat, her digits rubbing out uncontrollable swells of electricity, she spilled over into her release, collapsing as her limbs turned to noodles beneath her.

Somewhere between her blissed-out, sex-drunk mind and consciousness, she felt Slade pull her up his body, cradling her against his chest. He stroked her back with a repeated delicate motion meant to soothe her into sleep. Without much coaxing, she allowed herself to fall into the slumber Slade's touch was leading her to. The last thought crossing her mind was a question she wasn't prepared to answer.

How in the hell am I expected to live without this?

12

Mandisa walked slowly along through the open path that began in the back of Slade's house. After two weeks at Havenheart, she'd become familiar enough with the land to walk unaccompanied on some parts of the grounds.

She'd kissed a sleeping Slade this morning, pulling herself from his naked warmth to walk amongst the foliage. It was painful leaving him there, especially when her body wanted nothing more than to snuggle closer to him.

Her mind had shaken her awake with an amazing idea that was scratching at the back of her consciousness. It was there, something brilliant, but she could only make out the blurry edges of the image right now.

This always happened when her chemist's mind began to build something unique and beautiful. But she needed to work out the details by embracing solitude, freeing her mind from the need to think. Her skin prickling with creativity, she'd thrown on some walking clothes, grabbed her fully charged cellphone, and headed for the wild of Slade's backyard.

She walked until she reached the first line of trees in her sight. She pulled the cellphone from her pocket, opened a note-taking app, and used the phone's stylus to write out plans and sketch designs for this new thing, coming together one component at a time in her head.

She'd just saved her work to the cloud when an unknown number flashed on her screen.

"Hello," she answered with the slightest bit of annoyance in her voice. She wasn't out here to talk to anonymous folks —she just wanted quiet. Unfortunately, her fear of missing out didn't allow her to ignore notifications like ringing cellphones for very long.

"Doctor Avery, this is Bull Hamilton. How are you doing this morning?"

Mandisa released the breath she'd been holding while waiting for her caller to identify himself. That's what happened with anonymous calls. They could be anything from a telemarketer to emergency services. Not knowing which she was going to get always kept Mandisa edgy until the anonymous caller made their identity and purpose known.

"Mr. Hamilton, did we exchange numbers?"

He laughed loudly, the sound making her skin prickle with restlessness.

"Sweetheart, a man like Bull always knows how to contact a beautiful woman he has his eye on. I hope I'm not calling at a bad time, but I figured I'd better catch you before you get started with your busy day."

She caught the sly reference to Slade's flimsy excuse for refusing the man's company during their last meeting. Bull obviously knew it was bogus, and he didn't appear gracious enough to let it go, either.

"Is there something you needed, Mr. Hamilton?"

"I was hoping to invite you to dinner this evening. It

would give me an opportunity to see how negotiations are going between our two companies."

Negotiations were going great as far as she was concerned. She'd spent the better part of last night "negotiating" her way up and down Slade's pole. She was certain he wasn't referencing those particular events, so she forced her mind back on the conversation at hand, trying to keep her lecherous memories in check.

"Slade has been very easy to work with. We've made a lot of leeway in the last two weeks. I'm looking forward to the culmination of dialogues next week."

"Good, good. I'm glad to hear it," he answered. "But I'd be remiss as the head of Logan Industries if I didn't spend any time with such a valuable asset. I insist you have dinner with me tonight."

His words brought a chill to her. She didn't like the weight he put behind the word "insist." It made the hairs stand up on the back of her neck. It also made her want to ask him, "Who the hell you think you're talking to?" She checked her Brooklyn long enough to attempt to feel things out.

Bull Hamilton was a very important man in the world she worked in. Having a bad interaction with him could cause irreparable damage to her reputation and her business. Two things she could ill afford to have happen.

She smiled to herself when she heard her mother's voice in her ear. *Play the man's game, but play it better.*

Mandisa smiled as she pressed the phone against the side of her face. "We'll be more than happy to have dinner with you, Mr. Hamilton."

"We?"

"Yes, Slade and I, of course. This way you'll be able to get a complete picture of where we stand right now."

The pause filling the line told her exactly what she

needed to know—she'd won this round. Bull found his voice a few moments later, agreeing to her suggestion and providing her with the address to the restaurant they'd be meeting at. She gave her salutations to the business tycoon and thought about what she was doing.

If history was any measure, Slade wasn't going to be happy about this dinner meeting.

Slade, big, burly and lovably loud. It was almost comical how those same qualities could probably be applied to Bull too. Maybe that was the problem between the two men? Maybe there was too much tension between them because they were so alike.

Mandisa rubbed her arms with her hands, trying to get rid of some of the chill Bull's phone call had left her with. Slade was going to be pissed, but maybe this dinner was an opportunity for her to do some good with her remaining time in Texas.

Let's hope.

It had been a few days since Aaron had left for New York. Slade hadn't heard a word from him since he'd departed. Constantly wondering if something was going on was making him jumpy, and if he didn't get a handle on it, Mandisa was going to notice. Hell, Mama Indy already had. Shaking her finger at him, telling him Slade's dirt would come to light sooner or later.

He hoped to hell that wasn't true. He was trying to protect Mandisa and save his company at the same time. She didn't need to carry around this stress—that's what he was for.

"So where's that no-'count scoundrel been hiding at?"

Slade looked up from his cup of coffee, blinking until he'd processed what Mama Indy had said. "Who, Aaron?"

"How many other no-'count scoundrels you know on this ranch?"

Slade laughed. He'd never get enough of watching his mother and his best friend.

"Mama, why are you so hard on Aaron? You know he loves and respects you just as much as I do."

"Hush. This is just how we are. That boy knows I love him. Now tell me, where is he?"

That certainly wasn't an easy question. Partly because Slade didn't truly know where Aaron was, not specifically anyway. Slade had been Mama Indy's son long enough to know she wouldn't be pleased with whatever he and Aaron were mixed up in. She'd begged Slade to leave Bull be a long time ago. Let the old coot have the business if he wanted it.

Slade wished it was that simple now—just a matter of letting Bull have what he so desperately appeared to want. But Slade couldn't, not now. His legacy aside, Slade couldn't place Mandisa in that man's clutches. If Slade walked away now, there would be no one there to protect Mandisa from Bull's manipulations.

"Boy, I know you hear me talking to you. Where is Aaron, Slade?"

"He's taking care of some business for me. With Mandisa leaving next week, I didn't want any more of my time with her to be lost on Logan Industries business. Aaron is just handling something for me."

His mama watched him closely. Like she had when he was a kid, and she was attempting to gauge if he was telling the whole truth of a matter. "You care for that gal, don't you?"

Slade grabbed for his coffee cup, using it as a small barrier between him and the all-seeing woman sitting before him. Although he hated when she used her skills on him, he couldn't curse her ability to read non-verbal cues. Hell, she'd taught him to read people, a trick that proved useful in both his professional and personal lives.

The eyes will always tell the truth, even when the lips lie, Slade. Always watch the eyes.

He pulled his gaze from his coffee cup and allowed Mama Indy to see his truth. She placed a hand over her heart as she walked closer to him, pulling his head into her bosom as she cooed, "Oh, baby, you've gone and fallen for that pretty thing. Haven't you?" She didn't wait for Slade's response—she already knew it was true. "You know she's leaving next week. What are you going to do when she leaves?"

"*If* she leaves, Mama. I still have a few tricks up my sleeve. I'm hoping one of them will get her to see I'm worth giving up New York for."

His mother sat in the chair in front of him, keeping her eyes locked on his once she was comfortably seated.

"Slade, you are worthy of her staying for you. She knows that, and you should too. But that girl has a life of her own, one she seems deeply attached to, one you knew about before you brought her here."

She was right, he'd been aware of Mandisa's life when he'd made that wager. He'd questioned his own sanity in making that bet, wondering why he would go through so much trouble to get Mandisa on his own turf.

He could lie to himself and say it was all about winning. But the truth was, he hadn't thought about business at all when he'd begged her to take him up on his offer. The only thing filling his mind were thoughts of their one night together, and the emptiness that threatened to smother him when he thought of never having her near him again.

"Slade?" Mama Indy's voice was filled with love as she

called his name. It was a balm meant to soothe the raw spots in his soul.

"Mama, I know what I'm doing. Whether she stays or not, we've both agreed to keep seeing each other. She wants this, and I want her."

Indira nodded and patted a time-weathered hand over his. "I know you care for her, baby. I knew you did the moment you brought her home. But I don't quite get the feeling that her life will be easily dismissed. She doesn't seem wrapped up in that shallow glitz most city folk seem to be so concerned with. It runs deeper than that, bone deep in fact. You and I both know the only thing that runs that deep is family. If she's anything like you, she's never gonna leave her family."

Slade saw truth in the old woman's gray-blue eyes. Her truth rang through his soul, summoning a sadness he didn't want to acknowledge. A sadness that beckoned to swallow him whole whenever he thought of Mandisa's impending departure.

The sound of wood creaking behind them let Slade know Mandisa was entering the room. He ran a hand through his hair and took a fortifying sip of his coffee. "Whatever her decision, I'll deal with it when the time comes. Right now, I'm going to enjoy every second I have left with her and figure out a way to make this work for the long-term."

"You do what you feel is best, Slade. But be careful. Understand that isn't just an old mama's concern for her son, that's my concern for Mandisa as well. That beautiful soul doesn't deserve the hurt that could come her way if this ends bad."

"Good morning," Mandisa sang as she stood in the doorway of the back door. She walked into the kitchen. She looked around the room for a second, then offered Mama Indy a warm smile as she approached. "I see you haven't started breakfast yet, Mama Indy. I was hoping you'd be okay with me making breakfast for you this morning."

Slade regarded Mama Indy carefully. This kitchen was her domain, and she didn't allow anyone else to tinker with it. Slade almost felt sorry for the letdown Mandisa was about to experience.

"Mandisa, honey," Slade primed. "Mama Indy doesn't allow anyone in her kitchen."

"I'm sure she doesn't if her only choices are you and Aaron. I've seen you fumble with the microwavable popcorn in the evenings when Mama Indy isn't here to serve you. But unlike the two of you, I actually spent my formative years at my mother's side as she cooked."

Slade watched Mandisa kneel between them, turning her gaze to Mama Indy's as she spoke.

"I know it's not easy to let someone you don't know into your space. But you've been so kind to me, serving me and waiting on me hand and foot since I arrived. I'd feel terrible if you didn't allow me to repay the favor at least once before I left."

Mama Indy placed careful eyes on Slade, a gentle smile cresting slowly on her lips as she stared at him. Her truth shone through the shimmer reflected in her eyes. He wasn't going to be the only one missing Mandisa if she left this place. His mother would feel her loss too.

Mama Indy closed her eyes briefly, as if she needed a moment to gather her emotions. After a few soothing breaths, she opened them again. She then took her hands and placed one on each side of Mandisa's face, rubbing her thumbs across the apples of Mandisa's cheeks.

"Your mama raised you right, chile. Now come on and let me show you where everything is in the kitchen."

Ten minutes later Mandisa was fully entrenched in her meal preparation. While mixing a buttermilk coating, she heard the slide of Slade's chair as he stood up. With a few long strides he was standing at the kitchen counter with Mandisa and his mother. He kissed Mama Indy on the cheek and then dipped his head to place a chaste kiss on Mandisa's lips.

It was a quick peck, but the fact that he'd kissed her on the mouth in front of his mother made all sorts of bells ring inside her. That one act meant more to her than any words Slade had given her since they'd met. No man kissed you in front of his mama unless he was serious about having you around.

When he'd asked her to continue their relationship beyond her three weeks here in Texas, she'd thought it was just the heat of the moment driving him. But sharing such a simple gesture with her in the presence of his most treasured family member—that meant something.

"I've got to handle some things with the hands in Aaron's absence. I should be back in time for breakfast. Looking forward to it." He smiled at her, then nodded to Mama Indy before leaving through the back door.

Mandisa went back to preparing the ingredients for their meal by rote. Her mind was still replaying Slade's display of affection in front of his mother and the significance of it.

"He really cares for you. You know that, don't you, Mandisa?"

Mandisa's smile sobered. She recognized the beginnings of the what-are-your-intentions-toward-my-son conversation that hung in the air.

"I know," Mandisa responded shyly. She kept her gaze fixed on the bowl in front of her as she hyper-focused on stirring its contents. "The feeling's mutual."

Mama Indy placed a gentle hand on hers, bringing her power-stirring to a halt, forcing Mandisa to look up from her task and face the older woman.

"Please understand I don't mean no harm when I say this. But, you're leaving in a little over a week. I can't help but see the heartbreak waiting for the two of you."

Mandisa closed her eyes, trying desperately to hold on to the simple joy of a few moments ago. Reality had arrived right on schedule, waiting to burst their little dreamy bubble.

"I know, but Slade and I have both agreed we want to try to build something. There's only a four-hour plane ride between us. We can make this work. More importantly, we both want to make this work."

Mandisa could still see skepticism coloring Mama Indy's eyes. She understood. Long-distance relationships didn't have a reputation for working out. She couldn't be upset with Mama Indy's forwardness. She was protecting her son.

Mandisa recognized how deeply this woman loved Slade when she'd first arrived at the ranch. But standing in front of Mama Indy, watching her struggle with liking her son's choice in a woman but hating the circumstance that would rip them apart, solidified any doubt Mandisa could ever hold that this woman—despite her lack of shared biology with Slade—was his mother.

"Mama Indy, I care so much for Slade. He's such a wonderful man. But I can't break my promise to my mother. I can't just abandon my company and my employees. I'm not saying I'll be in New York forever. I don't get the feeling that I could stay away from Slade indefinitely. But I can promise you I'm going to do all I can to take care of him, to keep his heart safe."

The sorrowful look marring the older woman's face told Mandisa she wasn't exactly thrilled with her answer. But the gentle nod she gave Mandisa implied her acceptance.

Mandisa wiped her hands off on a nearby towel and pulled Slade's mother into a full embrace. Hoping the hug would give the woman reassurance that her son's heart was in careful hands, Mandisa held tightly to the matron in her arms.

"Now, these chicken and waffles aren't going to make themselves," Mandisa chided. "So you go rest while I get to work."

Mama Indy gave Mandisa one more squeeze, then headed off in the direction of the family room.

Mandisa lost herself in the preparation of the meal, her mind still buzzing with nervous energy. Slade walked through the door just in time to see her plating up the food. He washed his hands, dropped another quick kiss on her lips, and carried the heavy platters in to the table.

There wasn't much conversation. Slade seemed to be very engaged in cleaning his plate, and Mama Indy seemed equally interested in her food. Relieved her meal had passed inspection, Mandisa relaxed enough to eat too.

When they were done, Mandisa watched Slade rub his stomach, a sure sign that he was happy and satisfied. She took a fortifying sip of Mama Indy's coffee before she began speaking. Hoping to somehow keep the mood light and pleasant, she shared her news.

"When I was out on my walk, I received an interesting phone call."

Slade cleared the table and headed for the sink to rinse the dishes. He turned to the side so he could still provide eye contact as she spoke to him. "Yeah? Who was it?"

"Your dad."

Mandisa and Mama Indy looked at one another when they heard a loud clattering noise in the sink. Mama Indy stood up, leaving Mandisa at the table, and shooed Slade out of the way as she took care of the dishes.

Slade motioned for Mandisa to follow him into his office. His movements were stiff and calculated, obvious displeasure coursing through him. He remained quiet, stoic, not speaking a word until the door was closed behind them and he was leaning against his heavy wooden desk that sat in the middle of the room.

"How did Bull get your number?"

She shrugged. She honestly didn't know.

"What did he want?"

"To invite us to dinner."

Slade crossed his arms against his chest and lifted a skeptical brow. "He wanted to invite us to dinner, or you?"

Busted.

"Look, Slade, the man has a vested interest in talking to me. I can't ignore him. Even if this deal collapses, I still need to make certain I walk out of this thing with my name intact. I don't see where sharing a meal with the man will cause any harm."

"Of course you don't see, because you don't know anything about my father. I specifically told you I didn't want Bull anywhere near you. Why couldn't you just respect that?"

Fire began to simmer in her blood, and not in the usual sexy way his words often incited. Especially the way he'd said the word, "told."

She took a few steps closer, meeting his gaze with her head slightly titled. "You told me?" Her words were quiet but sharp. She didn't want to argue, but she wasn't about to let Slade believe he could say shit like this without any opposition. "Do I look like one of your lackeys, or better yet, your child? The man called my damn phone, Slade. What exactly did you expect me to do?"

"How about telling him to go to hell?"

Mandisa looked around the room, searching for the hidden camera that had to be recording her. This had to be some ploy created to catch her acting out of character. When her perusal of the office yielded nothing, she took a long look at Slade's carved features, the stiff set of his angled jaw screamed how serious he was.

"I can't believe you're acting this way, Slade." Her statement seemed to throw him. He shook his head and stood up from his desk, his full height towering over her.

"Mandisa. You've got to believe me. You don't know Bull. I'm trying my best to keep these negotiations on track. Bull's way of doing business isn't something you want to deal with. Just let me handle it."

"What the hell is that supposed to mean?"

She threw her hands up before he could answer. This conversation was veering left, and she needed to yank it back to the middle of the road before they ended up crashing and burning.

"It doesn't even matter. I promised the man we were having dinner with him. Show up, or don't show up, but I'm keeping my word."

She stormed out of the office, making sure to give it a good hard tug as she made her way to the front door and out of the house.

If Slade wanted to be an overprotective jackass, she'd let him. But what she wasn't about to let him do was ruin her chances of succeeding in the business world. Like she'd told him in the beginning—no piece of dick was so good that she'd let it rob her of her family's legacy.

13

Mandisa inspected the final touches to her makeup. Her face was flawless. She couldn't very well convince someone to buy her product if she didn't wear it herself. She looked at her outfit, a fitted black three-piece pantsuit. It was her power suit. It screamed sexy, confident professional who wasn't to be fucked with. It was absolutely the impression she was attempting to make as the creator and owner of a cosmetics line.

She grabbed her red pumps and matching clutch to finalize the ensemble, satisfied her appearance would be acceptable for the country club Bull chose.

She was placing the vampire-red lipstick she'd used in her purse when Slade stepped out of his closet wearing a suit that fell somewhere between a tuxedo and a business suit. It was crisp black, and tailored to enhance every manly curve he possessed, Mandisa was entranced by the sight of him.

"You're going?" She managed the two-word question despite the dryness in her mouth.

"Of course I'm going." He took careful strides across the room until he was standing in front of her. He reached out his hand and lifted her chin carefully with his finger. "I'm sorry for the way I behaved earlier. I was completely out of line."

The remorse filling his voice eased some of the tension between them. They'd spent the day in their separate corners, ignoring the problem, pretending it didn't exist. It hadn't worked, not for her anyway. Her pride kept her from extending some sort of peace offering, but standing here, with him touching her again, she was more than happy that he wasn't as stubborn or juvenile as she.

"You were, but so was I. I shouldn't have made plans for us without discussing them with you first. Especially since I knew you didn't want Bull around. I was just trying to do what I thought was best. For me, my business, but also for you, Slade."

If the strange spark in his bright blue eyes were any indication, he was surprised by her statement. "What made you think this was best for me, Mandisa?"

She pulled his hand from her chin and laced their fingers together. "Slade, it's obvious to me that there's something off between you and your dad. I know I haven't been here long enough to get all the info, but I hope you'll realize you can trust me with those details soon. I just wanted to give you an opportunity to hang onto something I can't."

"What's that?"

Mandisa raised her eyes to his, hoping he would see sincerity resting in them. "A living parent."

Slade closed his eyes before pulling her into his embrace. He leaned back slightly to place a soft kiss on the back of her hand.

"Darlin', that's sweet of you. Knowing how much you miss your mama, understanding what it feels like to bury a parent myself, I'm flattered you would attempt to do something like this for me. But, Mandisa, Bull isn't a parent. He has never loved or cared for me. I haven't lived in his home since my mother died when I was a child. We may share blood, but we are not family. Sitting down to a meal with him will not change that."

She raked a careful hand through the hair at his nape, pulling him down for a quick peck. Her heart ached for him. Mandisa and her mother hadn't seen eye-to-eye on what was feminine. Mandisa's love of all things science often baffled Sadie King. But there was never a moment in her life that Mandisa questioned whether her mother loved her. Did Mandisa question whether Sadie approved of her choices, whether she was proud of the things Mandisa did? Yes, Mandisa would always question that, but there was no doubt in her mind that Sadie King loved every fiber of Mandisa's being.

"Let's go eat and see what Bull has to say. After that, we'll spend the next week cuddled up together, forgetting about the outside world."

He nodded and offered her a sweet smile. "I guess that's a fair compromise. Let's get to it, darlin'."

The sound of his pet name for her, the smooth way it slid across his lips made her tremble. Bull Hamilton be damned, Mandisa wasn't going to allow anything or anyone to hinder what she and Slade were building.

Slade walked into the country club with a possessive arm around Mandisa's waist. He couldn't care to be concerned by how Bull would react. Slade was done running from this son of a bitch. He was done hiding and hoarding what joy he could and praying Bull wouldn't come snatch it away from him.

He spotted Bull right away, his stomach knotting up with

anger as he saw the flawlessly beautiful blonde woman sitting next to his father at a table in the corner.

"Looks like Bull brought a date. Is it me, or does she seem a bit young for him, Slade?"

Hell, yeah, she was a bit young for the old man—more than thirty years Bull's junior if Slade remembered correctly.

"She's not his date," Slade grumbled as the greeter escorted them to Bull's table.

"Slade, Dr. Avery, glad you two could make it." Bull exchanged a quick handshake with Mandisa and motioned for her to take the seat next to him. He then offered a short nod to Slade as a greeting. He pointed to the young woman sitting across from him at the square table, his bright smile gleaming with perverse pride.

God, he's a sick bastard.

"This is my wife, Macy. When I told her you and I were going to talk business, she insisted on coming to meet you," Bull explained.

"It's very nice to meet you," Mandisa responded. "Please forgive me if I stare, but you seem very familiar to me, Macy. Have we met before?"

Slade watched Macy's pink, glossy lips curve into a smile while her long lashes fanned repeatedly. Slade had seen that exact combination of gestures before, had thought it sweet the first few times he'd witnessed it. In less than a year he'd learned the truth of what that expression meant. It was fake. Used to manipulate and mislead unsuspecting spectators into believing there was a genuine and humble human being behind it. It was the mask Macy used to conceal her venom from her would-be victims.

"I'm certain you probably recognize me from my work as the Venus Cosmetics spokesmodel. I've been the face of Venus for the last ten years."

Slade watched Mandisa assess Macy carefully. He wasn't

quite certain what she was thinking, but he could tell by the squinting of her eyes and the lines on her brow that her mind was working overtime.

"No, I spend most of my time in a lab or in an office running a business. I wouldn't know you as a spokes model."

Slade damn near choked on his laughter, turning it into a cough when Macy's sharp gaze cut across the table and landed on him. Saved by their server's arrival, they sat quietly as the young man filled their wineglasses with white wine, then deftly recorded everyone's order for the evening.

"So, Dr. Avery, my Bull here tells me you make makeup? Is that true?"

"That's a pretty broad description of what I do. I create beauty products, not just makeup. I use science to create formulas to address cosmetic needs for women of color."

"Just women of color? That seems like a very small market share. Wouldn't it be wiser to cater to all skin tones instead?"

Their server returned with their selections, and the conversation was abated for a few moments. When the server was gone, and they had each taken their first bites of food, Slade hoped Macy's ignorant line of questioning would recede. But after another glass of wine, the young woman found her courage and continued to press Mandisa.

"Take Venus, for example. Our brand caters to everyone."

Slade was ready to jump in and defend Mandisa's honor when he saw the edge of Mandisa's lip lift in a cynical half-smile that told him she had this. A celebratory gleam in Macy's eyes caught Slade's attention. He shook his head. Macy was so pleased with herself, she didn't see what Slade saw—Mandisa's brilliance preparing for the battle ahead.

"Actually, Macy, Venus does not cater to everyone," Mandisa countered. "Venus makes products that cater to mainstream America. If you're white, blue-eyed, and blonde,

Venus products will work gloriously on you. But if you have the slightest bit of melanin in your skin, Venus products will make you look like you learned cosmetics application at a clown school.

"It's a fact I think your husband is well aware of. That's probably one of the reasons he wants me to come work for him. Without a line that caters to women of color, Venus is leaving money on the table. Besides failing to cater to an entire population demographic, there's also the greater problem of Venus' contribution to the historical and social issue of perpetuating the idea that only white, blonde women are beautiful."

Slade let an uncaring smirk rise unchecked on his face. Watching his woman educate Macy on a business, financial, and social issue wasn't just hilarious, it was sexy as hell. Mandisa sent him a cavalier wink across the table. Game, set, match, she had this, and everyone at that table knew it, especially Bull.

For the rest of the evening Mandisa watched the bitter bitch sitting next to her hoover multiple glasses of wine while Slade, Bull, and Mandisa talked business. To anyone watching it seemed cordial, but Mandisa could see Slade was doing his level best to keep from slitting Bull's throat every time the man tried to find a different method of pressuring Mandisa for a final decision on the deal.

Mandisa was unmoved by Bull's tactics. She didn't respond to bullying. She needed Bull to know that if she was going to make this deal, it would always be on her own terms. When she was tired of the boardroom back and forth across the dinner table, she excused herself to the ladies' room.

She used the restroom, washed her hands, and sat down in front of an empty seat at the vanity station. Satisfied most of her makeup was intact, she retouched her vibrant red lipstick that had been sacrificed to the meal they'd eaten.

"You're sleeping with him, aren't you?"

Mandisa looked up in the mirror to see Macy standing behind her. Mandisa calmly placed her lipstick in her purse and continued checking her reflection, unbothered by Macy's question.

"Seeing how you're married to Slade's father and Slade's a grown man, I don't understand how that's any of your business."

Mandisa saw a spark of jealousy streak across Macy's face, leaving her lips flattened into thin strips and her eyes squinting. Considering all the plastic surgery Mandisa could detect on the human doll's face, she was thoroughly impressed Macy could scowl at her like that.

Mandisa would be amused by Macy's reaction save for the fact that the woman was Slade's stepmother.

Why the hell would she be jealous over Slade?

"I hope you don't think it's serious. You're not exactly his type."

"And let me guess. Who is his type? You?"

When Macy squared her shoulders and placed both hands on her tiny waist, Mandisa knew she'd hit the nail on its head. This foul bitch was really jonesin' for her husband's son.

If this ain't some nasty soap opera shit.

"Listen Macy, I'm not concerned about what you do or don't want from Slade. The fact is you're married to his father. The man I know, however briefly, would never cross that line. So whether I'm sleeping with Slade or not is irrelevant. Even if I weren't a factor, he still wouldn't touch you with a ten-foot pole."

Mandisa pulled a bill out of her purse and made a deliberate show of shoving the folded paper into the bathroom attendant's tip jar. She gave Macy a parting smile and made certain to add a little extra sway to her full hips as she walked away.

Slade grabbed his glass of water and emptied it. He could feel the contents of his stomach rising, a frequent event whenever he was in his father's presence for longer than a few moments at a time.

"I'll give you one thing, boy." Bull's voice held a lascivious tone that made Slade's jaw tic. "You've always had fine taste in woman. That one right there is smart as a whip and sexy as sin. Please tell me you've tasted that at least once."

Slade squeezed his fists together, shaking with the need to let them fly across the table at Bull. It was only the room full of witnesses that kept him planted in his seat.

"Bull, I'm going to give you some advice." Slade leaned closer, his voice dropping lower as he spoke. Slade watched Bull's Adam's apple bob up and down as the man swallowed deeply. "You can talk about that tramp that you're married to like that, but don't ever let me hear you speak about Mandisa that way."

"Seems I've touched a nerve."

Bull was right—he had touched a very raw nerve. Mandisa was completely off limits. She wasn't about to be a casualty of Bull's senseless destruction. Not on Slade's watch.

"I never believed you were capable of such depravity until Macy came along. I'm telling you now, I've learned from that situation. I'm not some naïve young buck you can step all over anymore, Bull. If you come anywhere near Mandisa, I promise I'll ruin you."

Slade watched the shocked-still features that made up his father's face. The man's quick-moving eyes considered Slade carefully—more carefully than Slade had ever witnessed before. Bull could try Slade if he wanted to, but Slade meant every word he'd said. He would decimate Bull if he came anywhere near Mandisa.

Satisfied that his point had been made, Slade stood up, removed his phone from his jacket pocket, and sent off a quick text to Aaron.

Send me something quick to end this now.

Once the text was sent, Slade replaced the phone in his inside pocket and pulled enough money from his wallet to cover the bill. He didn't want to owe Bull anything, not even the cost of dinner.

Resolute in his desire to get as far away from Bull as possible, Slade looked up and directed his sights toward the corridor with one thought resounding in his head.

Where the hell is my woman?

Slade must have been waiting for her to emerge from the restroom. He was standing in the corridor leaning against the wall. When their gazes met, he took a few strides and was at her side. He placed a comforting hand at the small of her spine and directed her toward the exit.

The valet brought Slade's car to the curb and was rewarded with a generous tip from Slade's billfold. He helped her into the car and joined her shortly, pulling quickly into traffic. Mandisa said nothing for the hour-long trip from Downtown Austin. She was equally quiet as they entered the house and climbed the stairs to Slade's bedroom.

She remained quiet, removing her jewelry and clothing, then heading for the shower. When she was dried, wearing shorts and a tank top, her usual uniform for bed before she began sharing night space with Slade, she stood in front of a sitting Slade and crossed her arms.

"So tell me, Slade. Exactly how long have you been sleeping with your father's wife?"

14

"Shit," Slade muttered under his breath as he pinched the bridge of his nose.

"Was that an admission of guilt?"

Slade shook his head. He'd known the moment Macy had suddenly needed to go to the ladies' room a few moments after Mandisa that his scandalous stepmother was up to no fucking good.

"Darlin', however Macy made this seem, I'm sure she didn't provide you with an honest picture of what really happened."

Mandisa nodded and sat down next to him on the bed. "So, there's a story behind you sleeping with your father's wife? Good, let's hear it."

Slade stood up from his perch on the mattress. He walked away from Mandisa, keeping his back to her. God, he didn't want to relive this shit again. No matter how he explained things, he'd come off looking weak and shameful. He never wanted Mandisa to think of him in those terms. Not her.

Mandisa was bright, beautiful, and awe-inspiring. For some reason, she saw him in a similar way. Slade knew deep within himself all that would change if Mandisa knew the truth. Unwilling to compromise her view of him, he kept his gaze fixed on the wall before him while she stood behind him.

"Mandisa, I'm not the kind of man to sleep with my father's wife. I would hope you would be able to tell that much about me in the time you've spent here in Austin."

"Slade, there's something going on that I'm not aware of. I don't like feeling as if I'm walking into an ambush. That's exactly what Macy did to me. She ambushed me in that bathroom. I just want to know how to protect myself, protect you."

His heart jumped at those words. He was six-feet-four, a hulk of a man—he shouldn't need protecting from anyone or anything on this earth. Yet the sound of those words on her lips gripped him so tightly he had to steady himself.

"Please," he whispered. "Just let this go."

"Slade, I'm sorry, but I'm not comfortable—"

"I said drop it!"

He whirled around, his lungs tight with anger as he struggled for air. He regretted his outburst the moment he saw her step back from him, folding her arms across her chest, retreating into herself.

"Darlin', I'm sorry." He attempted to step closer to her, but she retreated, deliberately maintaining what felt like a chasm between them. "Mandisa, I'm sorry. I didn't mean to speak to you like that. Talking about my father and his wife is very difficult for me. There's a lot of family drama and history that I just don't want to dredge up. Please, can you respect that?"

He watched her chest lift as she took in a deep breath through her nose. When she looked at him again, the anger he saw building was replaced by a slight wariness. She blinked a few times, her dark, full lashes fanning her cheeks.

When she opened her eyes again, she walked to him, taking his hands, wrapping them around her body, and burying herself in his chest.

"For now, Slade," was all she said before going up on tiptoe and placing a soft kiss on his cheek. She stepped out of his embrace and climbed into his bed. When she was settled, she held up the end of the bedding and gazed at him. "Coming?"

Mandisa knew she was alone in bed before she opened her eyes. The now-familiar way Slade blanketed her with his body was gone. He literally curled around her, covering almost every inch of her with his big, warm physique. She always felt so secure and treasured when the early rays of the sun pulled her from slumber. Not so today, though.

Whatever this deal was with Slade, Macy, and Bull, it made all Mandisa's warning signals ring in her head.

She reached over to the nightstand and grabbed her phone. Opening a browser, she was just about to type all their names in the search engine when she heard the pain in Slade's voice from the previous night.

There's a lot of family drama and history that I just don't want to dredge up. Please, can you respect that?

Guilt began to set in. She'd promised him to leave it alone, and here she was not even a full day later looking to get the goods on the internet. Whatever this thing was had changed their easygoing dynamic, and Mandisa didn't like it one bit. *Really, girl? spying on him? If you can't trust him with this, how are you going to do it long distance when you go back home?*

She closed the browser and tossed the phone back on the

nightstand as she made a final decision. Whatever this family drama was, she wasn't about to let it change what was quickly becoming something significant between her and Slade. He meant too much.

She pulled herself up against the headboard and crossed her arms. "All right, Slade. We'll play it your way…for now."

She swung her legs out of the bed, showered, dressed, and headed downstairs. In desperate need of a hit of Indira's coffee, Mandisa headed directly for the kitchen.

Her first footfall into the room, Mandisa met a smiling Indira holding a cup of the treasured brew.

"Please tell me that's for me?"

Mama Indy waved Mandisa to the table, placing the cup carefully in front of Mandisa when she was seated.

Mandisa was halfway through the glorious first sip of the warm nectar when she heard Mama Indy mutter, "Rough night?"

Mandisa blinked away the haze the addictive elixir created and focused on a suspicious Mama Indy. She was standing next to Mandisa, a cup of her own raised to her lips, as the squint of her knowing eyes regarded Mandisa carefully. All that was missing for a classic "I'm waiting" posture was Mama Indy tapping her foot in impatience. Convinced that was the next gesture to come, Mandisa took a quick sip of coffee to fortify herself and returned her gaze to the waiting matron.

"Slade and I had dinner with his father and step-bimbo last night. It was…interesting."

"I'm surprised she could pull herself away from her shopping and traveling to be bothered." Mama Indy pulled out the chair across from Mandisa and sat down.

"I get the feeling she lives for as many chances as she can get to be in Slade's face," Mandisa answered.

"Did something happen at dinner?"

"No, everyone seemed on their best behavior, but it was obvious something wasn't right. If the Hamiltons are anything like my family, no matter what the issue is, you don't act out in front of company."

Mama Indy pressed a firm hand on top of Mandisa's, the elder woman's gaze locked firmly on her as she leaned in to speak. "You are not company to Slade. You mean more to him than anyone at that table last night. If he sat at a table with those two, suffering their company for longer than a second, it was because he cares very much about you."

Mandisa dropped her gaze to sidestep the woman's stare. Even without those words, Mandisa knew they were true. Ever since they'd met, every interaction she and Slade shared was always about Slade taking care of her. He was gentle, caring, and always concerned with her wellbeing. Whatever this thing was about, him asking Mandisa to drop it wasn't about keeping her in the dark.

"Strangely enough, I know that, Mama Indy. I just feel like he needs my help, and I don't understand why."

"Slade has suffered a great deal of loss, most of it at his father's hands. In Bull's twisted mind he's making his son stronger. In reality, he's forced Slade to lock himself in a bubble of protection. The only people Slade's allowed in are Aaron and me, and now you. I'm sure you want to know all the details, but let him come to you in his own time. Pushing him right now will only alienate him when he needs you more than ever."

Mandisa circled a single finger around the rim of her coffee mug as Mama Indy's words weighed on her. Two weeks ago things had been light and fun, and that had scared the hell out of Mandisa. She hadn't completely trusted all of the lightheartedness she'd experienced in Slade's presence. Last night was the first time she'd seen him as a real person and not some godlike figure who could make the impossible happen with a wink and a smile.

"Last night was the first time he'd ever allowed me to see him when his control was slipping. He's always got this million-dollar smile plastered on his face. It's hard to imagine anything ever bothering him. But last night I saw a glimpse of who he is when things aren't perfect."

"Did it make you want to run?"

Mandisa could hear the motherly concern in her question.

"I will return to NY because that's where I live, where my life is. But I'm not leaving Slade. The only thing last night accomplished was to show me that even a giant needs protection sometimes. Bull may have taken more things than he should have from Slade, but I won't be one of them. And as for Macy, if she wants a fight, she'd better recognize that a Brooklyn girl ain't ever scared to take off her earrings and put grease on her face."

Slade's back ached with the repetitive motion of bending and shoveling as he cleaned each stall in the stables. If it had been just the stalls alone, he probably wouldn't feel it as much, but before that he'd moved fresh bales of hay into the barn as well.

Sore, hot, and sweaty, he thrived on the physical ache and the emotional release it gave him. Aside from his family and his horse, the ability to lose himself in the upkeep and work of the ranch was one of the things he loved most about owning his spread.

Whenever Bull pissed him off, or stomaching his father's presence became too much of a burden to bear, Slade would work from sun up to sundown until his body had burned every ounce of anger out of him.

After last night, he'd needed an outlet. He'd allowed his anger at Bull to affect Mandisa. Too afraid it would happen again, he woke before dawn and started on the morning's chores to help himself get a grip on his emotions.

The gentle vibration in his back pocket made him lean his shovel against a stall door to answer his phone. "Aaron?"

"Slade, we've got a problem."

"What do you mean? Is something wrong with our plan for Bull?"

There was a brief pause over the line before Aaron answered. "No. We're still a go with that, but I won't be able to be there physically for it. You're going to have to include me on the meeting via phone or webcam. I can't leave Brooklyn right now."

"Aaron, what the hell is going on?"

"I finally located Bull's man, but by the time I did, it was too late."

Fear began to swell in Slade's chest. His father was treacherous, and if Aaron was concerned enough to delay his return to Austin, something dreadful must have happened.

"What did Bull do?"

"His lackey vandalized Mandisa's Pitkin Avenue store. He waited until Mandisa's friend Kandi was alone at closing and forced himself in. He tied her up and destroyed the store. I got there in time to subdue him before he could bring any harm to her, but he'd already done his worst to the store by then.

"Is Kandi all right?"

"Yeah. She's shaken, but all right."

"Is she there? Put her on the phone."

"She's in the back trying to catalogue things. I'll go get her."

The line was quiet for a few moments before he heard a hesitant voice whisper into the phone. "Slade?" He could hear her voice shake with uncertainty as she spoke.

"Kandi, are you all right?"

"Yeah. Thank God you sent Aaron here to track this guy down. I don't know what would've happened if he hadn't been here. Slade, why would a perfect stranger want to destroy Mandisa's store?"

"Kandi, I don't want you to worry about anything. Aaron and I are going to take care of this. He's going to stay there with you until the store is up and running, and I'm sure you're safe."

"It will take weeks, even months for the store to be fixed. It's a pile of rubble. We have stock coming in next week, but there will be no place to put it. I need to talk to Mandisa so we can figure out what we're going to do."

"No," Slade barked.

"Slade, whatever the terms of this bet you have going with Mandisa are, she has to be told."

Slade massaged the back of neck as he quickly attempted to think up resolutions to this situation.

"Kandi, we both know Mandisa will leave the moment she learns of this. She's down here brokering a deal to expand her company. If she leaves now, she'll never secure the funds for the expansion. You know how much that means to her."

"Slade, she needs to know."

"Kandi, it's a week. That's all I'm asking. I'll hire and pay for a crew to fix everything up. You handle the execution; I'll cover the cost. Just don't tell her anything about this until this deal is signed and she's secured the funding she's been trying to raise."

"You're asking me to lie to my best friend and my boss."

The pitch and volume of Kandi's previously shaky whisper increased.

"Kandi, please, a week, that's all I'm asking. In a week, this deal will be done, and she'll get everything she's been working so hard for all this time."

The line was quiet for longer than Slade was comfortable with. He'd do whatever he could to keep Mandisa with him until he neutralized Bull. Neutralizing Bull was the only permanent answer to saving them all.

"A week, Slade. That's all I can promise. If this deal isn't done in a week, I'm calling her and telling her everything."

"A week is all I need, sugar."

He closed the phone and shoved it back into his pocket, hoping to God his statement was true. He had one week to win over Mandisa and snatch his company back from Bull. Slade closed the empty stall he'd been cleaning and headed out of the stables. As much as he loved working his land, right now he had to exchange his cowboy hat for his corporate one. It was time to end this ugly saga with his father.

15

Mandisa sat on the back porch swinging lightly as the music from her phone filled her ears. Eyes closed, with the sexy groove of LUV by Tory Lanez blasting through her earbuds, she allowed the emotion of the song to slowly spread through her. With each bop of her head and snap of her fingers, ideas would blossom, forming the building blocks for the scent she was creating in her head.

To the average person, scent was something handled solely by the nose. However, for the chemist in her, scent always began with ideas about what she wanted a scent to represent, and what ingredients she'd need to build it the way her mind imagined it.

This scent was inspired by the man she'd cradled in her arms for the last few nights. The memory of Slade, resting his head on her chest and letting her stroke the dark strands of his hair until his choppy breathing turned into a quiet bristle of wind against her skin, warmed her.

He'd scared her the night of their dinner with Bull.

Not in the physical sense. She had no fear of him bringing

her physical harm. But watching him battle whatever this fucked-up situation was between Slade and his father unnerved her. Slade was always calm, carefree. But when she'd asked him to discuss Macy, she almost hadn't recognized the man who'd walked into the bedroom with her.

Bull made Slade jumpy, uneasy, and wary, none of which were attractive qualities on the big man.

When he'd first lain in her arms, he was stiff, his body rigid with anger and pain. Pain he hadn't wanted to voice. But even though he hadn't revealed his pain to her in his words, the way the stiffness bled out of him as she stroked his hair and ran light fingertips across his skin told her everything she needed to know…for now.

That dinner had caused a tide to turn in their brief but intense connection. It was somehow deeper than before. In Slade's anger, Mandisa could see a glimpse of vulnerability she wanted to desperately protect. That vulnerability was just one more beautiful layer to the tender man she was getting to know.

A light flashed across the inside of her lids as aromatic thoughts burst behind her eyes. She pressed her finger over the home key of her phone and pecked away at the digital keyboard.

Strong, fun, sexy, spicy, sweet, intriguing, intelligent, and treasured, were the words swirling around her head and olfactory system. She could feel a wide grin dancing on her lips as she thought of ways to describe Slade. She couldn't say exactly when it happened, but at some point he had become a cherished part of her life. Someone she wanted to keep near at all times.

You live three thousand miles apart. How are you supposed to keep him close with that much distance between the two of you?

As the song played on repeat, the sensual tones sliding through her veins and stoking the bubbling emotions just beneath the surface, her mind created scenarios of how she and Slade were going to make a go of their relationship living in two different time zones. Her jam session hadn't given her a definitive answer to the how of their situation, but she knew they'd figure out a way in the end.

Satisfied about the direction of the relationship and certain she had the correct descriptors for the new scent she was planning, she needed to go shopping and play with a mixture of ingredients to make a scent that was uniquely him.

She finished jotting down her notes on her phone, turned the music off, and stood up, looking out at the beautiful expanse of Slade's land. Leaving this place, even with the knowledge she'd be frequently visiting to see it and its owner, created a small ache inside her heart. She shook herself, attempting to displace the heavy feelings trying to take over. Convinced her creative process had left her emotions exposed, she took a deep breath and headed inside.

Why sit here lamenting leaving when you can be spending time with the object of your thoughts?

"Hey, cowboy." Slade looked up from his desk to see a smiling Mandisa leaning against the doorway. "For someone I sleep next to every night, I've seen very little of you over the last couple of days. I get the feeling the events of the infamous dinner with your father are still hanging over us."

Slade closed his laptop as Mandisa slowly made her way from the door to his desk. She kept walking until she was standing next to him, twisting his swivel chair until he faced her. She climbed into his lap and snaked an arm around his neck, tugging him until their lips met in a sweet kiss.

"You don't have to avoid me, Slade. I'm not going to hound you about the issues you have with your dad. You don't have to spend my last few days here dodging me because of it. Or does your avoidance have to do with our bet coming to an end? Is this the part where we transition from the pleasure part to the business?"

Slade closed his eyes, quickly attempting to hide the shame he felt welling up inside of him. She was right. Ever since Aaron had called with the news about the Pitkin Avenue store, Slade had been avoiding her.

Slade worked tirelessly to put his plan into action. Getting all the necessary players into position while keeping Bull in the dark hadn't been easy, but he'd managed to do it, and tomorrow he'd finally be able to cut his father off at the knees.

"Darlin', my scarceness doesn't have anything to do with you. A few days after you got here, I found out my father is trying to make a play to steal my company. I've been working overtime to stop him. Tomorrow I take back what's mine."

"Your company? Isn't Logan Industries Bull's?"

Slade shook his head. Bull certainly wished Logan was his, but Slade would never let that happen.

"Logan Industries was created and owned by my mother's family. My mother dying when I was a child left us a in a bit of a pickle when my granny died and I was still a teenager. Although she left me the ownership of the business, I wasn't technically old enough to run it. So she put the company in a trust for me until my fortieth birthday. Until then, Bull and two other trustees run it. I'm not supposed to take the reins for another five years."

Slade could see the questions swirling around in her warm chocolate eyes when she asked, "Why forty?"

"Granny didn't want to pressure me into taking over the business if I didn't want it. She was attempting to give me options. What she actually did was give my father another way to attempt to control me. Don't get me wrong—she put in failsafe contingencies to keep him from completely screwing me over, but for the last decade that I've worked under him, he's used his position to torture me."

Concern marred her deep brown skin and reminded him yet again why he couldn't let Bull's tentacles reach her. She should never look worried or saddened, especially because of something his useless father did.

"Slade, if my being here is a complication right now, why didn't you just tell me?"

Slade pulled her in for another kiss, this one deeper than the last. "You are never a complication. Work will always come second to you. That's why I've been down here late each night. It's over tomorrow. I was hoping you'd come join me for the meeting."

She regarded him carefully. The slow way her eyes appeared to be searching his face revealed her hesitation. "You don't want to come with me?"

"That's not it, Slade. Businesswise, I don't want to get caught in the middle of whatever this is between you and your father. Your company, your father, is a powerful man. I don't want to make an enemy of him."

"Mandisa, after tomorrow, you won't have to worry about it. Our deal will still stand, and if you decide you want to work for Logan, Bull won't be able to interfere with any of that. Please, come with me."

She touched soft fingers to his face, sparking a warm sensation that spread throughout his chest, into his limbs, stoking his need to touch her.

"I'll be there, Slade. But I can't walk into this meeting blind. I need to know what the real issue is between you and Bull. I haven't asked, because I wanted you to come to me in your own time. But, Slade, if this affects my business, or our ability to do business with one another, I need full disclosure."

He'd known it would come to this. He'd hoped to never have to recount these details, but realistically, he knew he'd have to come clean someday.

Slade took a breath, digging deep to pull up memories from a lifetime ago. Moments he'd fought like hell to bury so deep, he had to wonder sometimes if they'd actually happened. But just the sight of Macy at that dinner, clinging to his father while still flirting with him, brought the entire sickening ordeal to the surface.

"About ten years ago I fell for this cute flight attendant I met coming home from a business trip. She was sweet and fun and catered to every one of my whims. My oversized ego told me it was love. So, after dating and living with her for a couple of years, I proposed to her."

"That cute flight attendant was Macy, wasn't she? So, you lived with her here on the ranch?"

Slade shook his head. Thanking God yet again that Macy had never set foot on his ranch. She would have tainted it, prevented him from enjoying the land he loved.

"No, this happened just before I bought the ranch. At the time, Bull and I were still cordial to one another. I harbored a lot of resentment toward him for how he treated my mother when she was ill. Instead of being home with his dying wife, he was cheating on her with any floozy that showed interest in him or the things he could provide.

"Even though I didn't think he was worth a damn, I don't think I hated him at that point. It wasn't until I found him screwing my fiancée at our engagement party that my loathing of Bull began.

"I remember that moment clearly. I'd walked into the bridal suite to get Macy and found my father bending my fiancée over a damn table, fucking her from behind, and the two of them smiling at me through their reflections in the mirrored walls. I watched that disgusting whore come on my father's cock while I stood there paralyzed in the open doorway."

Slade closed his eyes as the memory flooded his mind. The smiles they were both wearing, their lack of shame, Slade's inability to react—all of it pressed to the forefront of his mind. By the time Slade had regained his ability to move, Bull was done riding Macy, and Slade's stomach contents were traveling up his throat.

Slade could still remember the taste of his own bile as he rushed through the wait-staff and stumbled into a private bathroom. He didn't realize he was heaving in the present until he felt Mandisa's familiar touch on his face.

"Slade, it's over. You're not there." She leaned down and kissed him, pressing her body into his personal space, using his senses to pull him out of the traumatic hold of his memories. "You're here with me, not with them."

He raised his hands to her arms, touching her, verifying her statement, making certain the right woman was in front of him before he opened his eyes.

"That was the moment I hated my father, Mandisa. The moment I watched him take another thing I loved from me. First my mother, then my company, then Macy. I knew then that if I didn't fight him, he'd steal it all away, and I'd have nothing left."

Mandisa rubbed her fingers through his hair, her nails scratching lightly against his scalp, soothing the tidal wave of emotion that threatened to take him under.

"None of what your father has done to you is your fault, Slade. And if Macy was willing to betray you like that, you dodged a bullet. You are a wonderful man, one that deserves so much love, because you give it so easily. You're the man I fell in love with from the first time he called me darlin' and made me tremble with his beautiful southern drawl."

"You love me?"

The question seemed to surprise her. He allowed quiet to remain between them as she appeared to contemplate his question. He wouldn't hold it against her if she rescinded her declaration. It wasn't logical that she would feel love for him yet. But Slade had no doubt if given the opportunity they were headed in that direction.

Everything from the way Mandisa held onto him at night when they slept to the way she treated his mama made Slade feel at ease, at home. When you'd grown up with so much hell and mistrust, security was something you didn't dare reach for or expect. But Mandisa made him foolishly want to believe in the cradle of security that only love could bring.

"The day after we made love, Kandi asked me why I was so hesitant to take you up on your offer. She wanted to know if something bad had happened between us in your hotel room."

That first night she'd shared herself with him had been heaven. He'd known from those few hours tangled together in his bed that one night wouldn't be enough.

He'd been secure in his assumption Mandisa felt the same. After all, she'd followed him to Texas forty-eight hours later. It never occurred to him that she might not have been as overjoyed about their first time as he was.

Slade swallowed the slight weight of fear that was attempting to settle in his throat. It would just about kill him to know that night had been a disappointment for her. He let his eyes fall from hers, not wanting to see it if she didn't feel the same.

He felt the warmth of Mandisa's touch radiate from the gentle fingertips she'd placed on his chin throughout every cell in his being. It quieted the growing uneasiness in his belly and called to him, giving him the strength to face her, even when his fear told him to shy away.

"I didn't understand why, but I told her the truth. I felt loved. It was a crazy notion considering you and I had only spent a handful of hours together. I didn't, and still don't understand how that could be, Slade. But in the three weeks since I met a handsome stranger in a lounge, I can't seem to remember what life was like before he called me darlin' for the first time."

Something broke inside Slade as he watched her. He'd been so busy attempting to make Mandisa stay that he hadn't even considered the fact that she would love him willingly. He knew they were connected, felt the undeniable chemistry they shared, but he hadn't recognized their need to be together for what it really was—love.

"I ought to thank that skank," she continued. "Macy was just a place-holder for me. Giving you something to play with until the real deal showed up."

He watched her tuck her bottom lip between her teeth and saw a brief flash of uncertainty.

"That is, if you want the real deal, Slade. I know we've talked about seeing each other once I go home. But I want you to understand I'm not just talking about casual dating. If you're truly serious about doing this long distance, I'm all in. All the way in. I just need to know you're equally as committed."

"We still have a few more days before this bet is over. After enjoying life with me on the ranch, and seeing what could be at your fingertips at my labs, you still won't stay? Isn't what I have to offer you enough? Aren't I enough?"

God, he hated the desperate sound of his voice. He couldn't help it. If begging was the only way to keep her near him, to keep what they shared at his fingertips, he'd spend any amount of time on his knees.

"The only thing that's taking me back to Brooklyn is my business, Slade. You are definitely worth uprooting my life for. But I can't. You knew that when you made this wager."

"I did know that. I just hoped that playing in face paint and making people feel pretty would pale in comparison to building a life with me."

He wanted to swallow those words as soon as they'd touched the air. He'd meant every one of them, but he knew they sounded harsh. "Mandisa, I didn't—"

"Yeah, you did," she answered. "But I'm not angry about it. I understand that you're coming from a place of loss. That just tells me I mean something to you. I know you don't want me to go, and honestly, neither do I. But I can't leave, at least not yet.

"I promise you, Slade, you and I are going to figure this out. But the best I can come up with right now is frequent flying by both of us. No matter how jet-lagged I end up being, I'm not willing to let this go. Can you say the same?"

A gentle smile tugged at his lips. Even though he wasn't thrilled about her plans to leave, he couldn't hide his happiness at the level of commitment she was proposing. "Darlin', I'm right here with you. All the way. If we need to fly back and forth to be with each other, then so be it. My pilot gets paid way too much anyway. It's about time he started earning the hefty salary he pockets."

"Good," she replied just before planting a quick peck on his lips. "Are you finished working for the day? Because if you are, I'd like you to take me someplace where I can purchase essential oils and other ingredients I'd like to pick up."

Slade didn't know essential oil from cooking oil, but he figured he probably couldn't find what she needed at the local market. "Let me do a little research. I'm sure we can find someplace to get you what you need."

He tried to stand up, but she wouldn't shift her weight off his lap. He remained seated when she pressed a still hand against his chest to keep him in place.

"I want the oils. But the only thing I need around these parts is you, cowboy. Remember that."

She moved from his lap and headed toward the door, the happy sway of her hips hypnotizing him as he watched her retreat.

Uncertain what good deed he'd done that had blessed him with Mandisa in his life, Slade understood one thing. No matter the cost, no matter the sacrifice, he could never let this woman go.

16

Slade woke to the most tantalizing aroma filling his nostrils. He pulled the source of the fragrance—a sleeping Mandisa—closer to him and buried his nose in her neck. A deep breath garnered him a lungful of the enticing mix of coconut and peppermint.

He was certain whatever she was wearing was something she'd made herself. He'd taken her shopping yesterday, and as requested had left her to her own devices when they returned to the ranch. He'd worked straight through dinner and crawled up the stairs to shower and lie down next to her when he'd finally completed his work. His reward was the delectable scent wafting up from her skin.

She smelled edible, and if he hadn't been so tired, he'd have shown her just how hungry he was for her. Another sniff of her skin, and he was convinced now was the time to make up for his exhaustion last night. But a quick glance at the clock told him there was no time.

Today was the day he rid himself of Bull Hamilton. The man had been a nuisance for years, and today, Slade would take back what was always his. He'd protect his family legacy and the woman sleeping in his arms right now.

He placed a gentle kiss on her bare shoulder and smiled as she snuggled into the press of his body. "Hey, if we're going to make this meeting, we should probably be up now."

She moaned seductively, and his traitorous cock jumped with excitement. *If she lived here full time, I'd probably never leave this bed.*

"By the feel of things, I don't believe that's what you really want to do."

She was right. There was nothing more he wanted than to bury himself in her right now. But he needed to take care of Bull, and if he didn't do it now, they'd both suffer the consequences later.

"All I ever want to do is lie in bed with you. But I promise, as soon as this is done, we can hightail it back here and spend the rest of your time in Texas in bed."

Mandisa turned in his arms, a slow smile curving her full lips into a perfect bow. "Well, that's an awfully tempting offer. You sure you've got enough stamina to live up to that promise?"

"Darlin', when it comes to you, I'll do whatever I must to keep you satisfied. Let's hope there's enough energy drinks left in the pantry from the last time Mama went shopping."

She kissed him quickly and crawled out of bed. When she reached the bathroom door, she gave him a questioning glance over her shoulder.

"Aren't you coming with me? Showering together would conserve time and water."

"We both know us together in a shower will only prolong our time in that water. We wash off, then get dirty, and then have to wash off all over again."

She threw her head back in laughter as she continued into the bathroom. Slade waited a few moments after he heard the shower running behind the closed door to grab his phone and dial Aaron.

One ring, and the call connected. "You just crawling out of bed, Hamilton?"

Slade's shoulders shook with quiet laughter. His friend was always at the ready. "Something like that. We're getting ready to head over to the offices in a few."

"You sure that's such a good idea? Bull might act worse in front of company."

"I know. She'll be in my office as we hammer out the details of Bull's extraction in the conference room. I'm not too keen on leaving her by herself ever since you called with news about New York. At least I know she'll be safe at the office."

"You think Bull suspects anything, Slade?"

Slade's answer was quick. "No. It's not like I called this meeting out of the blue. This is a normal quarterly board meeting. And being the taskmaster that Bull is, he always demands the board's presence in person or via teleconference. We're going to stick to the plan, let him run the meeting as he usually does, and then when he asks if there's any extra business to be brought before the board, we'll drop our bomb."

It was going to take all the patience in the world for Slade to sit through this meeting, knowing what he had planned for his father. But any change from the usual might tip Bull off, and he couldn't risk that.

"Just be careful, Slade. We have Bull dead to rights. He can't prevent us from ousting him today. But he's unpredictable and ruthless when he can't get his way."

Slade knew Aaron spoke the truth, but he couldn't allow the fear of what his father might do to prevent him from doing what was right. The best thing for all of them would be freedom from Bull and his callous ways.

"I'll keep that in mind. You just make sure you're sitting in front of that web camera at nine sharp Central time."

"Wouldn't miss it for the world," Aaron's stated.

Slade ended the call with his friend just in time to hear Mandisa turn the shower off and close the glass door to the stall. He stood from the bed and walked toward the bathroom door. His future was waiting for him. Time to get up and meet it.

Slade pulled Mandisa into his office, heading directly for the large wooden desk sitting in front of the floor-to-ceiling-window. He sat on the edge of his desk, pulling her into his arms as soon as he was seated.

The firm press of his lips against her mouth made her sink into the warmth of his embrace. He tore his lips from hers, peppering the sensitive skin of her neck with tiny electric nips that made her blood sizzle.

Her brain cloudy with desire, she clung to the last thread of clarity long enough to pull slightly away from him and look up into his eyes. Watching his gaze, full and heavy with need, only worked to frazzle the thin thread of restraint she was holding desperately to.

"Slade, we're in your office."

"I'm aware of that, darlin'. It is mine."

He leaned forward to capture her lips again. She turned her head just in time, his lips meeting her cheek instead of the intended target of her mouth.

Mandisa watched him as she tried to make sense of the moment. She wasn't certain why things felt off. Slade was an amorous man. He'd kept her satisfied since the first night they'd spent together in New York. But as much as he did to keep the fires burning between them, alarm bells were going off inside of Mandisa's head right now.

"I tried my best to keep you in bed for a little morning fun, and you turned me down. Now, you're practically painted on me. What gives?"

He tried to kiss her again, chasing her lips as she turned her face from one side to the other. "So you're complaining because I'm giving you what you want?"

He certainly was giving her everything her libido had been begging for this morning. His hands cupped the curve of her ass, pulling her closer to him, as his tongue and teeth laved and nibbled at her earlobe. She could feel her juices begin to coat her pussy walls and pool at her opening.

"Yes, I want this," she murmured as her eyes fluttered closed. "I'm not trying to give your staff a show, though."

He held her for a few seconds more before he lifted his head and looked down at her. This time she saw more than lust clouding his vision. There was reverence for her in his blue gaze. As if she was something vital and treasured to him, something of great value.

"Hey, we talked about this. Even though I'm going home in a few days, we are not done. Slade, you don't have to look at me like I'm the last slice of pie at Thanksgiving."

She snaked her hands up the firm planes of his chest, and they landed on his broad shoulders. She stood there, her hands still as his chest expanded with a heavy breath. "Why are you so worried?"

"Mandisa, long-distance relationships don't exactly have a great track record. We don't have a lot of history to anchor us."

"Why do we need history when the present is so damn wonderful?"

Her words seemed to erase the long crease running

between his brows. The stiffness in his shoulders remained, making her need to comfort him increase.

"Go to your meeting, take care of your business, and I'll be right here waiting for you when you're done. You do that, and we'll spend the next few days pretending the world doesn't exist."

Slade tightened his hold on her and leaned to place a quick peck on her lips. "How's a man supposed to resist an offer like that?" He granted her a crooked smile filled with delicious devilishness, making her skin hum with familiar excitement.

"That's the point—you're not supposed to."

The desk phone ringing behind him pulled his attention away long enough to reach behind him and press the speaker button.

"Mr. Hamilton, the board members are convening in the conference room. The meeting will begin momentarily."

"On my way," Slade answered and clicked the speaker off. He leaned in for another kiss, threading his fingers through her braids, keeping her mouth positioned exactly where he wanted it as his lips parted hers. He dipped his tongue in her mouth to taste her, moaning in sublime pleasure when his tongue touched hers.

The taste of Slade made Mandisa hungry for him. Kissing him was never enough. It always made her want to feel his skin on hers with no barriers between them.

"You'd better go before I tie you to this desk," she whispered as she broke the kiss, resting her forehead against his.

"Darlin', you never told me you had a bondage kink."

"I don't, but for you, I'll make the exception."

"God, woman," Slade uttered as he peeled her arms away from him and readjusted the firm bulge of his cock. He stood and fastened the buttons of his suit jacket before he walked toward the door.

He grabbed the doorknob, turning slightly toward Mandisa before he opened the door. "This isn't going to be a pretty meeting. Things will probably get ugly. Do me a favor —stay here and wait for me. If you need anything, get my secretary on the intercom. I don't want you to end up in the crossfire of what's about to happen."

The heated sizzle his touch had left her with was replaced by a wary chill that made her senses go on alert. The crinkled lines around his eyes and the tense planes of his face conveyed the concern weighing on Slade. She hadn't had enough experience with the corporate world to know if this was par for the course with business coups, but she would bet everything she owned his sense of dread had more to do with Bull Hamilton than whatever the status quo was for these types of situations.

She didn't say anything. She simply nodded in response and waited as he kept his eyes fastened on her. He took one more breath, then sighed in satisfaction, opened the door and stepped into the hallway.

She didn't know if it was the fact that she knew how deeply Bull had hurt and betrayed Slade, or if it was the uneasy feeling she'd had the few times she'd been in Bull's presence, but Mandisa was just as worried about Slade walking into that meeting as Slade seemed to be about her.

Bull didn't seem like the roll-over-and-take-it kind of guy. He seemed more like the fight-dirty-and-take-what-I-want type. Slade was honest—he wore his heart on his sleeve, and she worried Bull would crush it if given half the chance. She just hoped Slade knew what the hell he was doing. If he didn't, this was going to blow up in all their faces.

"Finally, my wayward son has decided to grace us with is presence," Bull snarled as Slade walked into the conference room. "I hope we weren't keeping you from something important."

Slade swallowed the venom attempting to rise in the back of his throat. Giving in to his need to argue with Bull wasn't part of the plan.

Get in, let him carry on as he usually does, and end it before he knows what's happening to him.

Bull eyed him carefully. He always did after landing a blow. It was how the old man gauged how hard he should come back with the follow-up blow. The glint in Bull's squinted eyes begged Slade to take the bait. But Slade sat quietly in his chair and greeted the entire board as he normally would, refusing to give in to Bull's tactics.

Slade could feel the heat of Bull's gaze following him. He calmly walked the length of the table and sat in his designated seat at the opposite end, facing his father. He tipped his head and leaned an elbow against the armrest as he watched Bull.

"Where's that no-'count leech you call a best friend. Isn't he going to fulfill his duties here today, boy?"

Slade raised the laptop screen and tapped a few keys before meeting his father's eyes again.

"If you're talking about Aaron, he's away on company business." Slade hit the last key, and then pointed to one of the flat-screen monitors hanging from the wall. "He'll be attending virtually."

Everyone in the room raised their eyes to the screen to watch Aaron tip his hat in greeting as he took his seat in front of the web cam.

Bull balled his hand into a fist, silently venting his frustration. This was a game, and the first point had gone to Slade. Bull wasn't happy about that at all.

"There's only one item on the agenda today I feel needs our attention." Bull leaned back in his chair as he spoke, giving a passing glance to the other board members seated at the table. "C.E. Stuart is looking to acquire Venus. I've laid out line by line the details of this deal in the individual copies of the prospectus sitting in front of all of you.

"Venus has performed well, but not as well as it should have. L.I. has had to plug in a good deal of money into it. If we take this deal, we relieve ourselves of a potential problem and make a killing in the sale."

Anger rose quickly in Slade. He wrapped his hand around his armrest and squeezed until he could feel the bite of the metal pressing into his flesh. The man couldn't even be bothered to spare the time to ease his bullshit down the board's throat. He was going to try to choke them all with it and steal Slade's company right off the bat.

Slade lifted his eyes to the monitor to get a glimpse of Aaron. The brief blink of Aaron's eyes was all the sign Slade needed to initiate plan B. Fuck sitting back and taking it. This fight was about to get ugly.

"I fail to see what potential problem you're talking about. Venus is one of our largest moneymakers. Why would you want to get rid of it?" Slade watched the other board members nod in agreement.

"Yes, it is making us money now. But if you knew anything about how business works, you'd be able to see the warning signs as early as I have."

"With an MBA in finance, I'm confident there isn't much I don't understand about business. What I find mysterious are your business practices, but I'm sure you'll be happy to explain them to me in detail."

Slade kept a straight face as he watched a muscle twitch briefly at the corner of Bull's eye. The old man was getting angrier, and Slade didn't much care. This was his family's heritage. Slade couldn't let Bull do this to him without a fight.

"Slade, I know you have a persecution complex. I know you think every decision I make is about you. But if you'd stop and realize that I don't run my business on emotion, you'd know this was a good deal."

"I think you mean *my* business, Bull. It's mine, always has been, always will be. And you don't get to steal it from me brick by brick."

Bull laughed a bit. The slick smile he wore when he thought he was winning climbed on his face. "As CEO, I damn sure can."

Slade picked up a nearby remote and tapped a button. Instantly, all of them one by one opened to a collage of documents displaying on the screens.

"Ladies and gentleman of the board. My father is right in his assumption that he can sell off individual bits of my company as he sees fit. He is in fact the CEO, and that's definitely in his purview. But what he can't do is use this company as a bargaining chip to secure lofty, personal business deals for himself."

Slade watched the same smug smile on Bull's face begin to waver slightly as he recognized the document on the screen.

"What you're all looking at right now is a detailed copy of this proposed sale. In exchange for the sale of Venus and its holding of Sweet Sadie's formula and stores, L.I. makes a very generous amount of money, and Bull gets a cushy corner desk over at C.E. Stuart, Inc."

Slade repositioned himself, leaning back comfortably in his chair and crossing one leg over the other. Bull was busted, and everyone in the room knew it. The only thing left was to take out the garbage.

A moment later Slade's secretary entered the room with an armful of folders, placing each one carefully in front of the seated board members.

Aaron cleared his throat, breaking through the deafening silence cloaking the room. "If you'd open your folders, you will see a copy of the email between C.E. Stuart, Inc.'s CEO and Mr. Bull Hamilton detailing the terms of Mr. Hamilton, Sr.'s future employment. The next page behind that is a copy of the trust Mrs. Logan created to be executed at the time of her death. The highlighted portions detail that Mr. Hamilton, Sr. can sell and purchase on behalf of the company. He is not, however, allowed to make deals that will only benefit him personally at the expense of the company."

"You hacked into my personal email?" Bull questioned.

"You've been sloppy over the last few years, Bull," Slade answered. "You've been so ensconced in your delusion that no one can stop you, you started making silly mistakes. That may be your private email, but you opened it and transmitted responses to it from an L.I. computer, using our network. If you'll look at the bylaws of the company, all communications over our server are subject to monitoring."

Slade could see Bull's ire rising as his complexion turned from pale to crimson. The old man knew he was caught, and he was pissed about it. As much as Slade was enjoying watching Bull get what he deserved, he was more concerned with getting him out of his building and his life.

"I don't know what you're trying to pull here, but there's no detriment to the company. It doesn't matter if C.E. Stuart is offering me a position. If L.I. makes a profit from the sale, there's nothing you can do to touch me."

"L.I. would be paid lots of money, but not a profit. Not really. If you'll all turn to the final page in your folders, you'll see an appraisal of Venus' assets and worth. When broken down into actual dollar amounts, the sum you agreed to is fifty cents on the dollar."

Slade didn't have to watch them to know the board members were scouring the appraisal affidavit. The undervaluing of the company in the sale would have cost them each millions. The board might follow Bull, but only if he was making them money.

"We'd lose our rights to Venus and its products and only make half of what it was worth. That's not a profit, that is a deficit. That means you were attempting to rob us. In your hurry to secure the position with our competitor, you didn't do your due diligence in figuring out the numbers. You fired yourself."

"Fired?" Bull huffed. "You can't fire me. Venus is one small part of this company. I have made so much money for this company. Who else will lead it? You certainly can't, not for the next five years. Your grandmother made certain of that when she created the trust."

"Actually," Aaron interrupted, "the trust doesn't actually preclude Slade from taking the reins of the company. It just says that he has up until the age of forty years to take his place as CEO. You had your lawyers interpret that as he can't run his own company until then, but really, it can be interpreted in several ways."

Slade pressed a button on the intercom and returned his attention to Bull. "Aaron has secured an injunction preventing you from making any more decisions as CEO and giving me control of my company. My first act as CEO is to take out the trash."

Two large men dressed in matching navy blue jackets walked into the office, flanking Bull on both sides.

"Security will escort you from the building. Any personal items you may have will be packed and forwarded to you.

Have a good day, Mr. Hamilton. Logan Industries thanks you for your service."

Bull's lip curled into a snarl. He looked almost ready to jump across the table to strangle Slade, but the two burly men standing beside Bull seemed to make him think twice about it. Instead, Bull rose slowly, taking a moment to glare at Slade before he walked toward the door.

"I promise you will regret this," Bull uttered before he walked through the doorway and was escorted to the elevators.

Slade rose from his seat, walked slowly around the length of the table and took the seat that used to belong to his father.

"If we're done with the entertainment portion of the hour, let's get back to business, shall we?"

Mandisa was bored out of her mind. She kept looking at the door like a diabetic does a fat slice of cake, like it was her saving grace and her downfall all wrapped into one. After spending so much time in the wide-open fields of Slade's ranch, being bottled up in his office made her twitchy.

Who would have thought three weeks of fresh air and a good man by her side would make her want to run from work? Well, she didn't want to run from all of her work. She'd enjoyed mixing up scents the other day for Slade. She couldn't wait to give him the final settled products tonight. He'd enjoyed the quick massage oil she'd made and used on him. But the body butter and cologne always smelled better once they'd cooled and settled for a few days.

She stood up, rubbing her restless hands against her legs, and walked to the window. The closer she got to the end date, the more she wanted to say to hell with it all and just lose herself in Slade and the world he offered her.

But you can't. They need you.

Before she could continue with her thought, she heard her phone ringing. The name "Ash," flashed across her screen.

"Hey Ash," she answered. "What's my friendly neighborhood contractor doing calling me?"

"Hey, Mandisa," Ash replied. "I was just about to go order the paint for the store. I know Kandi ordered the exact same color you guys have now. But the last time you and I spoke, you told me you wanted to revamp the store and go with that red-and-black theme I showed you. Have you changed your mind? Or should I just go with Kandi's selection?"

"I'm sorry, Ash," Mandisa answered. "I've been on vacation for a little while. Why don't you start from the beginning?"

"Well, since the break-in and vandalism, this would be the perfect time to implement the new theme. I just figured in all the craziness to get this place up and running as soon as possible, you'd forgotten to mention it to Kandi."

Break-in? Cold ran through Mandisa. What the hell was going on in New York?

"Ash, I know you always take before pics for your website. Can you forward them to me so I can make a final decision about the plans we talked about a couple of months ago? How long before you need my decision?"

"Uh, I can put it off until tomorrow. But your new business associate, Aaron. He's been hounding me to get things done ASAP. He hired three of my crews to get the store done by the end of the week. Frankly, he's a little bit scary, and I don't want to piss him off."

"All right. I'll text you tonight."

She ended the call and tapped the message notification on

her phone. In Ash's text, she tapped on the slideshow and waited with her breath caught in her chest as each pictured detailed the destruction Ash referred to.

Her mama's beloved store was reduced to rubble. Light fixtures were destroyed. The shelving was ripped from the walls. The floors were covered with glass and debris. It didn't look like the trendy store her mother had created with nothing but her backbone and sweat.

Mandisa was startled out of her shock by Slade's voice on the opposite side of the door. She wiped at her face quickly, attempting to compose herself.

"Hey, there," Slade called to her. "I'm finished here. You ready to get back to our plan of spending the next few days buried beneath the covers?"

"Sure, just let me put in a quick call to Kandi."

"What are you calling Kandi for?"

Mandisa watched Slade. Everything about him looked cool and confident. Nothing about his bright smile and open posture gave anything away.

"She's my friend and I miss her. Do I need any other reason to call her, Slade?"

Slade shrugged his shoulders. "I'm sure you don't. I just wanted to make sure you were adhering to the rules of our wager. No work calls."

"Of course. I mean, why would I need to call work? You promised that if something was wrong at work Kandi would call you and you'd tell me right away. If I've learned one thing in the short time we've been together, it's how honest and open you are. I know if something were wrong, you'd tell me right away. Isn't that right?"

She waited a beat, part of her hoping he would come clean, the other hoping he could create some plausible scenario that would explain away his deception.

He stood there, an easy smile glued to his face while he

pulled her into his embrace. He leaned down and placed a gentle kiss to her cheek as he said, "Of course I would, darlin'."

The image of Judas betraying Jesus with a kiss came to her mind. It felt like someone had taken a sledgehammer to her soul knowing that Slade deceived her. The bottom fell out of her stomach, and she had to swallow to keep the contents of it from racing up to her mouth.

"Hey, let's hurry and get back to the ranch, cowboy. I think I've had my fill of Austin for the day."

17

Something was off.

Slade couldn't put his finger on it, but something had shifted between them. For a moment Slade thought Mandisa somehow knew about the break-in at her store. He texted Aaron to find out if Kandi had spilled the beans. According to Aaron, he was certain Kandi hadn't called Mandisa.

It was probably his own guilt making him so jumpy. If she knew, there was no way Mandisa wouldn't have gone off on him. Now that he'd neutralized Bull, he could tell her everything and give her the opportunity to decide to work with L.I. with no monsters looming in the shadows.

He'd protected her. She'd be mad about it, but Slade was certain she'd see reason in the end about why he'd made the choices he had.

Slade swallowed the seed of guilt sitting in the back of his throat as he pulled into the gates of his ranch. This place, his land, was his redemption. He could remake himself as many times as he needed to on this land. He could be the man

Mandisa believed he was when his boots touched the soil of Havenheart.

Slade parked the SUV and was about to open his door when Mandisa jumped out of the car and ran up the front steps of the house. Puzzled, he walked in the house behind her, just in time to see her racing up the stairs toward the second level.

"What did you do, Slade?"

Slade turned his head to see Mama Indy sitting at the table sipping coffee.

"What do you mean? I just walked in." Slade walked into the kitchen, stopping as he stood next to the table where Mama Indy was seated.

"I just asked that child if she wanted a cup of coffee. She looked at me like I just asked her to cut off her right arm and ran upstairs. What did you do, Slade?" Mama Indy popped him on the arm to emphasize her desire for an answer to her question.

"Ow, Mama. I didn't do anything. She barely said anything in the car. She's probably just tired, that's all."

The older woman crossed her arms over her chest and squinted. She pressed two fingers to her temple as she gingerly massaged the area. "Good Lord. It cannot be possible that I raised a son this stupid."

She fixed her gaze to Slade and stared him down like she used to when he was a child. Whenever she'd caught him in the middle of some trouble he didn't belong in, whenever she was disappointed in him, she'd glare at him and make him feel like he was two feet tall.

He understood her ability to do that when he was a kid. But now that Slade was grown, it baffled him how she still managed to make him slump his shoulders in shame whenever her weighty assessment of him overran him with guilt.

"I like that gal, Slade. Whatever you did, you better undo. Now go fix it."

Slade eyed his mother carefully. Indira was a sweet and nurturing woman. But if you found yourself on her bad side, there wasn't a devil in hell that could protect you from her wrath.

His mother's concern for Mandisa's welfare grabbed at his heart. His fear of the older woman pushed Slade toward the staircase. Slade walked the stairs carefully as he recounted their morning together. There was nothing there that sent up red flags about Mandisa's current mood, but he kept searching through his memory anyway.

He knew something was wrong the entire way home, but he'd chosen to ignore it. Their time together was limited. He didn't want to focus on anything but the happiness they could steal in these next few days. His mother was right. Slade needed to find out what was going on.

He walked the few steps to his bedroom and lightly pushed the door open. Alarm bells rang inside his head when his gaze met an opened suitcase he recognized as Mandisa's.

"Mandisa," he called out into the empty room. "I know you like to get things done early. But don't you think packing three days before you actually have to leave is a bit much?"

The silence in the room was palpable. He was about to leave the room when he saw her walking out of his closet with her hands filled with her clothing. She didn't acknowledge his presence or the fact that he'd called her name. She just kept pulling things off hangers, folding them neatly, and resting them gently in her suitcase.

Her motions were eerily calm and calculated. Robotic and measured, her movements lacked any indication of emotion at all.

He stepped toward her, carefully placing his hand on her

shoulder to cease her motions. Mandisa took a step away from him, pulling her shoulder from beneath his hand and leveling a cool look that kept him from attempting to touch her again.

"What's going on, Mandisa?"

"It's called packing, Slade. I know someone with as much money as you probably has never packed his own bag, but us regular folks have to fend for ourselves."

Slade's eyebrow rose. Sassy-sarcastic Mandisa was familiar. She made him laugh and tickled him with her biting wit. Nasty-sarcastic Mandisa wasn't recognizable to him. This wasn't Mandisa joking. She was serious.

The good thing about being six-four was the long arms that came with his endless legs. He reached over Mandisa and closed the suitcase lid, forcing her to stop her folding and look up at him.

"What's going on, Mandisa?"

He watched her, looking for any resemblance to the fun-loving woman he'd spent time with. But she wasn't there. Instead, angry lines carved into the angles of her face as she glared back at him.

"I'm going home today, Slade."

"What the hell? We have an agreement. You're not due to leave for another three days."

She nodded, but somehow her agreement didn't soothe the panic that was building within him. "It's true. I was supposed to stay for a few more days. But, when I get a call from my contractor asking me what paint color I want to select for the renovations I apparently sanctioned after one of my stores was burglarized, I think it's probably best if I carry my ass home immediately."

His mouth suddenly dry, Slade swallowed slowly. It was both from physical need as well as an attempt to stall for time for him to get his bearings.

On some level, he'd always known this moment was coming. He'd assumed he'd have time to prepare her for it, get her to understand the purpose of his deception. Explain the role he played in this lie so he would look more like a savior than a sinner.

Not like this.

Like this, he could see the anger burning in her molten eyes. He could see the anguish of his lie in her rigid stance. With each labored breath she huffed, he could see the cracks in the foundation of their relationship.

"Darlin', you need to let me explain."

She squinted, sharp lines spreading on the side of her eyes as her steely gaze evaluated him.

"Let you explain what, Slade? The fact that you used our wager to hold me hostage in Texas while someone was ransacking one of my stores? The fact that you went behind my back and enlisted my best friend and employee to lie to me about something important going on in my company? Or are you going to explain how you could violate my trust the way you have? What exactly can you fucking explain to me?"

She stomped away from him, returning to the closet. When she re-entered the bedroom, she flipped the lid to her suitcase open and threw the armful of clothing in without bothering to sort or fold it.

The sound of the zipper closing pulled him out of the deep freeze he'd been standing in. He closed in on her, not caring if she belted him for invading her space. Lord knew he deserved it if she did. But he had to try.

"Mandisa, I know you're pissed. You have every right to be. I should've told you. But I couldn't."

"Why not?"

"Because your store being vandalized was just one step in Bull's plot to force you to accept his original terms of purchase. I was trying to protect you."

"Bull might run shit in Texas, but for damn sure he doesn't have shit to say about what goes down in Brooklyn. How was my store being vandalized going to force me to sell to him?"

Slade released a long, heavy breath, and sat down on the side of the bed. He moved the suitcase out of the way and motioned for her to sit next to him. It almost killed him when she looked at him as if he were asking her to jump off a ledge.

Not long ago she would've trusted anything he asked of her, but now a simple gesture was met with disdain and mistrust.

She took a moment more before her curiosity won out and she sat next to him. He went to rest a hand on her arm, and she pulled away. Apparently sitting beside him was where she drew the line.

"The Pitkin Avenue store was supposed to be the first of your stores to be hit. Aaron uncovered that Bull actually planned to have all of your stores destroyed. With all your stores gone, you couldn't've afforded to rebuild. The only thing you'd have left worth selling was the name and your formula."

Her eyes danced back and forth as her mind attempted to process Slade's revelation. He could almost see the pieces clicking into place for her in her head.

"Why is my formula so important to a place like Venus? It can't just be about tapping into the African American market? He could hire people to create a cosmetics line for him. Why does my formula matter so much?"

"It doesn't matter at all to Bull. But it matters to C.E. Stuart. They want your formula. It would take them years of study to develop what you'd already created. Buying the rights to all your research and your line would have saved them millions. Bull knew his time was coming to an end with my company. He was attempting to secure a cushy position with C.E. Stuart. He was going to buy your company, then sell it to Stuart before he left L.I.

"Once we discovered what Bull was up to, I knew I had to do whatever was necessary to protect you."

She stood up and walked to the foot of the bed, looking around at the room as if she was cataloguing everything. "You did this to protect me? That's what you're telling yourself?"

"Mandisa?"

"Slade, just stop. This is bullshit, and you know it. Yes, your father was apparently doing some sneaky, dangerous shit. Please explain to me how keeping me in the dark about it protects me?"

Slade understood her anger. But quite frankly, she was beginning to piss him off with the attitude. Yeah, he'd kept some shit from her, but ultimately he'd kept her safe and stopped the threat against her business.

He stood up, stalking around the end of the bed to meet her. Being as tall and big as he was, Slade was always aware of his body language. He was always afraid of others perceiving him as a threat because of his size. But with Mandisa standing directly in front of him, arms crossed, eyes wide, and chest heaving with anger and defiance, the only person in that room that was possibly in danger was him.

"Slade, I don't really want to hear your bullshit. You lied to me. That's all I care about. That's all that matters."

God, she was stubborn and headstrong. Those qualities had seemed so attractive when he'd met her in New York. Had made his blood sizzle when she'd unleashed her wit on Bull and Macy at the dinner table. But standing in her wake right now, Slade was torn between wanting to take her over his knee and throttle her hide and kissing her until the fire she directed at him was fueled by her passion instead of her anger.

"Mandisa, I know you're mad. You have every right to be. But I wasn't going to let Bull hurt you. I was willing to do whatever I had to do to ensure the safety of the woman I loved."

The raw sound of his voice shook the air around them, causing him to stumble slightly. He grabbed for one of the posts on the bed to steady himself as the surprise of his declaration washed over him.

Was Slade surprised that he loved Mandisa? No. He'd been privy to that little fact almost since the beginning. Certainly since she'd defended him in front of Bull and Macy. But he hadn't meant to say it the way he had.

In his mind, he'd imagined he would create some magical scenario where he bared his soul tenderly to her. He'd profess his love, she'd be overwhelmed with emotion, and they'd make love.

They weren't supposed to be arguing. And she certainly wasn't supposed to be so full of anger and mistrust that she couldn't even bear his touch.

How far was he from the vision he'd created in his head? His pulse was throbbing in his ears with anger and frustration while he was yelling his feelings at the woman he desired.

"This shit doesn't feel like love, Slade. It feels like control."

Her words hit him like a blow to the gut. He could feel his center tighten in response to them. "I never tried to control you, Mandisa. I was trying to help you. Control and manipulation are my father's game, not mine."

She threw her head back and laughed loudly. "You're delusional if you think Bull Hamilton is the only one that's a master manipulator. Slade, you thrive on bending people to your will. How did I end up here in Austin with you? You made a wager to get me down here when you didn't like the initial no I'd given you. You couldn't stand to lose. Once you got me down here, you did everything you could to convince me to stay here with you. Even though I'd made it clear I had no intention of leaving Brooklyn, no intention of selling my company to you, you still insisted Austin was what I needed."

"So I'm wrong now for being a persistent businessman and showing you a good time?" He walked over to the dresser, smashing his hand against the heavy wood of its surface. "I've always wanted you to stay with me. I've never hidden that. Why is it suddenly so wrong now, Mandisa?"

"Because, Slade, that's not love, that's control," she whispered. The acute softness in her tone alarmed him, drawing his eyes back to hers. "You thought of everything you could to keep me in Texas with you, even when I told you that wasn't a possibility. When my business was in danger, you kept that from me. Not because you were trying to protect me, but because you didn't want me to leave. That's manipulation, Slade. That isn't love."

She walked over to the bed, pulling her stuffed suitcase to the floor. She stood it on its side and extended the handle. She pulled it next to the door and then turned to him.

"Love would've had you trying to figure out how to meet me halfway. Love would've had you trying to come up with some sort of schedule where we could take turns traveling back and forth. Love would've had you attempting to calculate how long it would take for you to set up shop in your lover's hometown, so you could work and love in the same place. Love would've made you do anything to make this work for the both of us. Instead, the only person you worried about this working for was you. If it was really love, you would've thought about all of these things, Slade. I know, because I thought of every single one of them."

The anger painted across her face melted into anguish. Her eyes glassed over with tears as her voice thickened with pain. His first reaction was to go to her, to fix it. But, when he moved toward her, she took a step back.

When did we get to the place where comfort wasn't welcomed?

"Mandisa. I run a multinational corporation. I have to be here. I can't just let Logan Industries fall to waste. You just—"

The moment he let those two words slide from his lips, he regretted them. He watched her stiffen against them, straighten her back, and square her shoulders as she left her suitcase at the door and stepped back inside the room to move closer to him.

"I just what? Play in face paint? Make people feel pretty? Obviously, in the real world, in your world, that has no value. The successes I've had are meaningless because my work isn't as important as yours? And there is the real problem, Slade. You don't see value in what I do in comparison to yourself, so therefore it makes perfect sense for me to give up my entire world to love you. But Slade, if you ever loved me, if you even know what love is, you'd have done anything to be with me. Even concluding that maybe the only way you could love me was by leaving your world behind and following me to New York. Real love is ready to sacrifice anything, not just manipulate things to make it convenient for you."

She returned to the door, standing there in the doorway without turning around as she spoke.

"You've shown me you can't be trusted, Slade. If I can't trust you, I can't do business with you. Whatever deals you had on the table, please consider this my official notice of intent. I will not be authorizing the sale of any percentage of my company to you. As for the debt I owe you for the renovations, I'll have my attorney contact you about repayment of those funds."

Before he could tell her there was no debt, she quietly slipped out of the room and closed the door behind her. One fuckup—albeit the mother of all fuckups—and she was gone. What the hell was he supposed to do now?

18

Slade swallowed the strong amber liquid sitting at the bottom of his glass as he waited for Aaron to enter the room.

"How is she, Aaron?"

Aaron sat down in front of Slade's desk, taking his time to cross his legs and smooth out the wrinkles on his clothing.

"Hello to you too," Aaron answered.

"I'm not in the mood, Aaron. I asked you a question. Answer it."

Aaron met Slade's cold gaze with an unyielding one of his own. Slade had been around Aaron long enough to recognize his *you're-getting-on-my-damn-nerves* look. But the despair resting in Slade's gut was so pervasive, he couldn't bring himself to give an actual fuck.

"I've been in New York every week for three weeks straight checking up on Mandisa because you're too chicken shit to do it on your own, Hamilton. I'm your lawyer and your friend. I am not your errand boy. You want to keep tabs on her? From now on, you do it yourself."

Aaron stood up and headed for the door. Never one to

speak more words than necessary, he'd said his piece, and now he was on his way. When he reached for the doorknob, Slade lifted his eyes from the empty tumbler in his hand and looked at his friend's back.

"I can't, Aaron."

He hated how small his voice sounded to his own ears. He was a charmer. Everything about his personality and physique was larger than life. How could he sound so weak and fragile now? How could Mandisa have ruined him so thoroughly?

"She doesn't want me. She left me. I can't just go to her."

The pain sitting in his chest grew with each syllable. If he kept it all inside, then maybe it wasn't real. But hearing those words vibrate through the air into the universe made them as solid as the wooden desk he sat behind.

"You are an idiot, Hamilton. She wants you. She just wants you to stop being a selfish prick. You know everything she said to you was true. You manipulated her for your own gain. No, it wasn't for money. But manipulating someone into staying with you is still manipulation."

Aaron's words did nothing but dig a bigger hole inside Slade's gut. Everything and everyone in his life that he loved, he'd lost at the hands of his father. He could label Bull the big bad monster responsible for all those tragedies. But this one, the most important loss of his life, was all on Slade's shoulders.

"I know Aaron. I was afraid, and I let my fear get the better of me."

Slade walked to the mini bar in his office and poured himself another two fingers of scotch. He stood in front of the window looking out at his beloved Downtown Austin, and he ached. Even the beauty of his city couldn't dull the hurt of loss.

"She sees me as tainted. I don't want to bring her any

more hurt. I just need to know she's safe. Bull may be out of this company, but that doesn't mean he won't aim his sights on her to get back at me." Slade turned around to watch his friend still standing at the door, waiting to get away from the pity party Slade was hosting for himself. "Please." His voice quivered. "Just watch out for her for me. I need to know she's safe."

Aaron kept his back turned to Slade as he released a loud huff of breath into the air. "Fine, I'll make sure she's all right. But if this is what love does? Turns a man into a sorry, whiny version of himself? You can keep that shit."

Slade walked to his car in the executive parking lot. Fire singed his skin when he saw his father leaning casually against his vehicle.

"Hey there, boy. Bet your daddy was the last person you expected to see waiting for you today."

"I'm busy, Bull. What do you want?"

"Oh, I've got everything I want. The question is, do you? That's no by the looks of that hangdog expression dripping on your face. What happened? Your pretty little Dr. Avery leave you?'

Slade was too tired to attempt to pretend. He couldn't muster up enough strength to play the bluffing game with Bull. "I'm sure it makes your day to know that she did."

Bull let out a loud cackle of laughter. "Actually, it does."

Slade held on tighter to the keys in his hand, trying to weigh the consequences for smashing them in Bull's face. "Why does it bring you joy to steal from me? I can't think of anything I've done that would ever justify all the hate and venom you've poured into my life."

Bull shrugged his shoulders in a nonchalant fashion and

pushed his hands into his pockets. "You were born. Your birth signaled the loss of everything that ever mattered to me. Your mother and I had decided to be a childless couple. Not for selfish reasons—your mama was born with a congenital heart defect. She was supposed to stay home, and I was supposed to run her father's company. But she decided she had to have a child, no matter the cost. She stopped her birth control without me knowing and hid the fact that she was carrying you until she was too far along to do anything about it.

"The strain of giving you life took more of a toll than she'd figured. And once you were here, your grandfather had a natural heir to give his company to. He didn't need me any longer.

"But even after all that, I was happy to have a son. If I lost my wife and business because of it, I still had a boy of my own."

The sincerity of Bull's words sat on Slade's chest, making it difficult to breathe. He'd never heard Bull speak of him or fatherhood in any way that was remotely endearing. But the soft smile on his face coupled with the distant look of happiness in Bull's eyes were proof that he was actually telling the truth. He'd been happy about Slade coming into the world.

"Then where did it go wrong, Bull? Because I can remember you hating me from a very early age."

Bull's gaze dropped for a minute. When he lifted it again, the faint gleam of happiness faded, and cold hatred remained. "Even though I stood to lose everything I loved—and despite what you may think, I desperately loved your mama—I had a son born of my own flesh. Boy, I don't know a man alive that can't be happy about that. But that was stolen from me too."

Slade narrowed his gaze at Bull as he searched for clarity. "What does that mean?"

"It means if I'd been smart enough to do the calculations, I'd have realized I was out of the country for nearly two months when you were conceived."

"You lying son of bitch. Are you really going to try to tell me my mother ran around on you?"

Slade watched for any telling actions that would prove Bull a liar, but there were none. The man stared Slade in the eyes. His face was open, not a hint of subterfuge present.

"If you don't believe me, Slade, ask Indira. She was your mother's closest confidant. She was there for all of it. But if you want proof, all you have to do is look at our blood types. I'm A, your mother was B positive, you're O positive. It's a biologic impossibility that she and I could've produced a child with your blood type. Your mama told me you were premature because of her heart condition. I didn't discover the truth until you were three months old. In one moment my entire world was taken from me. Your birth had taken a handful of years from your mother's life. I'd lost my place at the company because you were a natural heir to the Logan empire, and then I was robbed of the last thing I ever held dear, my son. The last straw was your grandmother robbing me in her will. I promised I'd never let you steal another thing from me."

Slade was cold with shock. If he believed what Bull was telling him, his entire life was a lie. It was impossible. What Bull was suggesting was crazy. Still, when Slade thought about every incomprehensibly evil thing this man had done to him, them sharing no blood made sense.

"I've worked hard to make you feel the bitter cut of loneliness all these years, Slade. But in all my dealings, I've never come as close to seeing you look as destroyed as the dear sweet chemist has managed to. Hell, if I'd known she'd be the key to your destruction all this time, I would've sent you to New York a long time ago. Who knew that I all had to do was wait for you to screw up to make my dreams come true?"

Bull stood up and slapped a hand on Slade's shoulders. His crooked smile made his round face appear even more sinister. "Now you truly know what it is to be me, boy. To know that you somehow had a hand in your own destruction. Enjoy that feeling. Make use of it. That feeling is what makes me who I am. And you know what? I can already tell by that bleak mix of sadness and anger swirling around in your eyes, it's going to do the same for you, my boy. I guess you're gonna be a chip off the old block one way or another. Just like your *daddy*."

Slade lifted his eyes and met Bull's gaze. The fear and panic spinning around inside Slade's head must have been visible, because Bull started laughing all over again. That sickening sound echoed off the parking lot structure walls as Bull walked away from Slade and out of his sight.

Dear God, am I really turning into him?

Slade walked into the apartment, longing for a hot shower and his bed after his brief encounter with his Bull. The day had been grueling. Between work and the oppressive emotions Bull had stirred up, Slade barely had enough energy to breathe, let alone make it up the stairs to his loft.

He walked into the cold, empty space and shivered. This place had been just a roof over his head during the work-week to minimize his commute. But since Mandisa left Havenheart, Slade hadn't been able to bring himself to set foot on the ranch.

Memories of her were all over his beautiful land, lying in wait to assault him if he even thought to set foot on the property. All he had to do was close his eyes, and he could see her all over the ranch. In the stables, in the fields, by the brook, where they'd made love at the bank of the stream, at Mama Indy's kitchen table—she was everywhere.

Feeling weak, he dropped his briefcase, cellphone, and keys on the hall table and walked the rest of the way into the loft, leaning against the wall. He stripped as he walked, leaving a trail of clothes from the door to the bathroom.

He turned the water on as hot as he could bear it and let the shower fill with steam. He stepped into the spray, hoping the water would wash off the layers of pain and disappointment he wore like a second skin.

He'd done this, and yet he still couldn't come to terms with the outcome. He'd taken things too far by trying to keep Mandisa in Texas. He could accept that. He was wrong. There was no getting around that. But knowing Mandisa and everyone else in his family likened him to Bull—that infected his heart like venom. That knowledge kept him weak, bitter, and angry. He didn't know how to save himself from it.

He washed himself and wrapped a towel around his waist, collapsing onto his bed as soon as he stood next to it.

He turned his head and saw the bottle of scotch he'd opened last night to help him sleep. It was half empty, and the remaining liquid called to him like an elixir. The contents of that bottle told him it was okay to be who he was. Told him that being compared to Bull in this context wasn't such a bad thing.

He pulled himself up so that his back rested against the headboard and reached for the bottle with a shaky hand. It was the only thing in his life that understood him, understood why he'd done the things he had. It whispered soothing truths into his ear.

The bottle beckoned him to open and empty it. Slade was

about to oblige until it told him there was nothing wrong with being like Bull, that he should accept it, not fight it.

He sat there looking at the bottle in his hand, listening to the siren-like call in his head begging him to succumb.

"I'm nothing like him," he whispered. "I will never accept being like him." The sounds in his head became distorted, pulling him from his bed. He dropped the bottle back on his nightstand and backed away from it slowly. He knew this was all in his imagination, but that didn't make the experience any less real.

If you're nothing like him, then prove it.

"How am I supposed to prove I'm nothing like Bull?"

Are you really asking a bottle of scotch that question? Even better, do you really expect an answer?

Slade stumbled the few feet to the kitchen area and held on to the counter for dear life. He wasn't drunk, hadn't had a drop of liquor since the last glass he poured that afternoon when Aaron was in his office. The possibility of insanity dangled in his mind, but he soon pushed it away. A talking bottle of scotch might have been the object he'd focused on, but he knew the questions were coming from deep within him.

He poured himself a glass of cold water and guzzled it in one swallow as his mind raced for answers. He couldn't live this way, not when he'd experienced better. Not when he'd known what it was to be genuinely loved by the person lying next to him.

He found the cordless handset and pressed the third number on the speed-dial list. Two rings, and he heard the crisp and professional voice of his pilot.

"Good evening, Mr. Hamilton. What can I do for you, sir?"

"I need to be in New York as quickly as you can get me there. I'll be at the airstrip in twenty minutes."

"Then wheels up in thirty, sir."

Slade disconnected the call and headed to his closet. He pulled a pair of jeans, a fitted T-shirt, and a blazer from the racks and dressed quickly. The last items he grabbed were a pair of socks and his boots.

He headed for the door, grabbing his cellphone, wallet, and keys on the way. He wasn't worried about luggage. The only thing he needed was already in New York. He'd pick up anything else once he arrived.

He waited until he was in the car to make another call. When the other end of the line clicked, and he heard his mama's "Hello, baby," on the other line, he grinned.

"Hey, Mama. I just wanted you to know I'm gonna be out of reach for a few. I'm headed to the airfield now."

"Where you got business now?"

"New York."

He heard a brief sigh of relief pass through the line and could only imagine the smile coloring the older woman's face. "What business you got in New York?"

"The only business I should've had there in the first place, Mama."

"You going to fix things with our girl?"

That was his mama. Once she claimed you, didn't matter if you were around or not, you were hers. She hadn't seen or spoken to Mandisa in three weeks, yet she still claimed Mandisa as hers.

"I'm sure gonna try, Mama."

"Slade, to try is to fail. Don't try. Get it done."

Mama Indy had been a force in his life. She'd pushed him beyond his comfort and forced him to do the hard things, even when he didn't think he could. She was right. There was no room for failure in this. Mandisa wasn't an option. She was a necessity, and he couldn't just sit by idly and let her disappear from his life.

For a slight moment Slade thought to question Mama Indy about his paternity. But as he pondered the idea, he realized it didn't matter if Bull was telling the truth or not. The man had never been a father to Slade. Discovering they shared no biological connection didn't change that fact. He resolved at that moment to leave the past where it belonged —dead and buried. His only focus from here on out would be his future with Mandisa.

"On my word, Mama. I'll get it done."

19

Mandisa sat on her chaise lounge pretending to compile quarterly reports. The truth was she'd been reading the same set of numbers for the last three hours. Knowing a miscalculation would cost her company somewhere down the line, she shoved the papers aside and gave in to her need to obsess about the thing she was attempting to avoid.

Slade.

God, how she ached with need for him. Walking away from him, his family, his land had taken every drop of strength she'd had. Abstaining from picking up the phone to call him and see how he was doing was only possible because she exhausted herself with work.

Since returning, she'd set about restructuring her company. She'd given Kandi more responsibilities as executive manager. It was her job to oversee all the stores and their supervisors and staff. Mandisa kept an eye on things from a distance, but she no longer micromanaged every detail.

For the last three weeks, she'd spent her time in her lab, creating. The joy of working in her lab was the only thing that made her separation from Slade bearable. Getting lost in the science kept her afloat in the stormy sea of heartache.

Mandisa looked around the apartment she'd once adored, wondering why it didn't feed her soul the way a beautiful patch of dirt in Austin, Texas did.

Her internal jaunt down misery lane was interrupted by the ringing of her cellphone. Mandisa reached for the phone, her hand hovering over the accept icon when she noticed the caller's name.

"Mama Indy? I was just thinking about you." It wasn't a lie, not completely. Thinking about Slade meant thinking about everything and person she'd encountered on that ranch.

"That's good to hear." The old woman's voice beamed with warmth. "That means I'm gonna live a long time."

It was Mandisa's sincerest wish. Living in a world where this woman didn't exist wasn't an idea Mandisa wished to entertain.

"I hope I'm not bothering you. But I just wanted to share something with you if you'll let me. I promise it won't take too long."

"You take as long as you'd like, Mama Indy. How can I help you?"

"I was having a cup of coffee, and I got to thinking I'd never given you the recipe. I'd intended to give it to you before you left, but…"

Mandisa's heart sank when she heard Indira's voice trail off. The echo of pain in the air made her heart ache more.

"Mama Indy. Forgive me for asking, but did Slade put you up to this?"

"No, Slade wouldn't ask me to share my secret with you. He knows that kind of trust has to be freely given."

Mandisa wasn't certain Slade understood that. However, she wasn't about to disparage him to his mother. "You don't have to do this. That secret is something that should stay in your family."

Mandisa could hear a light chuckle over the line. "Baby, you are my family."

Mandisa sat quiet, letting the power of Indira's words surround her like a warm hug. In three weeks this proud but gentle old woman had reminded her how wonderful it was to be mothered again. The loss of that crippled Mandisa in ways she couldn't verbalize.

Indira must have sensed Mandisa's need for time to internalize her statement. A few moments passed before the matron began speaking again. "In the short time you were here, I watched you love my son like I'd always dreamed someone would love him. I make no secret that I hope y'all can smooth things out. But, whether you do or not, there will always be a home for you on this ranch. Family can always come home."

What little resolve Mandisa possessed simply melted away. She wrapped her arm around her knees, pulling them to her chest, aching so desperately for Slade's mama. When she was finally able to compose herself, hold her tears back enough to keep them out of her voice, she flipped one of the folders on the chaise over and grabbed a pen.

"All right, Mama Indy. I've got a pen. Tell me the recipe."

A slight zing of excitement sparked a smile on Mandisa's face. She was finally going to be able to satisfy her addiction to this woman's coffee.

She listened carefully, too afraid to miss one detail. When Indira was finished dictating the grocery list, Mandisa was puzzled by what she saw.

"Whole beans, cinnamon, nutmeg, spring water. Is that it, or did I miss something, Mama Indy?"

"No baby, that's it."

"But that sounds pretty standard for any cup of coffee. There's gotta be a secret ingredient."

Mandisa could hear Indira chuckling on the other end of the phone. The sound was contagious, making Mandisa smile as she reveled in the reverberation.

"The special ingredient is love."

"Love?" Mandisa was pretty certain she couldn't find love on the shelf at the market.

"Yes, baby. Love makes everything in life better. See, the care you take when making something special for someone you love, that will make even the simplest of ingredients taste gourmet. I grind those beans, cinnamon, and nutmeg by hand. Yeah, I could get a machine to do it all for me, but it wouldn't add that perfect blend that love does. When you love something, you have to tend to it to keep it strong."

There was a lesson in there. It was glaringly obvious to Mandisa. She just wished she and Slade could've garnered this wisdom before everything fell apart.

She ended the call with Indira and transferred the ingredients to her shopping list app on her phone. First thing in the morning she was running to the market. If she couldn't have Slade, his family, and the Havenheart ranch, Indira's special blend of coffee wasn't a bad consolation prize.

A tap on Mandisa's door pulled her from her musings. She padded to the door in socked feet, asking who was there as she reached for the knob. Hearing, "Darlin', it's me," coming from the other side of the door knocked the wind out of her.

She thought about pretending she wasn't home. You already asked who was at the door. He knows you're home, idiot.

She peeked through the peephole and saw a blurry version of the man she knew. She could feel excitement bubbling in her heart. But then reality reminded her why she'd been without Slade for so long.

"What do you want, Slade?"

"Darlin', please, let me talk to you face-to-face. We can have this talk in the hall with your neighbors listening, but I'd rather talk privately. Please, let me in."

It never failed. Every time she heard the word "darlin'" fall from his lips, it was like the sweet lure of honey. It was decadent, and something sticky that she couldn't easily break free of.

She leaned her head against the door, touching it as if she could feel him on the other side. She'd craved him for so long. Knowing he was there, just beyond her reach, played havoc with her willpower.

Her mind told her to stay away from him, to keep her resolve. But her resolve reminded her of the cold, lonely bed waiting for her, the empty life she'd been living since she'd left the ranch, and the pain that followed her into her dreams every night.

You want him to make this right. If there's even the slightest chance that he can, don't you deserve that?

She felt a single tear singe the skin of her cheek as it made its trail down her face. She wiped it away and straightened her spine. She was right. This wasn't about privileges Slade had earned. This was about what she wanted.

Being with him had shown Mandisa she should have someone love her completely. Yes, he'd screwed it up, and she didn't see how he could fix it. But, hadn't she warranted the chance to let him try? If he succeeded, it wasn't just him winning. Her happiness was at stake too.

Why should she lose out because of his stupidity? Why should she allow herself to suffer just because Slade had channeled his inner asshole?

"You'd better not fuck this up, cowboy."

She backed away, turning the locks and opening the door. Seeing him standing in her doorway dug up so many emotions. Anger was the loudest of them, causing her chest to rise and fall in a quick, heaving motion. She had to make a concerted effort to calm her breathing so she could hear herself think.

But then as he stepped into her apartment, and she allowed her gaze to settle on him, her anger began to bleed away and concern pushed its way through to the forefront of her heart.

His face was covered in scruff. Not the sexy beard kind of scruff. No, this kind indicated one couldn't be bothered to worry about his appearance. His hair looked unkempt, wild without the infamous cowboy hat that always kept it in place. Her eyes met with his, and her breath caught for a long moment in the back of her throat. The electric blue she'd spent hours gazing into was replaced by a dull, almost gray color that paired perfectly with the sallow complexion he was sporting.

What the hell have you been doing to yourself, cowboy? How the hell does someone look so pale when they live on a ranch in Texas?

He rubbed his hand self-consciously down the front of his T-shirt. She remembered that shirt. Remembered peeling it off him when they'd made love in his hotel room. With all his muscles, it had been a second skin. The now slightly loose fabric no longer showed the definition of his chest.

"Slade. What's going on? Why are you here? I thought we agreed—"

"You agreed, Mandisa. My guilt, my anger…I didn't even show up to the discussion. Not like I should have."

She waved him over to the eat-in counter in the kitchen. While he sat, she instinctively started looking for fixings for a quick meal. Loose clothing on a man that big was trouble. Something more than his feelings was hurting.

She pulled out a cutting board, grabbed a loaf of bread and the boneless barbequed ribs she had in the fridge.

"You don't have to do that." The softness of his voice stopped her movements. Her heart ached for the sadness she saw blanketing his face and hanging shoulders.

"If I didn't know any better, I'd think Mama Indy stopped feeding you."

He shook his head, dipping it a bit farther as a weak smile climbed his face. "No, Mama would be shoving food down my throat if I'd been near her. I've been at the loft in Austin since you left."

"They don't have food in Austin?"

He lifted a shoulder in a half-assed shrug as he adjusted the plate she'd set before him. "Yeah. I just haven't felt like eating. Had a lot on my mind."

She nodded her head and walked back to the fridge looking for something to drink. Water was a no-go. He needed calories, and probably some caffeine if the dark circles under his tired eyes were any indication.

She pulled out her stash of pineapple soda she kept pushed to the back of the fridge. She didn't indulge often, but whenever she had a craving, it was cold, crisp, and ready to go. She popped the top of a can and slid it across the counter to him.

With a tilted head his eyes scanned the can, and then lifted to hers. "Pineapple soda? You are aware I'm well over the legal drinking age, right?"

"Yeah. But, the fact that you turned up on my doorstep looking like a scraggly throwaway tells me you probably need to switch to something with less alcoholic content."

The paleness in his face gave way to a slight blush, confirming her suspicions he'd been drinking more of his meals than eating them.

"So, take a bite and unload. Why are you here, Slade?"

He took a large bite of the sandwich in his hands. His closed eyes sang his satisfaction, coupled with a deep hum emitting from between bites. Mandisa could tell the exact moment the flavor of the meat met his taste buds.

"God, that's good. Tastes like—"

"Heaven? It's my mom's recipe."

"I'll deny it if you ever tell her, but these are better than my mama's ribs."

Mandisa could feel her pride swell and spill into a wide grin. He wasn't lying. Her late mother taught her to make damn good ribs. She just hoped they were good enough to get him looking healthier.

She watched him clean his plate and finish his can of soda. When he was done, she put away the food and his dirty dish, then spread her hands wide on the countertop.

He must have recognized that she meant business, because he used a nearby paper towel to quickly wipe his mouth and fingers before turning to her and giving her his full attention.

"I was wrong, Mandisa. I thought I was doing what was best for you, but I was so wrong."

He looked up expectantly from his seat, as if hoping for her to throw him some sort of lifeline. She said nothing, just remained standing on the other side of the counter, continuing to watch him.

"Bull met me in the parking lot earlier today. I thought he'd come to threaten me about the company. What he actually wanted was to see me in my misery. He told me he'd succeeded, because the bitterness of loss was what made him the man he turned out to be. Now he could rest easy, because I was turning in to a chip off the old block."

She let out a slow breath through her nostrils, trying her best to release the weight of that statement. If it felt so heavy on her chest, she could only imagine the weight Slade must be carrying. Bearing a burden like that, recognizing the exact thing you hate in the mirror—it had killed lesser men.

From the moment she'd met Slade he'd been confident, so sure of himself and their connection that she'd had no choice but to follow him, to trust him. But seeing him here, with a dip in his shoulders and a sagging chin, all she saw was broken pieces of the man she loved.

"The moment he said it, I got why you left, Mandisa. Before that moment, I didn't. I won't even lie to you about that. But once I went home and tried to drink away all this hurt that's been sitting in my chest, I understood. You didn't want to watch me turn into that. You didn't want to see me become him."

He was right—watching him become bitter and callous wasn't on her lists of things to do. When you'd had the opportunity to experience something beautiful and natural, you didn't want to see how a poison like hate could mutate it.

"I know I fucked up. I know I was wrong. I know I don't deserve another chance, but I'm asking for one anyway."

She could see the spark of hopefulness trying to light behind his dim eyes. There was no doubt in her mind that he wanted this as badly as he did his next breath. But doubt plagued her. Her legacy had been threatened, and he'd hidden it from her. He'd lied by omission and attempted to play God with her livelihood. How were they supposed to come back from that?

The doubt clawing from her heart, out into her chest was trying to strangle her. But even though she was so overwhelmed by it, every cell in her body begged for her to give in.

She loved Slade, probably from the first time he'd traced his lips across hers in that lounge. Spending time at his ranch had ingrained him in her system. She hadn't thought about the cost of loving him then, but now, those consequences were all she could think about.

"Mandisa? Darlin', you haven't given me an answer."

How could she give him an answer when she couldn't produce one for herself?

Everything from the independent woman doctrine said when your man fucked up, you sent him packing. Breaking things off with Slade had been a knee-jerk reaction that felt expected in the moment. But, if she were honest, she'd never been at ease with it. How could she be when it was as if she was tearing off a piece of her body?

Was it weak to want to forgive the error of the person you loved, just so you could love them again? Was this the part where she was supposed to hole up in a room with a bunch of bitter Betties who would praise her for humiliating him and sending him on his way? Or was there the slightest bit of strength in forgiveness?

Too tired to continue the spiritual battle going on inside her, she stepped around the counter and walked into his arms. He wrapped himself around her, and she cradled his head on her shoulder and stroked it until the tenseness in his body seeped away.

"You look tired."

She felt him nod slightly against her shoulder. "I haven't slept well since you left."

She felt the truth of his statement. This wasn't just a line. Slade might have been a cowboy, but he was a pretty one. This disheveled thing he had going on was not his style. He was off his game, and she knew it was the tension between them at the root of it.

"I am too. It's late. Why don't we get some rest?"

She kissed the top of his head and held him close. Loving the feel of him in her arms, worried about how frail and raw he seemed.

"I don't have any answers for you right now, Slade." She leaned back, pulling out of his embrace so she could see his eyes. "Tonight, I just want to sleep, holding you. I want to know you're all right."

An open mouth and quickly moving eyes prepared her for his argument. But halfway between the words forming on his lips and his next breath, he closed his eyes and simply nodded.

He followed her down the hall to her bedroom. She asked him to sit on her foot bench, and unzipped and removed his boots and socks. When she stood, she ran gentle fingers up the length of his torso and pulled at the loose-fitting fabric of his shirt.

Next, she placed her hand on the wide belt buckle at his waist. Loosening it, popping the button on his jeans, and pushing them down his lean hips brought about more concern for him. A chill ran through her when she felt how prominent the bones were there. Slade didn't carry a lot of fat, but he had so many muscles, feeling bone on him was jarring.

She led him to the side of the bed, pulling the covers back, and motioned for him to lie down. When he did, she gave his arm a gentle squeeze and walked over to her dresser. She opened the top drawer and removed the glass jar she'd placed there three weeks ago when she'd left him on his ranch.

Standing next to him again, she sat on the edge of the bed, opening the jar, placing its lid safely on the nightstand.

"I made this for you right before everything blew up in our faces." She passed the opened jar beneath her nose and deeply inhaled the fragrant scent. "I chose sandalwood as the base scent, because it reminded me of you. Sweet enough to make life pleasant, strong enough to handle its ups and downs."

She removed a healthy dollop of the whipped body butter

and placed the jar next to its lid on the nightstand. Rubbing her hands together, she placed her coated palms on his chest and kneaded the moisturizer into his skin.

He was silent the entire time she rubbed him down, but she could feel the weight of his gaze on her as she paid deft attention to each section of skin she caressed.

She couldn't tell Slade how she felt, couldn't explain how seeing him so brittle and fragile made her want to care for him. She couldn't risk her words getting in the way, couldn't allow her ego to push him away, even though it was probably what he deserved. In this moment, the only thing she could do was take care of him.

She'd only finished his torso when she heard even breaths coming from him. He was in that strange place between sleep and wakefulness where his eyes were almost completely closed, only opening in slits when he felt himself falling to sleep.

She smiled to herself. She'd also placed chamomile in the body butter. In Slade's weakened state, the natural sleep aid took effect quickly. She rubbed the remainder of the body butter into his skin and closed the lid before she walked to the other side of the bed and climbed in beside him.

Almost instinctively, it seemed, he pulled her next to him. His arm around her waist, his legs tangled up in hers, his head burrowed on the pillows of her breasts. It felt calming, familiar, her senses relaxing into the remembered routine. Her mind shutting out the rest of the world, enjoying the safety of this familiar embrace.

With one last pass of her fingers through his wavy hair, Mandisa smiled as she kissed the top of his head. She may not have had any answers, but tonight, she'd have peace.

Slade felt the familiar heat of Mandisa's body against his.

He'd dreamt about her every night since she'd gone. Dreamt of feeling her beneath his fingers, of tasting the sweetness of her flesh again.

He let gentle fingers slide from her legs, up the curve of her ass until he reached the dip in the small of her back. She pressed the heat of her cunt against his aching cock. His tip, already leaking with need, throbbed as she canted her hips toward him.

Slade raised his head from the cradle of her breasts, decorating the skin on her neck with feather-like kisses that pulled sultry moans from her lips.

He was a man who enjoyed his sex just as feisty and energetic as the next man. But there was something about the subtle touches being shared in this moment that had him so hot, so turned on he could hardly think straight.

He pulled away from her briefly, just to savor the beauty of her desire. Her eyes closed, mouth slack and begging to be kissed, breath coming in heavy huffs. How could he have been foolish enough to do anything to push her away?

He brushed one of her long braids out of her face and let his thumb pass over the rise of her rounded cheek. When coal-black eyes opened to him, her desire shining in them like stars in the midnight sky, his mouth descended on hers, pressing until her lips parted, and she welcomed his tongue inside.

She tasted just as he remembered—warm, sweet, sexy, so full of need she took his breath away.

He let one of his hands travel down between their bodies, pushing between her legs and moaning his pleasure when he found her folds dripping with desire.

"God, you're so wet."

He licked his finger, reveling in the taste of her. He kissed her, sharing her essence with her as he returned his finger to her entrance and slowly slid it inside. He couldn't help the broad smile pulling at his lips when the hungry sounds of her satisfaction attempted to escape into the air. He swallowed those sounds. Keeping his lips fastened to hers, his tongue licking in and out of her mouth, nothing could pass between. Those sounds were his, and he'd been starved for weeks. He needed them.

He removed his finger, using his hands to spread her thighs wider. He may have lost some of his muscle, but there still was enough of him left that he needed space to work. He ground against her cunt, enjoying the slick heat of her juices wetting the soft fabric of his boxer briefs.

He wanted so desperately to be free of the material. In previous dreams, every time he broke away from her, he'd wake up, and she'd be gone. This morning he couldn't do it. He couldn't let her slip through the ether of his mind. He needed to feel her warmth, her touch, her desire for just a little bit longer.

She must have sensed his dilemma. She smoothed quick hands down his flanks, pushing the fabric below the curve of his ass. A relieved sigh escaped his lips as his rigid cock sprang free. The two of them shimmied around the bed until his boxer briefs were off and he was resting gently in her slit.

Fire burned through him, he was so close. The closest he'd been in weeks to joining their bodies together. It didn't matter one bit that this was a dream. If he couldn't have her in life, dreaming of moments like this would have to be enough to get him through his otherwise mundane existence.

He lifted himself just slightly, ready to position himself to enter her when he felt the stiff coolness of a foil wrapper being pressed into his hand.

"Hang on, cowboy. You forgot something."

He opened his eyes, looking at her for what felt like the longest time, even though he was sure it was mere seconds. She was lovely, so full of life, so real.

Too real.

"Mandisa?"

Bright, chocolate eyes lit up at the sound of her name, full lips pulled into a perfect bow. Could his memories, his dreams be this vivid?

"Please tell me you're real."

She took the condom, opened it, and slid it down his hard length, making him bite the inside of his mouth to keep from losing his control.

Sliding her closed fist up and down and applying pressure, she created the perfect amount of friction for him to fuck against. When he began moving his hips in earnest, she pressed her free hand against his hip, stopping his motions, and led him by the cock to her entrance.

"Is this real enough for you?"

She pulled him inside, and he fell into her depths willingly. He moved his cock in and out of her sheath, desperately trying to bury himself within her. The feel of his balls slapping her ass, the sizzle of fire that slid up his spine every time he felt her walls clamp down around him, edged him closer and closer to his end.

Lightheaded from pleasure overload, he gathered as much strength as he could, cradling her head and turning them until he was resting against the pillows, and she was seated deliciously on his cock.

He grabbed a handful of her ass and pulled forward, encouraging her to ride him.

"Fuck me," he whispered as he swiped his thumb across her bottom lip. She licked it, sucking it into her mouth and moaning as she swiveled her hips.

He pushed his thumb between her silky folds, moving it in a circular motion until it scraped across her clit.

She howled, bucking forward as if electricity were zipping through her body. He kept rubbing that spot, increasing the speed and pressure of his digit with each pass. Between the vise-like grip her pussy walls had on his cock and the decadent sounds she was making every time he rubbed her clit, this was going to be over soon.

The sound of her skin slapping against his had his nuts inching up. His body was ready to explode. His finger swiped once, then twice more against her clit, her muscles spasmed, and she splintered into pieces around him, screaming his name as her climax spilled over her.

He tumbled over immediately after her, locking his fingers with hers, needing an anchor to hold on to. When he'd trickled the last drop of cum into the condom, he collapsed against the cushion of the pillows, pulling her down to rest on his chest.

He held her there, allowing the quiet to soothe them both. He stroked the smooth skin of her hand, bringing it to his lips to kiss gently.

"I don't ever want to be without you, Mandisa. This is the first time in weeks I've felt...alive."

She closed her eyes as he spoke, turning her face away from him. It could have been simply because she was tired after their lovemaking. But, it felt more like avoidance, as if she'd closed a door in his face.

"Mandisa?"

"Slade. You asked me to give you another chance last night. The truth is, I don't know if I can."

He attempted to sit up, but she kept her weight pressed against him so he'd remain lying down.

"Mandisa, I know I made you mad. I know I deserve your

anger. I promise you I will never act the ass like that again. Believe me, darlin'. I don't want to be without you."

"Slade, you certainly did make me mad. But anger wouldn't've made me walk away from you."

Slade pulled shaking fingers through his hair, then scrubbed his palm down the length of his face. She was here, lying in his arms. They'd just made love. He'd felt every moment of her heart beating in unison with his. How could she still be uncertain?

"Last night was the first good sleep I've had in weeks, darlin'. Head's a lil' fuzzy. You're gonna have to break this down for me, nice and slow."

He felt himself flush as he heard his twang fill the air. Usually he played the good Southern cowboy to entertain her. But this wasn't an act. When he was worried—and right now he was deathly afraid of losing his heart—sometimes his Texas slipped through his defenses, and he started sounding more ranch hand than executive.

"Slade, when you sat in your office and told me what Bull and Macy did to you, you wounded me. I saw how much that pain affected you. More than a decade later, and you still bore the trauma of those scars.

"Knowing what they did to you, it hurt me. And to get back at the monster that caused you so much pain, you allowed your fear to turn you into him. Before my eyes, you became the man who'd hurt me most, because he'd hurt the man I loved. It would have destroyed me to watch you change completely into Bull, so I left."

Slade stilled beneath her touch. The guilt of her words pressed him down into the mattress, rendering him paralyzed beneath her as she continued to speak. He'd been so angry when they'd first argued and upset she couldn't see his perspective. The truth he was too proud to see then was crashing down over him right now. She'd loved him too much to watch him destroy himself, and he'd let her walk away as a reward.

"I don't think I could sit around and watch you become that monster, Slade. It would break me."

"It will never happen again, Mandisa."

"But that wasn't our only problem, Slade. There was the little issue of you thinking my work didn't meet the same level of importance as yours."

He shook his head and threw up his hands in mock surrender.

"That wasn't exactly true, darlin'."

"Slade, it is true. I want to get past this. I want to wake up like we did today, cocooned in one another's arms. But I'm not sure we'll be able to get beyond our hurdles."

He laced his fingers between her braids and brought her mouth down to his. Things worked much better for them when they expressed their feelings through touch. Words just seemed to muddy the waters between them.

"I promise you, I will do anything I need to, anything you ask, to make this right."

She passed her gaze slowly across his face as if she were looking for the truth in his words. He placed her hand on his heart, hoping she understood his promise was made from love, and not the words he'd used to express it.

Slowly, he saw a spark of something devilish in her eyes, a sexy twinkle that made his recently spent cock toy with the possibility of getting hard again.

"Anything?" The cocky lift of her brow gave him a brief pause. But even the slight whiff of concern that fanned across his senses couldn't make him deny her.

"Anything you want, darlin'."

"I want three weeks." Now he was intrigued. Before he could speak she placed a silencing finger across his lips and continued. "I want you to spend three weeks in Brooklyn, seeing what it is I actually do for a living, for my community. After that time, if I can see that you have an appreciation for the work I do, I'll give us another chance."

A broad grin swept against his mouth as he considered her request. "How will you be able to determine I've learned my lesson?"

She pushed her hand between them and cupped the growing bulge of his cock. "Don't worry, I have my ways."

Her ways hadn't disappointed him yet, that was certain. But considering everything they'd just been through, he wasn't sure if taking this bet was wise.

"You know how much I like to win, darlin'. It might not be such a good idea to enter into another wager considering how badly the last one blew up in our faces."

"What's the matter, cowboy? You scared you'll lose?"

He watched her smile light up her face as she used his words against him. Her smile shone until he could feel its warmth burrowing beneath his skin, directly to his heart. This woman was his lifeline, the only cure for the pain he'd carried around for so many years. Wasn't she worth everything? Weren't they worth everything?

She was throwing him a line. All he had to do was look beyond his doubts and grab hold of it.

"So what's your answer, cowboy?"

EPILOGUE

ONE YEAR LATER…

Slade walked in a circle as he inspected the last of the offices on the executive floor. The one he was standing in would be his. He needed to make certain the specifications he'd given to the Realtor and the contractor had been followed to the letter.

Glass walls and an open floor plan welcomed him. Bull had spent so many years hiding behind closed doors in his office, Slade never wanted to adopt the same policy in his new position as owner and CEO of Logan Industries.

"Is everything to your liking, Mr. Hamilton?"

Slade turned around and greeted the Realtor with a firm handshake and a smile. Tall, but still shorter than Slade by a couple of inches, with long dark hair that hung beyond his shoulders and bright blue eyes that flashed with contentment, Kenneth Searlington had come highly recommended for the project Slade was seeking to undertake.

"It's perfect, Searlington."

He'd met the man a little over six months prior, and now

they were closing the deal on what would cost Slade millions, but net him the world upon its completion.

"I have to admit," Kenneth responded, "I wasn't sure we could find you the perfect space and have it ready in under six months, but even in real estate, miracles do happen. You must love New York to invest so much in this location."

Slade shook his head. "Frankly, it's a little cold, crowded, and noisy for my tastes. But, the woman I love lives here, so it's where I need to be."

"If the size of the check you just wrote me is any indication, you must love her tremendously."

Slade could feel the ridiculously huge grin tugging at the edges of his mouth. He was a grown man. You'd think he could mask his feelings for his woman while in a business setting. But even here, standing in front of a man he had no personal connection to, he couldn't help the joy he felt whenever he thought of Mandisa.

"You have someone special at home, Searlington?"

Slade chuckled a little when he saw a matching smile climb onto Searlington's face. "Yeah, married to a beautiful woman. She's all heart."

Slade nodded. "Then you know there isn't a thing I wouldn't do to make her happy. In the span of six weeks, she showed me how to live a life I'm proud of. This project is just me showing her what she means to me."

The Realtor pulled a folder from his briefcase and a pen from his pocket, handing them both to Slade. "Sign here, and your project is complete."

Slade scribbled his signature on the offered paperwork and returned the documents and pen to the man in exchange for a key ring with three shiny keys.

"As big as this building is, I'm only getting three keys?"

Kenneth laughed. "Most of the doors on the building are key-code or keycard access. Your security firm has been given the current access codes, and I'm certain they will begin changing everything immediately. The only door that needs actual keys is the front door."

Slade nodded and tipped his hat toward the Realtor. "Thank you, sir."

Kenneth stretched out his hand and offered it to Slade. "Thank you. Enjoy your property, Mr. Hamilton."

Slade watched Kenneth Searington exit the room and pulled his cellphone from his jacket pocket. He tapped on Mandisa's icon and waited for the phone to connect on the other end.

"Hey there, cowboy. How are you?"

The smooth sound of her sultry voice made his cock jump. "Missing my doctor lady something terrible. Are you on your way?"

"Yes, Slade. According to the driver you sent, we should arrive at this mystery place within the hour. Are you going to tell me what this is about?"

"Now, why would I ruin your surprise like that?"

Slade said his goodbyes and walked over to the window to look out across the city. A year ago he wouldn't have thought he'd be here. But loving Mandisa had changed so much about him and his life. All those changes enriched his existence and made him a better man.

She asked him for three weeks to teach him the error of his ways. What she'd done was shown him how to love on more than just a superficial level.

The first week she'd made him work with one of her younger employees in the Pitkin Avenue store. Carmen was the first in her family to go to college. Although she received financial aid, she could barely afford to eat and buy her textbooks. The job Mandisa provided her meant she didn't have to choose between starving and studying. Mandisa also made certain her hours were flexible and didn't interfere with her class schedule.

Watching that young woman work diligently to help customers, stock inventory, and keep the entire store in immaculate condition gave Slade a new respect for the humble little store and its employees. Slade paid his executives more money than Carmen would probably earn in her lifetime, and yet she worked so diligently for Mandisa not because of the whopping check she received every two weeks, but because her boss had invested in Carmen, and Carmen's future, and she wanted to make Mandisa proud.

Watching Carmen made Slade see Sweet Sadie's for what it was. Not a smalltime shop that sold insignificant things, but a lifeline for those struggling to make a better life for themselves in a community the world often forgot about.

The second week of their wager, Mandisa took Slade to a rehearsal at a local community center. Inside, he met a dance group made up of local kids. He thought they were cute, and talented as hell. They moved in ways he'd never be able to command his body to, with such ease and confidence. But he didn't understand how being there would help him appreciate Mandisa's work more, until he spoke to the director of the community center.

Apparently, these kids were part of a program initiated to keep local children from ending up on the streets. The program offered afterschool care for kids whose parents wouldn't be able to afford to send them to activities. The kids did homework, played, and worked on talents, skills, and hobbies that helped their development.

This particular group of dancers was practicing to perform in the Labor Day Parade. The director told him their costumes and all fees associated with their entry into the parade had been covered by Mandisa's company every year. She'd walked him over to a bulletin board where pictures of the previous year's parade were pinned up. Their little faces were all bright and happy, covered in expertly applied makeup. Mandisa donated more than money—she donated her product and her time.

Outside of that place, the streets were waiting for those children. Ready to swallow them whole and spit them back onto the cold, dangerous concrete. Mandisa's patronage was the best thing in their arsenal to defend those kids against the harsh realities of their current existence. Suddenly, Slade's job didn't seem so important. How many lives had he touched directly sitting in his office? Certainly not enough.

The third week, Mandisa sent him to the Atlantic Avenue store to help with a seasonal promotional event. Of all the requests she'd made of him, this one grated on his nerves slightly.

The store was always busy. He'd barely had a moment to take a breath, let alone learn whatever lesson Mandisa intend to teach him. It was hard to see the intrinsic value of the place when all he could focus on was a different woman asking him for help finding a particular shade of lipstick or the new scent in the body lotion line every two minutes.

Slade was just about to take his assigned lunch break—even though he wasn't on the store's payroll, Mandisa insisted he follow all the employee handbook rules regardless of the fact he was technically a volunteer—when he glimpsed a woman standing in the lipstick section.

She was short and curvy, with deep mahogany skin. He'd directed her to that section almost fifteen minutes ago. He couldn't imagine that anyone could be staring at lipstick that long. It was like selecting a crayon color for your face—pick one you liked, and move on.

Curious, he walked over to her, and asked politely, "Are you finding everything you need?"

Her brown eyes fluttered slightly, and she dipped her

head a bit before answering him. "It's just so hard to wear red with my skin tone. I want to wear a really bright red, but I don't think I can pull off any of these colors."

Slade ran his fingers through the reds and stopped when he came across the shade labeled, "Damn."

"My lady friend wears this one all the time. It's one of my favorites on her."

She smiled shyly. "No offense, but your girlfriend and I probably can't wear the same shade of lipstick."

"You'd be surprised. Mandisa's skin tone is like yours. Rich and deep, I love this red on her."

"Mandisa, the owner? She's your girlfriend?"

Slade nodded. "Yes, ma'am. You know her?"

The woman smiled as she gently took the tube of lipstick from Slade's fingers. "Most girls learn to wear makeup as teenagers. I didn't begin my studies until I was nearing thirty. All my life I'd been told I was too dark to wear anything but dim, drab colors. Only pretty girls with light skin could wear things like pinks, and golds, and reds. When I stepped inside of this store two years ago, fumbling through each aisle, Mandisa stopped and helped me. An hour later, she'd shown me how women like me, the ones who don't quite fit the world's standard of beauty, could be just as glamorous as the mainstream models on TV. Stepping into Sweet Sadie's, I learned I was beautiful too."

She looked down at the lipstick in her hand and rolled it between her fingers, holding it as if it were something sacred, precious. "You wouldn't happen to know which lip liner Mandisa wears with this, do you?"

Slade chuckled. He only knew the name of that particular shade of lipstick because he'd been part of the naming process. Mandisa had worn the prototype for one of their dates. When he saw her, lips bold, bright, and luscious, the only word that had spilled out of his mouth was "Damn."

He'd laughed a month later when she'd handed him the tube and turned it upside for him to read.

"No, sugah." His twang tinged the edges of the word. "I'm afraid the sum of my knowledge of lip color rests in your hands."

While sitting in the back of the store, eating takeout, he thought about the sadness in that woman's eyes when she'd said the world told her women that looked like her weren't beautiful. He wasn't a woman of color, had no clue what it was like to be a woman of color attempting to buy beauty products. But he knew that every famous makeup model that worked with Venus' products was Caucasian.

He hadn't thought much about that until this point. If Logan Industries was doing it, he was certain, his competitors were as well. If all you saw was blonde hair and blue eyes associated with things deemed beautiful, wouldn't that become your definition too?

Slade realized then all the things he was missing before. That cosmetics were about much more that people looking pretty. They were about making people feel pretty on the inside. Her work was much deeper than what went on top of someone's skin. He realized why she couldn't leave Brooklyn. Sweet Sadie's was part of the community. It helped her little corner of the world thrive.

What a fool he was. Up until that moment, he was so stuck on himself and his way of life, Slade hadn't figured that Mandisa's presence in her community, in her customers' lives was as significant as his title of CEO of L.I. The sick feeling of regret floating at the bottom of his stomach told him how wrong he was.

Slade made money for a living—lots of it. But Mandisa touched people's lives. In that moment, Slade had to wonder when was the last time he'd impacted someone's life the way Mandisa had.

Love moved Mandisa to sacrifice the things she wanted for the people who needed her. It was time for Slade to do the same.

He blinked his eyes clear of the memories of their challenge and smiled at the results of those life-affirming lessons. He was standing here in this empty office building, waiting for the woman he loved more than his next breath, simply because he'd learned he wasn't the most important thing in the world.

A knock on the door pulled him away from the window and caused him to turn toward the entrance. A smile bloomed on his face when he saw Mandisa stepping into the large office.

"Hey, cowboy. Any reason why you had me meet you in an empty office building?"

He walked in her direction, pulling his hat off his head as he reached her. He dipped down, stealing a quick kiss from her lips before placing his hat back on his head.

"Yes, ma'am." He smiled, kissing her again before pulling his cellphone out of his pocket and swiping his finger across the screen to wake it up.

She took the phone from him and glanced down at it. He could see her assessing the photo, turning his phone sideways to get a better view from the landscape position.

"This looks like the front of this building. But with the L.I. logo?" She looked up at him, the smile dropping from her face as she met his gaze. "Slade, what's going on?"

"In the last year, you and I have racked up so many frequent flyer miles we could both travel the world twice. I'm tired of feeling as if I must steal time just to be with the woman I love. I closed on this building today. It will probably take a couple of months, but this is going to be the new headquarters for Logan Industries."

Her eyes, wide with unspoken questions and the sheen of

unshed tears, outshone the twinkling lights in the darkening sky. She closed her eyes, and the tears she was holding back spilled onto her reddish-brown cheeks.

"Hey, I hope those are tears of happiness?"

She bit her bottom lip, trying to conceal the self-conscious quiver it displayed. "Slade," she whispered. "I would never have asked this of you. I would have continued traveling to meet you all over the world if it meant being with you."

He pulled her into his arms, tucking her into his chest and resting his chin atop her head. "Darlin', I know you didn't ask."

"But what about your mama, Slade?"

"She doesn't want to come here. Believe me, I tried, but Texas is her home. She gives us her blessing and says we can visit her as often as we want."

She wiped a nervous hand across her damp cheeks to dry them. He smiled when he saw fresh tears reappear. "Are you sure, Slade? This is a lot to commit to for a relationship."

He leaned down to kiss her, slowly pressing his lips against hers, savoring her sweetness. She wasn't asking if he was making a sound business decision, she was asking him if he was certain about them.

"I did this because I'm a selfish bastard at heart, and I wanted to wake up every morning with you next to me. Now, I'll still have to travel a good bit. Especially while moving our base from Austin to here, but I get to come home to you. Is that something you think you can live with, Dr. Avery?"

She lifted her face from his chest, stepping back a little before she gave him a full smile.

"Oh, I can definitely deal with that, Mr. Hamilton." She stepped completely out of his embrace, walking around him slowly, her fingertips grazing his chest as she moved from one side of him to the other. "The question is, can you?"

"Is that a challenge?"

She lifted a brow, glancing at him from her periphery. "Well, since Texas has lost both bets to Brooklyn so far, I thought I'd be gracious and give you a chance to win some of your money back."

She closed the distance between them, pressing her body into his, wrapping her arms around his neck and pulling him down to her. She traced his bottom lip with her tongue, the heat searing him, making his flesh tingle with excitement.

"So what's your answer, cowboy?"

He tried to steal a kiss, but she backed away from him just in time to deny him.

"Missy, you like playing with fire, don't you?

She shrugged, snaking a hand down his chest, across the firm expanse of his abdomen, until she was cupping his heavy balls.

"What's the matter, cowboy?" she whispered slowly as she caught his earlobe between her teeth. "You scared you'll lose?"

He seared her lips with his. The taste and feel of her against him made every one of his nerve endings crackle with need and excitement. He pulled her closer to him, his hand branding the curve of her ass, stamping his ownership across the firm globes.

The kiss was hard and dirty, his tongue prying her lips open, forcing its way inside. Tasting her wet warmth made him ache for a flat surface to devour her on. Overwhelmed by love, lust, and need, he didn't give one single damn that they were surrounded by glass walls. If Searlington or some random passersby saw them, they could either enjoy the show or leave.

His body was on fire. But more than that, more than the

physical desire coursing through his veins, he was content. He'd never had that in Texas, never understood what it was to not be in a constant state of worry about the future. In his woman's arms, he had no questions about his place in the world, or his purpose.

From the moment they'd touched, Slade knew he was meant for one thing, and one thing only.

To love her.

He tore his mouth away from hers, smiling as he felt her deft fingers unbuckling his belt. He leaned down, raising her chin with his finger, locking his gaze with hers, and uttering the two words that only a fellow competitive spirit such as his would revel in.

"Bring it."

The End

ABOUT THE AUTHOR

LaQuette is an erotic, multicultural romance author of M/F and M/M love stories. Her writing style brings intellect to the drama. She often crafts emotionally epic, fantastical tales that are deeply pigmented by reality's paintbrush. Her novels are filled with a unique mixture of savvy, sarcastic, brazen, and unapologetically sexy characters who are confident in their right to appear on the page.

This bestselling Erotic Romance Author is the 2016 Author of the Year Golden Apple Award Winner, 2015 Swirl Awards Bronze Winner in Romantic Suspense, and 2015 Georgia Romance Writers Maggie Award Finalist in Erotic Romance. LaQuette—a native of Brooklyn, New York—spends her time catering to her three distinct personalities: Wife, Mother, and Educator.

Writing—her escape from everyday madness—has always been a friend and source of comfort. At the age of sixteen she read her first romance novel and realized the genre was missing something: people that looked and lived like her. As a result, her characters and settings are always designed to provide positive representations of people of color and various marginalized communities.

She loves hearing from readers and discussing the crazy characters that are running around in her head causing so much trouble. Contact her on her website, LaQuette.com, or via email at LaQuette@LaQuette.com.

NEWSLETTER SIGNUP

Hello,

If you're interested in staying current with all of the happenings with my writing, previews, and giveaways, sign up for my monthly newsletter at LaQuette.com.

COMING SOON...

LOADED LONGSHOT

Kandi Adkins is the executive manager of Sweet Sadie's Cosmetics. With her roots planted firmly in Brownsville, Brooklyn, Kandi knows what it's like to have nothing. Education and her friend's late mother, Sadie King, pulled her out of the mire of poverty, and enabled her to grab hold to personal and professional security. It was a debt Kandi would never be able to repay.

Didn't mean she wouldn't try, though.

Restitution came in many forms. For Kandi, it meant keeping a promise to her late benefactor that would never allow her to dream beyond the borders of Brooklyn, or her position in Sweet Sadie's company no matter how her deeply-buried desires called to her.

She'd accepted her place in life. There were worse fates than having a permanent position in a thriving cosmetics company. She was content. As long as she didn't allow herself to dream, she'd be satisfied for the rest of her life. Too bad the stoic, but sexy Aaron Nakai makes it hard to keep her heart grounded, and her head from asking, "What if?"

Aaron Nakai plays his cards close to the vest. Life has taught him that reaching for more than you need only invites trouble into your life. That's what happened to his father, a man who died young attempting to make his mark on the world. He finds comfort and security living in his adoptive brother, Slade's shadow. Aaron refuses to allow lofty dreams to rob him of the gains he's made in life. Being Slade's lawyer and right-hand man suits him just fine.

When Slade needs Aaron to step out of the background and take care of an unexpected problem in New York, Aaron's quiet existence back in Texas is blown to bits by a quick-witted, sassy-mouthed fireball named Kandi. Their attraction is just as palpable as their distaste for one another, making the decision to wager their hearts and their careers is a high-stakes game with potentially disastrous outcomes.

Will they fold? Or will they reach for it all in a game of double or nothing?

OTHER TITLES BY LAQUETTE

Heart of the Matter: Queens of Kings: Book 1

Divided Heart: Queens of Kings: Book 2

Protected Heart: Queens of Kings Book 3

Power Privilege & Pleasure: Queens of Kings: Book 4

His True Strength: Queens of Kings: Book 5

Lies You Tell

Bedding The Enemy

My Beginning: Trinity Series: Book 1

Love's Changes: A Losing My Way Novella: Book 1